"I'm sorry."

"Sorry?" Her voice sounded high and breathless. "You said so already."

"I know," Armand murmured. "I said I was sorry my actions had caused you grief. But it's more than that. It's everything. I am sorry for everything."

Hardly daring to breathe, Armand brought his lips closer to hers. Dominie did not say a word to prevent him. Nor did she turn her face away. Nor raise her hand. But when his lips finally found hers, with a tentative, whisper-light touch, he felt them tremble beneath his.

From somewhere he summoned the control to draw back, though he could hardly bear it.

"Don't stop!" For a moment Armand could not be certain whether the fierce whisper came from Dominie or from his own banked desire.

"You went away without a parting kiss." She passed her hand over his chest and up his neck. "I claim payment...*now!*"

* * *

The Last Champion
Harlequin Historical #703—May 2004

Deborah Hale

The Last Champion

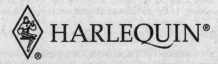

HARLEQUIN®

TORONTO • NEW YORK • LONDON
AMSTERDAM • PARIS • SYDNEY • HAMBURG
STOCKHOLM • ATHENS • TOKYO • MILAN • MADRID
PRAGUE • WARSAW • BUDAPEST • AUCKLAND

ISBN 0-373-29303-8

THE LAST CHAMPION

Copyright © 2004 by Deborah M. Hale

This book is dedicated with admiration and love
to my fellow Harlequin Historical authors,
"The Hussies," who are the unswerving champions
of my Muse, my mental health and my joy in life.
Thank you for always being there!

Chapter One

Norfolk, England, 1143

Armand Flambard is alive.

The realization quivered along Dominie's veins as she caught sight of Breckland Abbey, its cloister walls standing tall and austere between a swath of orderly tilled fields and a tangle of wild green forest.

Armand, alive? Was it possible? Dominie De Montford had asked herself that question a hundred times since setting out three days ago on the risky, roundabout journey from Harwood. Or had Father Clement seen some sort of bizarre vision while accompanying her mother on a pilgrimage to Breckland's holy well? Dominie could not afford to be absent so long from her family estates, chasing a will-o'-the-wisp of futile hope.

And yet…

If it were true, if she did find Armand Flambard here at Breckland, it could mean the difference between survival and starvation next winter for her family and vassals. Those people were her responsibility now, but they had once been his. Before he'd forsaken them…and her.

A rustling sound in the tall grass behind her drove those bitter memories from Dominie's mind, sending her diving for cover into a small copse of hazel and beech trees. Her pulse pounded so fast and loud in her ears, she half feared the holy brothers of Breckland might hear it while at their prayers.

When a small grouse took to the air from out of the heath, Dominie exhaled a shaky breath. After three days traveling through the English countryside in stealth, she found her senses tuned to a quivering pitch. So was her appetite.

A faint breeze from the direction of the abbey tormented her with the aroma of roasting meat. Dominie's mouth watered and her stomach let out a piteous growl. Dropping to her haunches, she rummaged in the cloth pouch attached to her belt and pulled out a hard heel of bread. As she gnawed at it, she tried not to think about the hungry winter everyone at Harwood and Wakeland would face if they failed to keep the wolf from their door.

Eudo St. Maur. Former Earl of Anglia. Wolf of the Fens.

Please let Armand be here! Dominie begged, though she knew better than to hope God would heed her desperate plea. Perhaps, as some impious folk claimed, he and all his angels were asleep. If they had been awake and heedful, surely they would not allow such wickedness and strife to stalk the land.

Just then, a bell pealed from the tower of the abbey chapel, summoning the monks of Breckland from prayer to work. Not long after, the cloister gate swung open to let out a party of brothers and lay brothers in rusty black habits. Each one carried a hoe, spade or other farming tool.

Though her hunger was barely dulled, Dominie dropped

the remainder of the bread back into her scrip. Step by stealthy step, she made her way through the stand of trees, drawing closer to the abbey work party. Her gaze ranged over each man in turn, fastening at last on the tallest.

He had the firm, spare build she remembered of Armand Flambard, and the brisk, purposeful stride. His head was not shaved in a monk's tonsure, which must mean he had not taken his final vows…yet.

Perhaps God had stirred in his sleep and heard Dominie's desperate prayer, after all.

Without a word, the men dispersed among the various fields and garden patches to begin their hours of labor. The tall one moved steadily in Dominie's direction, as if drawn by her intense scrutiny. Or possibly nudged by some unusually obliging higher power.

When he reached the edge of the garden, the lay brother hefted a billhook and began to tend the hedge fence, cutting new saplings and bending them down to weave among the others. He was still far enough away, with his head bent over his work, that Dominie could not be certain his was the face she remembered.

Get on with it! she chided herself. One way or the other, she must waste no time finding out. Yet something made her hang back. Fear, perhaps, that this last hope might be snuffed out, like so many others.

Gathering her courage, Dominie stepped from the shelter of the trees and walked toward the fence. Intent on his task, the lay brother paid her no heed, until nothing separated them but the narrow barrier of felled brush.

''Armand Flambard?'' Her words erupted in a hoarse croak, for she had not spoken aloud in the three days of her journey, and her last drink had been some hours ago.

The man's head snapped up, and the stroke of his billhook fell awry, contradicting his gruff answer. "You'll find no man here by that name, lad."

Lad? For an instant the word bewildered Dominie as much as Armand Flambard's denial of his identity. For when he'd looked up and spoken, her heart had given a giddy lurch of recognition.

To be sure, he had changed a little in his appearance since she'd seen him last. His face was more deeply tanned than it had once been, and any suggestion of boyish roundness had been hewn away by the years, leaving a profile of rugged, masculine beauty.

His shoulders were as broad as ever, his limbs lean and hard as iron. His hands looked larger and more powerful than Dominie remembered them. Yet his fingers moved with a deft, virile grace that had once caressed haunting music from a lute...and soulful sighs from a certain maiden.

Thrusting that bedeviling image from her mind, Dominie took stock of her appearance. No wonder Armand had called her *lad!*

She pulled the Phrygian cap from her head, letting a thick, tightly braided plait of dark auburn hair fall down over her shoulder. "Look at me again, and see if that does not jog your memory...brother."

In their younger years, she had sometimes called him that. Only in jest, of course. Though he'd been fostered at Wakeland, with the De Montfords, she had never felt the least bit sisterly toward Armand Flambard. Nor did she now.

When he glanced her way again, Dominie forced herself to smile, the better to help him recognize her. Though she could neither forget nor forgive what he'd done in the past, her people needed his help now. Whatever she must do to gain it, she would.

"Dominie?" The billhook slipped from his slack fingers, falling to the ground with a soft thud. "How did you find me? Why have you come here?"

So he did recognize her. Dominie tried in vain to subdue the foolish rush of pleasure that surged through her.

"Father Clement came to the abbey on a pilgrimage not long ago. He thought he recognized you, so I came to see if it was true. We'd heard you were dead, Armand." Dominie could not keep a sharp edge of rebuke from her voice. "Killed at Lincoln, like my father and Denys."

How she had mourned for him. All the longer and more bitterly because she'd tried so hard not to. It had felt disloyal to her father and brother, grieving for one of their fallen foe.

Armand's handsome features contorted as Dominie had sometimes seen them, years ago, during sword practice, when he'd taken a hard blow.

She guessed what his expression meant. "Had you not heard they were killed?"

"I'd heard." Armand glanced over his shoulder toward the rest of the brethren. They were all too far away and too deeply occupied with their own tasks to pay him and Dominie any mind.

"I was killed at Lincoln, too." He stooped to retrieve his billhook. "Part of me, at least."

What did he mean? Had he taken some grave wound that did not show, but which had destroyed his ability to fight?

A chill went through Dominie. Then she reminded herself she was not expecting Armand to tackle St. Maur's forces single-handedly. It was his tactical skill as a warrior and his leadership she needed, though an extra stout sword arm would not go amiss.

"You look hale enough to me." At least for her purposes.

Armand shrugged his shoulders and started cutting more brush.

Perhaps the time had come to answer his second question. "I sought you out because I need your help, Armand."

He stiffened. "Please don't call me by that name. I'm Brother Peter now…or soon will be."

Not if she had any say in the matter, he wouldn't!

"By whatever name you call yourself, you *must* help me." The words came out in a half pleading, half demanding tone. "The king is doing what he can, but too late and not enough, as is his way. Eudo St. Maur is the trouble. Have you heard what that cur has done since King Stephen was fool enough to let him go free?"

"I've been in a cloister," Armand snapped, "not in a crypt! Of course I've heard. We have brothers here at Breckland who are refugees from some of the holy houses to the east that St. Maur has despoiled."

The fierce outrage she heard in his voice heartened Dominie. Holy brothers didn't speak in such tones.

Warriors did.

"Then you know he's picked clean the land for miles around his camp in the Fens."

Armand froze, as if he'd been struck by a blade much larger than the one he wielded. "Harwood?"

Dominie nodded. "Near the end of the winter, a raiding party of St. Maur's attacked one of our outlying manors. The tenant and his family barely escaped with their lives."

"The devil take him!" Armand muttered through clenched teeth.

"One day the devil may oblige us," replied Dominie.

The earl had been excommunicated for his violence against the clergy. "Until then, someone must defend the innocent against his rabble of outlaws."

He must have understood what she was asking, yet Armand did not answer. Instead, he continued to hack away at the saplings.

Dominie tried again. "As the tenant and his family rode away, St. Maur's men taunted him that they would be back when Harwood and Wakeland had more worth taking. We cannot let those reavers plunder our harvest, or people will starve!"

Armand straightened to his full, daunting height and turned his formidable blue gaze upon her.

Sighing a prayer of thanksgiving, Dominie choked back tears. Her hazardous, hungry journey had not been in vain, after all. Armand Flambard, flower of a line of righteous warriors stretching back to the days of Charlemagne, would stand as their champion against the Wolf of the Fens.

And he would prevail. Dominie knew it with all the hero worship of her girlhood.

At last Armand spoke. "I will pray with all my soul for the deliverance of Wakeland and Harwood." He shook his head, regretful but resolved. "More than that, I cannot do."

"Pray?" Dominie shrieked, not caring how much attention she drew from the other Benedictines. If she could have laid her hands on Armand's billhook, she might have taken his head off with it. "I don't want your prayers, Armand Flambard, I want your sword!"

Murderous rage should not look beautiful in a woman's eyes.

In the thousands of times Armand had imagined Dominie De Montford during the past five years, never once had she worn an expression other than one of angelic innocence. And when she'd spoken to him in his dreams, it had always been in the sweetest, softest whisper.

Now she stood before him, dressed in a boy's long hose and tunic, with hard emerald fury in her glare and scornful wrath in her voice. And he wanted her with a fierce, urgent lust that shocked him speechless.

Five years ago, when honor had demanded a wrenching choice from him, Armand Flambard had reluctantly left behind a girl. Now he faced the woman she'd become.

And such a woman.

Hair the rich fertile hue of fuller's earth. Eyes that mingled the warm brown and vivid green of a forest in summer, with flecks of shimmering gold like shafts of sunshine that often pierced the woodland canopy. None of her features, taken separately, suggested beauty—high cheekbones, angular jaw, full brows and wide, lush lips. Yet they melded together in a look of such arresting charm, Armand could scarcely tear his gaze away.

"Is there some trouble here?" From behind Armand, the deep voice of Brother Ranulf, the cellarer, rolled like approaching thunder. Yet again, Armand thought what a fine sergeant-at-arms the man would have made.

"No trouble." Armand shot Dominie a look that demanded her cooperation.

The old abbot had continually denied his request to take vows, on the grounds that Armand had not completely abandoned his former life. The new abbot seemed more amenable, and might soon be persuaded…as long as Dominie did not stir up a fuss.

Armand turned to face the cellarer. "Brother Ranulf, this is Lady Dominie De Montford, my foster sister from Wakeland. She's come to Breckland…"

He grasped for what to say next. Deceiving a fellow brother would not only be dishonorable, but downright sinful. To blurt out the truth might lead to all manner of questions he could not bear to answer.

"I've come to Breckland on a pilgrimage, Brother Ranulf," Dominie declared in a tone of perfect sincerity. "To visit your holy well." She gave the cellarer a guileless smile, like the one she had worn so often in Armand's dreams.

Brother Ranulf proved no match for her charm. "All the way from Wakeland, by yourself? Child, that was a perilous undertaking! What ails you?"

The tone of his question implied that she did not look ill. Armand agreed. The lady looked *too* well for his uneasy peace of mind.

"Sharp pains in my belly, Brother." Dominie clutched her arms protectively over her middle. A look of mute suffering twisted her features, convincing Armand she spoke the truth. "They have troubled me for some time. I pray Our Lady will be able to intercede for me. Otherwise…"

Dominie, dying? A grim, bottomless ache settled in Armand's belly. True, he'd had no contact with her in five years. He'd earnestly prayed they would never come face-to-face again. Then why did the notion of a world without her grieve him so?

Another thought struck him. What a noble lass she was, to plead with him on behalf of her vassals without once mentioning the personal affliction that had brought her to the abbey. Armand despised himself for the carnal desire that had flared in him. Perhaps the old abbot had been right, after all, in denying him full brotherhood.

Brother Ranulf shook his tonsured head. "I pray you will find healing in our house, child. Come 'round the hedge and I shall direct you to Brother Alwyn, our hosteler.''

''Thank you.'' Dominie gave a little cough. ''Would it be too great a boon to beg that Armand…er, Brother Peter…might show me the way? When we were young, he was as dear to me as any true brother. Finding him here, unlooked for, feels like a small visitation of grace.''

Her air of wistful sweetness would have moved a stone saint. A wave of grateful relief washed over Armand as he realized Dominie did not mean to cause him problems with his superiors. Yet something about her words troubled him vaguely. She had not found him at Breckland by accident, or by grace.

Only moments ago, Dominie had told him she'd come on purpose, looking for him.

Brother Ranulf had no such reason to doubt her sincerity.

''Bless you, my child. Whatever you wish.'' His forceful voice had never sounded so gentle. Catching Armand's eye, he nodded toward the abbey. ''Fetch the young lady to Brother Alwyn. He'll make sure she's settled properly.''

Armand accepted the order with a slight bow to signal both his obedience and his thanks. Having seen Dominie in the flesh for the first time in five years, he could not bear to be parted from her again so soon. Even if she stirred up feelings he had long struggled to subdue.

He pushed aside some of the brush to make an opening for her to enter. When she scooted in with a lively step, Armand had trouble wrenching his gaze away from her slender, well-shaped legs, on which a pair of green woolen hose clung tightly. He managed it, at last, only to find himself staring at the soft curves of her figure, which even the baggy folds of her tunic could not disguise.

When had his paragon of virginal innocence become the embodiment of feminine temptation?

It was no fault of hers, Armand's conscience protested. Dominie had done nothing but stand and speak and smile. He was the one who had entertained sinful thoughts—all the more wicked if the poor girl was ailing.

As he shoved the brush back into place, Armand considered cutting a switch with which to flay himself, later, for his wickedness. Then he remembered the new abbot did not hold with such practices.

Straightening again, Armand set off toward the abbey with a brisk stride. Behind him, he heard Dominie scurry to catch up. He forced himself to slow his pace.

Without turning back to look at her, he asked, "Why did you not tell me you were ill?"

"It makes no difference," she heaved a weary sigh.

Armand pushed open the abbey gate. "It does to me."

"Does it?" Dominie lofted a glance at him as she breezed by to enter the abbey.

She passed so close he could smell the earthy musk of the forest that clung to her garments. It made his nostrils quiver. He followed her through the gate, pushing it shut behind them with greater force than he'd intended.

With no warning, Dominie checked her stride and swung around to face him. Armand barely escaped blundering into her.

"Is there somewhere private we can talk?" she asked. "Before you deliver me to the hosteler?"

Though he knew his answer should be a regretful but firm no, Armand cast a furtive look around the courtyard. He saw none of the monks or lay brothers. At this time of day, those not at work in the fields would be busy in the scriptorium, the infirmary or wherever else their usual duties took them.

Armand glanced back down at Dominie, and felt himself tumbling headlong into her bewitching hazel gaze. She stood so close, he fancied he could feel the warmth of her body. No woman should stand that near a man unless he had some claim upon her...or she upon him.

Raising his hand, he pointed toward the cloisters. "Down there, we can talk." Monastic discipline reasserted itself. "But only for a moment, mind."

"I don't need long." Dominie nodded in approval. "We can't afford to tarry."

Her use of the word *we* stirred a bittersweet sensation in Armand's heart.

Breaking from their intense gaze, Dominie turned and strode down the covered walkway that ran beneath the brothers' dormitory.

"What are you doing in an abbey, Armand Flambard?" She made an impatient gesture toward the line of graceful pillars that supported the outside edge of the cloister, serene and beautiful in their regularity. "When we were young, I never once heard you speak of wanting to enter the church."

Of course she hadn't. That notion would have been the furthest from his mind, back then. For as long as Armand could remember, his had been the creed of the sword.

"I was the only son." He offered an explanation he hoped she would accept. "I had other responsibilities. The Flambard lands, our people."

He didn't mean his words to sound so curt, but that was how they came out. Dominie's sudden advent, with her intrusive questions and problems, had shaken the tenuous, hard-won peace of mind he'd found in these quiet cloisters.

"You still owe a duty to that land and those people,"

she reminded him, in a tone of rebuke that rasped against his overwrought emotions.

"No!" Armand swept his arm in a slanting motion that signaled denial. "All belong to your family now. A reward for your father's oath-breaking."

Even after his years in the abbey, the injustice of it still rankled—that those dearest to him should have stolen his birthright. "How dare you come to me now that your people are in peril, demanding *my* help, invoking *my* sense of duty?"

"Oath-breaking?" Dominie clenched her fists, and the flecks of gold in her eyes glittered like hellfire. "Why, you arrogant ass! My father, God rest his soul, cared more about his vassals than he did about some daft pledge the old king bade him speak. He knew those simple, hard-working folk needed an able lord to govern and protect them, more than Empress Maud needed his service at arms."

Fie, but it was like contending with old Baldwin De Montford all over again!

An estimable man in many ways, Armand's foster father had always kept his eyes trained on the ground, rather than gazing high, toward the stars. He'd never looked beyond the limited scope of his own interests, or the mundane matters of sowing, reaping, eating, drinking and building, to loftier ideals.

How Armand remembered the arguments between them, when the time had come to declare their allegiance to one of the claimants for the English crown. Arguments that had spun around and around in a downward spiral of bitter rancor, drowning their powerful bond of fosterage.

"If your father didn't mean to keep his word, he should not have given it!" Armand clung to the reassuring certainty that he had done right, no matter how loudly his conscience protested otherwise. "An oath of fealty is not something that binds a man only for as long as it is convenient. If all the earls and lords had honored the oath they swore to the empress, England would not be the embattled, lawless place it has become."

For an instant, Dominie appeared ready to fly at him in a rage. Instead, she squeezed her eyes shut and drew a deep breath. Her willowy body trembled as she battled the severity of her passion. Or could there be some other cause?

Her illness! How could he have been such a base knave to forget that, in the grip of those old grievances he should have long since let go?

"Dominie!" Armand reached for her, and to his surprise, she did not struggle to escape his embrace. "Forgive me. I should have held my tongue and not vexed you when you're ill."

Her eyes flew open. "Ill?"

It felt so good to hold her again, Armand knew it must be wrong. He tried to convince himself it was an innocent gesture of compassion, and nothing more. "The pains…in your belly."

"Oh, those." She sniffed the air. "A good meal or two from your refectory would work a miracle on my affliction."

"What?" Armand's hold on her slackened.

She raised her hand and clouted him on the shoulder. "I'm *hungry,* you daft clod!"

Armand backed away from her. "You told Brother Ranulf you had pains."

"So I do. You try making a journey of three days on a small loaf and a bit of cheese, then see if your belly doesn't pain you at the end of it!"

"But you said you'd come to find healing at the holy

well.'' This deceitful creature could not be his sweet, virtuous Dominie, no matter how much she might look like her. ''You made Brother Ranulf believe you were mortally ill. Made me believe it, come to that. How could you palm off such a bald falsehood on a holy brother?''

Shaking her head, she treated him to a look of perfect scorn. ''The truth will bend further than you suppose before it breaks, Flambard. I needed to talk with you, in private, and that seemed the readiest means. Now, about Eudo St. Maur—''

Just then, Armand heard the sound of approaching footsteps and voices out in the cloister garth.

''Come.'' He grabbed Dominie by the arm. ''If you have not journeyed to Breckland in search of healing, but only to pester me, then you must be gone at once, for I cannot help you.''

From lack of practice, his fighting reflexes were not as sharp as they had once been. Somehow, Dominie managed to twist her lower leg around his in midstride. Then she threw her slight weight against him, to aim his fall. Before he had time to react, Armand found himself spun around and pinned to one of the cloister pillars, with Dominie's hand held firmly over his mouth, her leg pressed snug between his.

He could have fought free of a male opponent in a trice. But against Dominie, his body betrayed him. His own long-denied urges held him to that pillar with greater force than a slender girl could muster.

''Listen to me!'' she hissed. ''For my part, I would as soon walk out of this abbey and henceforth consider you as dead as I believed you to be until a few days ago.''

Her words felt as cold as an iron blade thrust deep into his belly.

''But the people of Harwood and Wakeland need a

champion like you, if they are to survive. High principles won't feed their hunger next winter, nor shield them from St. Maur's torture. What I must do for them, I will, no matter how distasteful. If you come back with me and help us fend off St. Maur, I vow to see the Flambard lands restored to you.''

A holy brother should have few personal possessions beyond the robe on his back. Nor should he want more. Yet Dominie's impossible offer set a deep hunger gnawing at the marrow of Armand's bones. He'd been raised from the cradle to look on those lands as his destiny. Contrary to what Dominie might think, he had not surrendered them without a turbulent struggle.

He jerked his mouth free of her hand long enough to gasp, "How?"

What means did she have to give back what the king had taken?

The hand he had shifted from his mouth clung to his cheek, almost in the manner of a caress, and her voice took on a note of beguiling tenderness. "By wedding you, how else? Those lands are my dowry now."

Fire joined the hunger in Armand's bones, for his marriage to Dominie had also been destined and desired. Renounced only with bitter reluctance.

The footsteps and voices from the courtyard were coming closer. Armand thought he recognized the reedy tenor of Prior Gerard, his confessor.

He struggled to free himself. But how could he make much headway when every movement sent delicious flames of perdition licking his flesh? When he tried to push Dominie away, his hands closed over the generous swell of her breasts, and no amount of will could budge them.

It bewildered and horrified Armand to realize that the

softness of her womanhood held him hostage in a way no man's strength could have done.

"What is this?" cried Prior Gerard, as the footsteps pounded toward them.

Armand rallied his will to break free. But not before the hand that caressed his cheek snaked around his neck, pulling his face toward Dominie's. As she lunged up to meet him, her lips parted for a kiss that felt more like the last crippling strike of combat.

"Brother, what is the meaning of this?" The indignant demand did not come from Prior Gerard, bad as that might have been.

Armand managed to wrench his hands off Dominie's bosom, then grip her shoulders to push her back. When their eyes met, for the briefest instant, hers glittered with mocking triumph.

"I can explain, Father Abbot!" he gasped, making a deep reverence to the man beside Prior Gerard.

"Can you, indeed?" Abbot Wilfrid looked from Armand to Dominie and back again. "Then I think you had better try, my son."

Chapter Two

Let Brother High Principles talk his way out of this!

Dominie leaned back against a pillar to watch Armand squirm as he tried to explain how he'd come to be caught kissing and fondling the breasts of a young woman in the abbey cloisters. To make matters all the more scandalous—a young woman dressed as a boy.

"F-Father Abbot, Brother Prior, this is Lady Dominie De Montford." Armand flashed her a wrathful glance warning her to hold her tongue. "Her family fostered me and we were betrothed from childhood."

The shorter and elder of the two monks nodded, as if Armand's account was nothing new to him. He looked Dominie up and down with a gaze that seemed both shrewd and compassionate.

Though she reminded herself she'd had no choice but to compromise Armand this way, a clammy sensation of shame settled over her, as though someone had emptied a bucket of slops over her head.

The abbot paid her no heed at all. "What became of this betrothal of yours?" he asked Armand.

"The same thing that became of so much else, Father Abbot—this war for the throne. Dominie's father declared for King Stephen, I for the empress. All my lands were forfeit. I could not have maintained a wife, even if her father would have consented to let her wed an enemy.''

A likely tale! Dominie could feel her lip curling in a sneer. Armand Flambard had turned his back on her, as he had on every tie with her family and his people. How dare he pretend he'd considered her feelings in the matter?

Even to save her people from Eudo St. Maur, Dominie wondered how she could stomach being wed to a man who set so little store by her. Bearing his children. Sharing his bed.

Ah, but her flesh had quivered at his touch just now. Even though she told herself he'd meant nothing by it.

The abbot fixed Armand with a stern look. ''That is all very well. But it does not explain what the lady is doing here, or what the two of you were doing together.''

When Armand ventured to tell him, however, the abbot raised his hand for silence. He looked up and down the length of the cloister, then craned his neck to peer out into the courtyard.

Apparently satisfied that there had been no other witnesses, he lowered his voice to an ominous murmur. ''I will not have Breckland Abbey brought into disrepute over this incident, whatever its cause. Those self-righteous brothers of Citeaux are already stirring up trouble enough, accusing our order of laxity and corruption.''

He beckoned to Armand and Dominie. ''Let us go to my parlor where we may talk more about this in private.''

The prior hung back to let Dominie follow on the abbot's heels. When she glanced over her shoulder, she saw that he had placed himself between her and Armand.

As she trailed behind the abbot, Dominie thought about what he had said. A spark of sympathy for the man kindled within her, along with a sweet flicker of hope. Like her, Father Abbot knew what it meant to defend something with which he'd been entrusted. Skillfully managed, he might be a formidable ally in her cause. She would not scruple to exploit every possible advantage, if it promised to help her gain what she needed.

The abbot's parlor was not very grand for so large and prosperous an abbey, Dominie decided when they'd reached the room. It had a small hearth and a window that looked out onto the cloister garth. The only furnishings were a low table and three chairs, one considerably larger and more elaborate than the others.

The sole signs of extravagance were a pair of wonderfully embroidered tapestries on the outer wall, flanking the window. They looked to portray events in the lives of English saints. Dominie thought they must help keep the abbot's parlor snug in December, when North Sea winds swept over the East Anglian plain.

On this clement spring afternoon, winter must seem endlessly distant to most folk. But Dominie could already feel its icy chill on the back of her neck.

The abbot strode toward the larger of the three chairs and seated himself, while the prior poked his head out the door to check if any of the brothers or abbey servants might be lingering within earshot. Apparently satisfied, he closed it behind him and took a seat beside the abbot.

The two of them sat for a moment, staring at Armand and Dominie.

Suddenly self-conscious of how she must look, Dominie twitched her cloak from behind her shoulders to cover herself more modestly.

At last the abbot nodded to Armand. "Go ahead, Brother. Out with the rest of your story."

Armand held himself still, though Dominie suspected

it was the taut stillness of a lute string too tightly wound. "What more do you wish to know, Father Abbot?"

That was better.

Dominie had feared he would blurt out every damning detail in some misguided bid to unburden his conscience. She knew from experience that the truth, like rich food, was better doled out piecemeal, each morsel only by request, and garnished to make its best appearance.

She pictured a plump pheasant, slowly roasted, glazed with a mixture of fruit and honey, bedecked with its own long tapered tail feathers.

The thought of such a feast made Dominie's mouth water and her stomach squeal like a stuck pig.

The abbot and the prior exchanged a glance.

"When did you last eat, my child?" asked the abbot.

Tell him a day! her stomach urged her. *Tell him two!*

She should be able to do it without a qualm of conscience, for what little she had eaten since then could hardly count as a meal.

"I had some bread, Father, while I waited for the brothers to come out and begin their field work."

Before she could figure out what daftness had kept her from bending the truth, even an inch, Armand spoke up. "Lady Dominie walked all the way from Harwood, Father Abbot, more than thirty miles, with nothing to eat but a loaf and some cheese. If she took bread a short time ago, it could not have been any great quantity."

Armand had spoken up for her? After the trouble she had landed him in with his superiors? Dominie couldn't decide whether to be touched or contemptuous.

Would she have done as much for him if their positions had been reversed?

"Thank you, Brother." The abbot spoke in a crisp tone that suggested Armand should henceforth answer only when bidden. Then he shifted his gaze to Dominie. "Is this true, child? How much bread did you eat?"

"This much, Father." She pulled the crust from her scrip and held it out to show them. "And the other is true, about my journey from Harwood."

Both monks wrinkled their noses at the sight of her bread. Again they looked at each other and some wordless exchange passed between them. The prior rose from his chair.

"Go with Brother Prior, child," the abbot bade her. "He will see that you are fed a decent meal."

Dominie took a step or two after the prior, then froze. What might Armand tell his Father Superior in her absence? Might he somehow contrive forgiveness for his indiscretion?

"My thanks to you, Father Abbot, but I would rather stay here." Her stomach squealed again, in protest. It must be as bewildered and vexed by her behavior as she had been by Armand's. "You asked for an accounting. My lord Flambard can only tell you his half of what happened."

The abbot nodded. "And you can tell me yours once you've eaten, daughter. I would not have you swooning of starvation onto the floor of my parlor."

"I'm not as hungry as all that." Her declaration strained truth to the breaking point. "I don't mind staying."

"A generous offer, but hardly necessary." The abbot waved her toward the door. "I have found that when there is trouble involving two or more parties, the most effective way to ferret out the truth is to question them separately, then tally their accounts against one another."

"Then you won't make any decision until I've had a chance to tell you my story?" She pictured Armand smuggled away to some distant Benedictine house, where she would never find him, let alone in time to stop Eudo St. Maur from pillaging their harvest.

"I give you my word," said the abbot.

As Dominie passed by Armand on her way to the door, he caught her eye. The challenging look he shot her asked what would become of the world if all men gave and broke their word as it suited them.

The door had scarcely closed behind Dominie and Prior Gerard when the abbot fixed Armand with a stare that seemed to see clear down to his stained, battered soul. Abbot Wilfrid clasped his hands before him and rested his chin upon them.

His bushy brows rose. "So that was the lady you left behind in the world? Quite a remarkable creature. A man could be forgiven, I think, if he had difficulty forgetting her."

Perhaps. But could he be forgiven the kind of indiscretion the abbot and the prior had recently witnessed? Or thought they had witnessed?

"Yes, Father Abbot," Armand murmured, hoping it would be taken for agreement in principle, rather than an admission of fault.

It eased him to find the new abbot so understanding of the frailty of a man's heart.

"It was never my intention to molest the young lady," he insisted. "I was escorting her back to the gate when I tripped and spun around against the pillar."

The abbot would never believe the truth—that Dominie had pinned him to the pillar against his will. Armand could scarcely believe it himself, though his skin still prickled faintly where she had pressed her body against his.

"Indeed?" The look of doubt on the abbot's forceful features could not have been more plain. "Perhaps it would help if you explain how the young lady got to be alone with you in the cloisters to begin with."

Armand nodded. "I was tending the brush fence around the west field when Lady Dominie appeared from out of nowhere. At first I thought she was a lad, for she had her hair tucked under a cap, and her voice sounded hoarse."

He went on to tell what had brought her to Breckland and how she had deceived him and Brother Ranulf into believing she was ill. Hard as he tried, he could not subdue his mounting indignation over her behavior.

"When she heard you and Brother Prior coming," he concluded, "she threw her arms around my neck and…as you saw. I believe it was done to make the incident look as shameful as possible, so you would turn me out of the abbey. Then I would have little choice but to fall in with her plans."

"Remarkable." The abbot rose from his chair and walked slowly to the window, where he stood silent for a moment, staring out at the cloister garth. "Your lady Dominie sounds like a young woman of some enterprise."

"With not a scruple in the world," Armand muttered under his breath.

If the abbot overheard, he refrained from comment. Instead, he wheeled about to face Armand. "Tell me, Brother, why are you so adamant against doing what she asks?"

Of all the questions Armand had been prepared to answer, that one had been nowhere among them.

He struggled to frame a reply. "I…have sworn to renounce violence, Father. I have pledged the rest of my life to the church."

"Yes. But why? Did it have to do with the breach between you and the De Montfords?"

Armand flinched, the way he had as a lad when the blacksmith at Harwood probed too near a sore tooth with his tongs.

"It did," he answered, after a moment of reflection to gather his thoughts and his composure. "Before I went to Harwood for fosterage, my father always encouraged me to be true to the highest ideals of honor, justice and virtue."

The abbot tucked his hands into the opposite sleeves of his habit. "The seeds sown during your childhood found fertile ground in your character, I believe."

"So I hope, Father." Armand bowed his head. Though he clung tightly to the belief that he'd done right, he took no pride in the way events had fallen out. "For many years those ideals served me well...until the succession came into question and I found myself on the opposite side of this conflict from those dearest to me."

Armand could not say more. He had told his confessor the whole of it and received absolution. Yet in his soul he did not feel absolved.

A soft rustling sound issued from the abbot, like a sigh wedded to a chuckle. "How much easier life would be for us poor sinful creatures if all our choices were between right and wrong. Too often we must hoe a stony path between two vastly different *rights.* Or commit some small evil to avoid a great one."

It was a singular blessing to be understood...but not *too* well.

Armand continued to stare at the floor. "That is why I came to Breckland, Father Abbot. Here, I do not need to wrestle with such choices. I have renounced worldly possessions and personal ties that lead to temptation. I obey my superiors, trusting your wisdom to direct me in the right.''

Poverty, chastity, obedience. They were the only way for a man like him. All the more for what they cost him.

The loss of his lands and vassals had maimed him no less than if he'd lost a limb in battle. For all that, poverty was the easiest of the three to bear. Obedience came hard to a warrior and lord, trained from his youngest years to command.

As for chastity...the fleeting memory of Dominie's sweet, firm breasts beneath his hands made his palms itch with temptation.

''You trust me to direct your actions?'' Abbot Wilfrid sounded humbly honored by Armand's faith.

''In all things, Father Abbot.''

''Even when the path I choose for you might be contrary to what you would espouse for yourself?''

''Then more than ever, Father Abbot.'' Armand had drunk deeply from the bitter cup of guilt, when his own honorable intentions had come to grief.

Abbot Wilfrid resumed his seat. ''Then have no fear, my son. All will be well.''

The warm reassurance of his tone prompted Armand to lift his downcast gaze and look the older man in the face. The benevolent, paternal smile that greeted him laid all his fears to rest.

The hot, nourishing meal in her belly *should* have restored Dominie's courage and optimism.

Why, the savory steam that rose from her heaping bowl of pottage was almost a meal in itself. Beans and barley, simmered for hours in a covered kettle with onions, garlic and herbs to give it a delicious, hearty flavor. The fact that she could eat without fretting over Harwood's dwindling stocks of food provided a sweet seasoning of its own to the dish.

A succulent joint of fowl followed and new bread, hot and crisp from the abbey ovens. All washed down with a light, clean-tasting ale. Such a feast alone had been almost worth the journey to Breckland.

But now, as Prior Gerard ushered her back into the abbot's sunny parlor, a foul dram of doubt settled in Dominie's belly along with the food, making her gorge rise.

For all Armand Flambard tried to maintain a proper bearing of meek humility, he wore an air of quiet confidence that troubled her. What had passed between him and the abbot while she'd been gone? Nothing to her advantage, she feared as her desperation began to mount once again.

She only wished she could read the abbot's countenance half so well.

He had nothing of the tall, patrician austerity she'd always fancied an abbot should possess. Though the thick fringe of his tonsure was pure white, his features looked younger than those of the prior. They were strong and blunt, more like those of a serf than a nobleman.

Unless she misjudged, the abbot was a man who would do whatever he considered needful to protect that which he held to be his—including a certain lay brother of his order. Taken with Armand's air of serene triumph, it did not bode well for Dominie's mission.

"Come in, child." The abbot beckoned to her. "I trust you ate fully."

"Aye, Father Abbot. Thank you. It was the most filling meal I've had in a great while."

She could not ignore a heaven-sent opportunity to plead her cause. "Unless things change back at Wakeland and Harwood, who knows when I may eat so well again?"

The abbot nodded. "Brother Armand has told me of your plight, child."

Dominie shot Armand a spiteful glare. "I beg your pardon, Father Abbot, but he cannot tell you half our trouble, for I had no chance to tell him more than that."

"All the same, I feel I know enough to render my judgment in the matter."

This was what she had feared.

"But you gave me your word!" Dominie dropped to her knees and clasped her hands together. "Please, Father Abbot, I beg you hear me before you decide!"

"Why, child?" The abbot motioned toward Armand. "Do you believe this man would tell me other than the truth?"

Necessity urged her to say whatever she must to influence the abbot in her favor. But to accuse Armand of deceit, when he was the most hopelessly truthful man she had ever known?

"No, Father," she answered in a grudging grumble. "If Armand Flambard tried to tell a falsehood, I think his tongue would turn to stone."

The abbot's broad mouth twitched at the corner, but he rapidly brought it back under control. "I am told you wish him to accompany you back to your estates to help defend them against the Earl of Anglia…that is to say, the *former* Earl of Anglia."

Dominie could not help thinking that the root of her people's trouble lay in those very words—*former earl*.

In response to some treachery, King Stephen had stripped Eudo St. Maur of his titles and lands. Unfortunately, the too-merciful king had then allowed the scoundrel his freedom. St. Maur had taken his revenge against Stephen by preying on the very people who had once paid him homage and looked to him for protection.

"Aye, Father." Dominie rose from the floor. Going on her knees did not appear to have swayed the abbot. "Without my lord Flambard's help, I fear many will be killed and more will starve after St. Maur ravages our harvest."

"Could you not marshal your own defenses? From what I've seen, you appear a most capable young woman."

Was he in jest? A light of admiration in the abbot's gray eyes declared otherwise.

"I am but a woman, Father Abbot," Dominie protested. "Even if I cared for warcraft, which I do not, many men of Harwood and Wakeland would resent taking battle orders from me. Just as many of the barons refused to follow Maud of Anjou, because she is a woman."

The abbot shrugged. "By all accounts, others would follow the lady into hell itself. And do not forget Stephen's queen, child. Again and again she has saved her lord's bacon from the fire into which he has thrust it."

The monk was going to send her away empty-handed. Dominie struggled to keep from weeping or cursing, neither of which was apt to win his sympathy.

Suddenly Abbot Wilfrid tapped his forefinger against his chin, as if his own words had spawned some new idea in his mind. "I fear our king would have lost his throne long since without the able assistance of his queen. And where would her grace the empress be without the generalship of the Earl of Gloucester?"

"I don't care!" cried Dominie. "I don't care which of them wins anymore, if I ever did. All I want is for them to stop pitting good men from both sides against one another to be killed. Then they'd have a few left to deal with the *bad* men like Eudo St. Maur!"

There. Now she'd done it. The abbot would probably

think her a traitor to King Stephen, and decide that whatever crimes St. Maur committed against Harwood and Wakeland were her just punishment.

"Well said, child."

She must have misheard him. "I beg your pardon, Father?"

"Well said," repeated the abbot. "If I had the ordering of it, I would lock Her Grace and the king in a small room with you. I believe the hostilities between them would be hastily resolved."

The abbot's words warmed Dominie. But she did not need his praise. She needed Armand Flambard. "I fear you give me too much credit, Father."

The abbot smiled. "I fear you give yourself too little, Dominie De Montford. Now, as I was about to say before you interrupted me, both sides in this conflict clearly demonstrate that when a man and woman of great ability work together, much can be accomplished."

A man and a woman. Could he mean…?

"Brother…" The abbot turned to Armand. "I bid you go with this lady and do all you can to aid her against that vile enemy of the church. If you wish to return to Breckland when your task is done to her and your satisfaction, our door will be open to you. But if you should have a change of heart about your vocation, we will understand."

Relief swamped Dominie like a warm, powerful wave. She dropped to her knees again, partly in thanks to the abbot and partly because her legs would no longer support her.

"But, Father," cried Armand, "you said—"

"I said not to fear, that all would be well. I pray that may prove true." The abbot rose from his chair and walked toward Armand. "Do not forget what *you* said, my son—that you trusted me to direct your actions."

Had he said that? Dominie felt a grudging flicker of sympathy for Armand. It sounded as though the wily abbot had caught him in a snare woven from his own ardent ideals.

"Of course, Father Abbot, but—" Armand now sounded as desperate as she had a moment ago.

The abbot interrupted him with a further reminder. "Even when the course I would bid you take might run contrary to your own inclination?"

Armand heaved a vast sigh. "Then most of all, Father," he answered in a tone heavy with resignation.

"Excellent!" Clearly the abbot liked getting his own way. "No religious house should be a refuge from temptation or the perplexities of the world, my son. Otherwise the souls in our care would grow weak and become easy prey for evil."

The prior had been silently watching all that had passed, from his place by the door. Now he nodded, to endorse the abbot's words.

"Though we ask for the obedience of our brethren," continued the abbot, "that is to confound pride and ensure the smooth running of our order. Not to rob them of their God-given choice between right and wrong."

"Yes, Father." Armand could scarcely have sounded more downcast if the abbot had sentenced him to death.

Dominie bridled. Would it be such a great hardship to resume the warrior's life to which he'd been bred? To regain the lands that had belonged to the Flambards since the Conquest? To wed a woman he'd once professed to love?

The way he looked at her now made Dominie wonder if he'd ever truly cared for her. Though she told herself it made no difference anymore, somehow that doubt gave her victory a faintly bitter taste.

Chapter Three

To think all these years he'd imagined himself still half in love with Dominie De Montford. More daft yet that he'd clung to some impossible ideal of her as a sweet, modest maiden. Armand had known hardened mercenaries more sweet and modest!

Not to mention less stubborn.

"I don't understand why we had to set off so soon," he grumbled as they trudged through the rolling Norfolk countryside. "It'll be dark in another few hours. Would it have done so much harm to have bided one night at Breckland, sleeping in a proper bed and setting out at first light with a good breakfast in our bellies?"

Scarcely two hours had passed since their audience with the abbot. Back at the abbey, his brethren would now be sitting down to supper. Doubtless they would note his absence, exchanging eloquent glances, perhaps even whispers, for the rule of silence was relaxed in Breckland's refectory during mealtimes.

Those who'd been working in the fields might tell of seeing him escort a boy into the abbey. Would Brother Ranulf share his intriguing information that the boy had, in truth, been a young woman…and a comely one?

Without a doubt, the wench was comely. In that, at least, Armand's memory had not erred. If anything, she had grown more alluring since he'd last seen her—worse luck! What a shame her disposition had not improved to match her face and figure.

"I told you we need to make haste." Dominie tossed the remark at him over her shoulder. "I want to reach the cover of Thetford Forest by nightfall."

How did she continue to stay ahead of him? Armand wondered.

He was keeping up a good brisk pace and feeling it, too. She hardly appeared to be exerting herself at all, on shorter legs, yet he continued to lag behind her.

It was not a position he enjoyed. His time in the abbey had tempered Armand's pride, not abolished it.

"If it's haste you want, why did you refuse the abbot's offer of a horse? Then we could have waited until morning to set out, yet still arrived long before we will at this rate."

Humph! It was well enough for Abbot Wilfrid to talk about a man and woman working together. The abbot had spent at least twenty years in the cloister. The only women of his close acquaintance were those from the scriptures.

"Travel the road? Are you daft?" Dominie retorted in a tone Armand doubted any biblical female would have used…except, perhaps, Delilah or Jezebel. "It runs through a corner of the territory St. Maur has plundered. If any of his brigands were watching the road, we'd be set upon and robbed of our mount, if not worse. I'd sooner go roundabout, the way I came, if it means we're more likely to arrive all in one piece."

The thought of a three-day journey in her company alarmed him. Not so much the *days,* when they would be traveling with only short pauses to eat. But the *nights*… those were another matter.

Too many nights, during his time in the abbey, he had tossed and turned on his narrow bed in the *dortoir,* battling to keep dreams of Dominie De Montford from plaguing him. How would he manage with her only yards, perhaps feet, away? The soft drone of her dozing breath calling to him?

"You doubt I could protect you if we were attacked?" Armand challenged her, forgetting the vow he'd sworn to forsake violence.

He forced himself to speed his step, so he would not have to stare at the back of her—the slender curves of her legs tantalizingly visible beneath the sweep of her cloak. "Yet you insist I am the only one who can save all of Wakeland and Harwood from the Wolf of the Fens? A contradiction, surely."

"That will be different." Dominie scurried ahead of him again. "You'll have a position to defend, then. One of the castles, a manor house, a barn. And some force of men to command. Out on the open road, beset by three or four, what chance would we have, with neither of us even armed?"

"Unarmed?" he scoffed. "If my staff had wits, it would be sore offended to hear you say so."

Hefting the pole of light, sturdy ash wood, he knocked off her cap, sending Dominie's long braid spilling down her back. He was already too much aware of her feminine charms for his liking. One more in view would make no difference.

But he had not reckoned with her swift reactions. Before the tip of his staff had swung out of reach, she grabbed it and pulled. Armand stumbled and barely escaped sprawling on the springy heath.

With her legs planted wide and her hands on her hips, Dominie laughed. "Your staff may have more wit than you do, Armand Flambard. Beware how you assail me, after this. I give you fair warning, I never let an affront to me or mine go unavenged."

Assail her? Affront avenged? If she had seized his staff and rammed the butt end of it hard into his gut, it could not have staggered Armand more than her words. Only hours out of the abbey, and already he was forgetting his vow, slipping back with dangerous ease into the character of a warrior.

With the months until harvest stretching before him, would he be able to resist the temptation to reclaim his old life? And an old love, the hope of which had perished by his sword?

The man looked as if he had taken a mortal blow.

"Is aught the matter, Armand? Are you ill?" Could that be the reason he'd taken refuge at Breckland? It would explain what a born warrior was doing in the cloister. And that queer remark about part of him having been killed at Lincoln.

A strange emptiness gaped in the pit Dominie's stomach, as though she had not eaten that filling meal back at the abbey. Not because Armand Flambard's well-being mattered to her, she insisted to herself, the way he'd pretended hers mattered to him. But for the practical reason that an ailing champion would be of less use to her people.

"Ill? No." Though his tone sounded certain, the breath behind Armand's voice seemed a trifle labored. "When I work at the abbey, I work hard, but many hours are spent in the stillness of prayer, which does nothing to strengthen the body. I'm not used to long walks like this anymore."

From the look on his face, Dominie might have thought

he was confessing a mortal sin. He had always held everyone to an impossibly high standard, she recalled from their younger years. No one more than himself. Admitting even so minor a weakness would vex him.

"It isn't much farther." She pointed ahead. "Over that rise we'll come to a brook. Once we ford it, we'll be able to see the edge of the forest. We'll have to pick our way more slowly through the underbrush, but it will be worth the delay to have cover."

"Very well, Mistress Commander." Armand squared his broad shoulders and drew a deep breath. "Lead on, then."

Dominie surged up on the tips of her toes. Shading her eyes against the sun, she peered around them in every direction, but saw nothing more threatening than a man far off to the east, who looked to be digging peat.

Caution appeased, she began to walk again, but slowed her pace, falling into step with Armand.

"I cannot understand why you refused to help us until Abbot Wilfrid insisted." Something told her she should not ask, but the question itched in her mind for an answer. "Are you so bitter because the king gave your lands to my father? You must have known it would come to that when you chose as you did. Would you rather have seen Harwood go to a stranger?"

She steeled herself for a sharp retort, but none came.

Instead, Armand heaved a sigh so deep, it seemed to well up from the soles of his feet. "If matters had fallen out differently, there was no one to whom I'd rather have ceded Harwood than the De Montfords. Our families had been allies since they first came to this country, and before that in Normandy. We'd always watched each other's backs, exchanged sons for fostering, stood shoulder to shoulder against any trouble."

Had he forgotten to mention the ties of marriage between earlier generations of their families? Or had he omitted it on purpose? Armand had turned his back on that and on everything else he'd mentioned, for the sake of a foolish oath all the nobles had been pressured to take, and most had been shrewd enough to break.

With difficulty, Dominie swallowed the anger that always choked her when she thought about Armand's betrayal. Abbot Wilfrid had said they must work together for the good of their people.

"This is a chance for the Flambards and the De Montfords to stand shoulder to shoulder again," she reminded him…and herself. "Heaven knows, our people have never faced worse trouble than the Wolf of the Fens."

"It won't be easy." Armand shook his head as he stared off into the distance. "Even if we manage to hold off St. Maur until the harvest is gathered, what makes you think his brigands won't come back again next year and the next, more savage than ever for having been denied?"

Had he forgotten?

"What if they do?" Dominie shrugged. "You'll be there to meet them, again, all the stronger for having another full year to prepare. Besides, the king is trying to curb the demon he unleashed upon us—building castles to hem St. Maur in, though not fast enough to be of any avail this year."

She glanced sidelong at Armand. The furrows on his brow cast a shadow of doubt over his face. A doubt she felt compelled to banish…for her own peace of mind as much as his.

"St. Maur is no different from any other bully." Except in his power and viciousness. "Once we bloody his nose he'll likely go in search of weaker prey, leaving our lands in peace."

"I hope he does." Armand sounded as doubtful as he still looked. "For all your sakes. I will do my best to train someone to take my place, but I serve you notice that the abbot's order binds me only until your harvest is safely in. After that I must return to Breckland."

"You'll what? To Breck—" Dominie sputtered. "See here, I thought we'd struck a bargain, Armand Flambard!"

Her *champion* shook his head. "You made an offer…while you had me pinned to that pillar. I never accepted it. I come with you now by the will of the abbot, not by my own. And then only until after harvest tide."

Why did his words provoke her so? Dominie asked herself. Marriage to Armand Flambard and the return of his lands was not something she'd wanted. It was a necessary sacrifice she'd been prepared to make in order to gain his help against St. Maur. She should be delighted to secure his services without having to surrender her lands and her hand.

The quivering tightness inside her did not feel much like delight. Perhaps it was only her worry about what would happen to her family and estates once Armand had abandoned them…again.

"Why would you want me for a husband?" Armand asked. "After how matters fell out between us in the past?"

Beneath his brusque tone, Dominie fancied she heard a muted whisper of regret. She would let him taste regret!

Ever since she'd first spoken to him at the abbey—and before that, when she'd been told he might still be alive—she had stifled her anger over what he'd done five years ago. For the sake of her people and their future.

Now, no show of outrage would release him from Abbot Wilfrid's command. No feigned good cheer would inspire him to stay beyond this one season.

Dominie swung about, planting herself in Armand's path. Though she had to stare up at him, she refused to give a hint that he intimidated her. "Don't flatter yourself that I'm some lovesick little fool, still swooning over a man who forsook me, Flambard!"

She stabbed her forefinger into his chest. Right where his heart would be...if he had one. "The only reasons I would wed you are practical ones. If you had no skill as a warrior and a leader, I'd want nothing more to do with you."

"So I thought." He gazed down at her, out of deep-set eyes so blue they might have been plucked from the spring sky.

That gaze could stir something dangerous in her, if she were daft enough to let it.

"Is *love* another of those fine ideals of yours?" She drenched the word in contempt. "Do you think it necessary for a man and woman to *love* one another in order to wed?"

Armand parted his lips to speak.

A quiver of fear ran through Dominie, that he might say something to convince her of a falsehood she could not afford to believe.

"Rot!" she cried, to answer her own question and to forestall him. "Marriage is a practical matter, too vital to taint with some foolish fancy."

Slowly, he raised a hand to her face. Dominie flinched as if she thought he meant to strike her. In truth, she had no fear of that. This man could do her more harm with tenderness than with temper.

"No, Dominie." His tongue fairly caressed her name as he spoke it. Though Armand did not touch her, neither did he let his hand fall. "Marriage is too vital an estate not to hallow with a higher purpose."

The rueful murmur of his words struck her harder than any blow Armand could have dealt her with his hand. It made her yearn for her old faith and innocence, now lost beyond retrieving. It made her want to believe she could find the answers to her heart's questions and the balm for her heart's hurts in his arms.

Dangerous folly—all of it.

"Higher purpose?" She tried to laugh, but stopped for fear she would weep instead. "Spoken like a man who hides from the world in an abbey!"

Having spewed out a little of the venom inside her, Dominie spun away from Armand and stalked the last few yards to the crest of a gentle rise. She refused to let him guess how much his desertion had hurt her. Nor would she admit to herself that he had not lost the power to hurt her again…worse than ever.

Was that all he'd been doing during his time at Breckland? Hiding from the world? Armand could hardly bear to ask himself that question, let alone give an honest answer.

He had been seeking refuge from a world that now ran contrary to every precept he'd been taught. A world where honor was no better than folly and no man's word could be trusted. A world where a man who strove to do right could suddenly find himself guilty of great wrong.

It grieved him to discover that the woman whose virtue he'd so long exalted had become so much a creature of that world.

"Is there no ideal that matters to you?" he bellowed after her.

"Not one!" Dominie flung the defiant retort at his feet.

"To sustain me and mine, I will do whatever I must, and toss scruples to the wind. What purpose do they serve, but to make a body feel needlessly guilty for doing what it must?"

A small, traitorous part of him envied her. If nothing else, she probably slept a good deal better at night than he did. Armand forced his heavy feet the rest of the way up the gentle incline. At the base of a long, easy slope on the other side lay the brook of which Dominie had told him.

Armand judged it no more than five yards wide at its narrowest stretch. Neither did the water look too deep, for three large rocks poked their tops above the swift, tumbling current. Beyond and to the south, Armand could see the green smudge of Thetford Forest against the darkening sky. It beckoned him with the promise of rest and concealment.

Dominie strode ahead of him to the bank of the brook. There she dropped to the ground and pried off her short leather boots. Then, much to his shock, she began to peel off her woolen hose.

"What are you doing?" He tried not to stare at the fair, willowy length of bare leg splayed on the lush cushion of spring grass.

When she glanced up at him, Armand spied a glitter of golden devilment in her eyes. She knew his weakness and she would not hesitate to use it against him, whether for a little vindictive amusement or for some more urgent purpose.

With a provocative show of ease, she began to roll down the other leg of her hose. "I am doing the same thing I did when I forded this brook on my way *to* Breckland. Taking off my clothes so they will not get wet when I cross."

While he was opening and shutting his mouth like a freshly netted herring, Dominie slid her gaze from his sandal-clad feet to the neck of his dark robe. ''I suggest you do the same.''

''I'll do no such thing!'' Armand wanted to shake her for taunting him with such a brazen suggestion, but he did not trust his hands upon any part of her. ''It would be ungallant.''

''You virtuous blockhead!'' Dominie balled up the length of hose and pelted him with it. ''I wonder how you survived in the world so many years?''

The ball of green wool hit Armand square on the nose. Though it was too soft to do him any harm, the tantalizing intimate scent of her wafted into his nostrils, which flared to catch it.

Dominie leaped to her feet, her tunic falling less than halfway down her thighs.

She pointed to the brook. ''This is the narrowest spot for miles and the only way across is to wade. The water was colder than a miser's charity when I went through this morning. I doubt it has warmed much since.''

Given the time of year, Armand could not gainsay her.

Dominie was not done with him, however. ''If we take off our clothes and carry them above our heads, we will be cold when we reach the far bank. But dry clothes and a little more walking will soon warm us again.''

''True enough, but—''

''If we keep our clothes on while we wade the brook, we will reach the other side cold *and* sodden. And we would never have a chance to dry out before night falls.''

Why, the lass could argue circles around St. Augustine!

''No.'' Armand clung to his principles. ''It would not be right.''

Dominie swiped her hose from the ground at his feet.

"I know how men are made, if that is what troubles your modesty. You have my word, I will be too much occupied with getting to the other side of the brook before I freeze to spare a glance at your fine form."

Armand hesitated. He had often heard cold water extinguished lust. Somehow, he doubted there was enough in the whole German Sea to quell his.

"You're asking me to trust the word of a De Montford?" It was an unworthy thing to say. Armand repented it the instant the words left his mouth, but he could not recall them.

Dominie's venomous glare flayed him. "If the folk of Harwood and Wakeland did not need you so sorely, I would push you into that brook, robe and all."

It was not only having her see him naked, and knowing beyond doubt the forbidden desires she roused in him. After all, she *might* honor her promise not to glance his way. Armand didn't dare make such a pledge to her, for he know he could never keep it.

"I can walk across on the stepping-stones." He struggled to subdue a foolish sense of desperation that swelled within him.

"Those are not stepping-stones." Dominie's vibrant features twisted into an expression of disbelief, sharpened with contempt. "They are chance-strewn rocks. From the bank to the first rock, you might step safely, and from the last to the far bank is nothing. But from either of those to the taller rock in the middle, even your shanks are not long enough to reach."

"I'll jump."

"You'll fall."

"I'm nimble."

"You're an ass."

Nothing could have stopped Armand Flambard then, for

he'd been challenged. "Then you shall hear me bray in triumph when I reach the other side."

Dominie said nothing more, only shook her head and heaved an exasperated sigh that proclaimed, "Fool!" as plainly as if she had bellowed it at the top of her lungs.

Armand knelt and untied his sandals. Then he stood up and pitched them across to the other side. His bare feet would grip the rock better. Next, he hefted his staff like a spear and threw it across the brook, too. He would need both hands free. Finally, he kilted up the lower part of his habit and let it fall over his rope belt, leaving his legs bare to the knee. He could not afford to trip on the hem of his robe, or have the length of his stride checked.

He did not dare try to toss his cloak over the brook in case it fell short. Pride would not permit him to ask Dominie's help in ferrying it across.

She made a point of ignoring him as she untied her own cloak and pulled off her tunic. Once she'd wriggled out of the light linen smock beneath, she rolled her garments into a compact parcel.

Wrenching his rebellious gaze away, Armand forced himself to concentrate on getting to the other side of the brook, fully clothed.

As Dominie had predicted, he reached the first rock with one long step. Finding the surface more slippery than he'd expected, Armand dropped to a crouch and steadied himself with his hands.

Behind him, he heard the sharp intake of Dominie's breath as she stepped into the cold water.

He made a mighty leap to the second rock and gained it, though his right foot slipped underwater for a moment. A great shudder ran through him at the numbing cold.

Beside him, he heard Dominie splashing as she waded across.

The third rock was not so far a jump as the last one, but its surface looked more uneven. Too late to turn back now. Armand clenched his teeth and lunged. He landed at an awkward angle, which his leg protested in pain.

What did that matter, though? He had made it. The far bank was no more than a step away.

As Armand took that final step, Dominie surged out of the water beside him. Her flesh had a bluish cast and was tight with cold. She held the bundle of clothing above her head, like some pagan priestess bearing an offering.

Lust caught Armand by the throat.

His foot fell too close to the edge of the shore. The earth beneath it crumbled under his weight, and he could not keep his balance.

He felt himself fall sideways. Just before he hit the unforgiving water, Dominie spun around and threw herself toward him.

But it was too late.

Chapter Four

For an instant that could have been no more than one hundredth part of a heartbeat, Armand's gaze sought Dominie's and locked, as she scrambled to reach him. Before she could grasp any part of him, he tumbled into the water, his arms flailing.

The brook was not very deep at that spot. But with Armand's sprawling fall and the weight of his sodden robes, he might not be able to gain his feet before the current dragged him deeper.

Time seemed to slow to the deliberate rhythm of the land itself, while thoughts rushed through Dominie's mind with the swiftness of the flowing brook.

She had known something like this would happen. She'd told Armand the only sure way across was to wade. Curse him and his monkish modesty for not heeding her! It would serve him right if he drowned or froze.

But she could not let that happen. Her people needed him too much. Yet, when her body rebelled against plunging back into the remorseless cold of the water, it was not only the thought of her vassals and Eudo St. Maur that compelled her.

Armand Flambard had once turned his back on her. He

might no longer be the man she'd once cared for. Perhaps he never had been as she remembered him. But she would never forget the grief that had gnawed at her when she'd believed him lost to her forever. She could not bear to lose him again, so soon. Not when she had the power to prevent it.

Besides, her body was numb already, so what would it matter?

Dominie discovered the answer, to her dismay, when she threw herself into the water after Armand. On her previous pass through the brook, at least her shoulders, neck and head had stayed dry. This time, they were the first to hit the water.

A shudder ran through her naked body. How did the poor fish stand it? If she'd been one, she would have wriggled out onto the warm riverbank, even at the risk of being gutted and fried.

Pulling herself out of her shallow dive, Dominie struggled to plant her feet firmly beneath her as she reached for Armand.

He caught her first. One large hand swiped against her breast, then grasped onto her upper arm.

It did not warm her. Dominie doubted anything short of hellfire could have. But for an instant, his touch made her forget the remorseless cold.

Clutching his arm with both hands, she dug her feet into the streambed and hauled Armand toward the bank with greater force than she'd believed she could muster. He shifted more readily than she'd expected, sending her hurtling backward.

Armand landed on top of her, pressing Dominie's head under the water. Like a wild thing, she battled to push him away. Battled to reach the surface so she could draw air. If the pair of them drowned in four feet of water, she would haunt his sorry soul in hell for all eternity!

Through all this, Armand had not loosened his grip on her arm. Now he took hold of the other one, though Dominie tried to squirm away. She lashed out with her knees, driving them into any part of his body she could reach. Panic surged through her with every lurching beat of her heart.

Just when every particle of flesh in her body screamed for sweet air, Armand rolled onto his back, thrusting her above the water.

Dominie choked and coughed, retched and gasped for breath. She heard Armand doing the same. She felt his broad chest quake beneath her.

As she managed to take in more air, her mind began to clear. By chance or by grace, she and Armand had reached the bank of the stream. Now he lay with his shoulders barely clearing the water, and she perched on top of him, stark naked.

"Come," she croaked, struggling onto the bank. "We'll freeze if we don't get moving."

Reaching back, she tugged on his arm. Without the water's buoyancy to help her, she would never be able to shift his weight if he could not.

"Move, Armand!"

He was still coughing hard and struggling to catch his breath. But the urgency of her tone and touch seemed to reach him. With obvious effort he rolled onto his side, then collapsed on his belly. Slowly, he began to drag himself out of the brook's icy grip.

Hovering over him, Dominie locked her hands under his arm. Each time he lurched forward, she pulled with all her might. Even if it only gained him a farther inch or two beyond what he could reach under his own power, the effort was worthwhile. By the time he had struggled completely free of the water, with her awkward aid, Dominie's limbs felt less like blocks of wet wood and more like they belonged to her body.

She crumpled onto the grass beside him, her chest heaving. If the sun had been warmer, and the daylight not waning, she would have been content to lie there until her strength returned. Instead, chattering teeth and puckered gooseflesh drove her to keep moving.

Her bundle of clothes lay just where she had dropped it—on dry ground, thank heaven. Dominie wriggled back into the linen smock, savoring its slight warmth. She had begun to fumble with her hose when she remembered Armand.

She turned to find him sprawled on the grass, coughing and trembling. In that sodden robe, the man was little better off than if she'd left him in the water. Dominie clenched her teeth to keep them from clacking together, and to bite back a curse at Armand for not minding her warning in the first place.

Perhaps she deserved a measure of blame, too, for not *making* him heed her. The notion struck Dominie a backhand blow, but she could not dismiss it. If she had persuaded him with gentle reason, instead of antagonizing him with orders and childish taunts, they would not be in this dangerous pass.

Armand had not fully understood the risk. She had.

For that reason, she should have used whatever means necessary to convince him, even at the expense of her pride and spite. Perhaps she was not as practical a woman as she claimed to be.

Dominie's conscience tormented her with more such thoughts as she approached Armand and began to tug up the hem of his robe.

He made an effort to bat her hand away. "What-t-t are you about now?"

With some effort, Dominie swallowed the scornful retort that rose to her lips. She forced a soft, coaxing note into her voice, like the one she sometimes used with her mother or her younger brother when persuading them to do something disagreeable for their own good.

"Come, now. You cannot stay in these wet clothes, or you'll perish. Bestir yourself to help me get you out of them, like a sensible fellow."

Expecting him to protest further about modesty, she marshaled her appeal.

It rocked her back on her haunches when he nodded and struggled to his knees. "This is a j-j-just penalty for my error. I sh-sh-should have listened to you."

Dominie took less satisfaction than she expected when she said, "Aye, so you should. But what's done is done, and all water under the bridge, as they say."

Water under the bridge? Dominie's conscience asked in a mocking whisper. Like his decision to support Empress Maud and everything that had followed? Armand could no more go back and change that than he could reverse his ill-fated choice to cross the brook by way of the rocks.

He collapsed onto his backside and began to fumble with the knotted length of rope that served as his belt. "At the v-v-very least, I c-c-could have let you c-c-carry my cloak across. Then it would have b-b-been dry to wrap around me."

"You might have thought of that if I had not taunted you." Dominie reached toward the stubborn wet knot that threatened to defeat his floundering fingers. "Here, let me help."

Chastened as Armand had sounded, it still surprised

Dominie when he let his hands fall away so she could work at the knot. A chill of fear settled in her belly as each precious moment of daylight slipped away. Unlike the numbing cold of the water that had leached her energy, this nipped her to action, propelling her clumsy fingers. At last the slick, tight twist of rope yielded to her persistent struggle.

As she helped Armand lift the heavy, sodden robe over his head, he stared up at her with a look of mingled gratitude and bewilderment that tugged at Dominie's heart. "You saved my life."

A tight and twisted knot inside of her began to work loose, as well.

Had the swift-flowing water scoured away the ill will between them? Armand wondered as he listened to the soft, cajoling murmur of Dominie's voice, and surrendered to her gentle but capable touch. Or had the cold purged his cursed pride?

He *had* been an ass to defy her, forging ahead with so little thought to the consequences. He'd deserved his dunking. What he had not deserved was Dominie diving in to his rescue when she must have been chilled to the bone from her first pass through the brook.

She looked taken aback by his acknowledgment of what she'd done. "I couldn't let you drown, now, could I?" Avoiding his gaze, she shook her head over the drenched state of his undergown. "Not after all I've been through to fetch you this far. A cold corpse makes a poor champion."

Of course, she had only rescued him for the sake of Harwood and Wakeland. Just as she had made the hungry, dangerous trek to the abbey. Just as she had offered him her hand and his old lands when she'd rather have counted him dead and forgotten. He'd be a fool to hope for any other reason.

With Dominie's help, he cast off his undergown. In some queer fashion, it felt as though he was shedding his identity as a Benedictine lay brother along with it. When he finally sat naked on the grass, with his knees tucked up to preserve a crumb of modesty, Dominie fetched her hose and began to rub the rough wool over his back and shoulders.

"In truth, I suppose we saved each other." Her voice sounded as brisk and practical as her actions, chafing away the foolish melancholy that had begun to settle over him. "I thought I was done for a minute, there. I hope I didn't hurt you when I tried to kick my way free."

Those cold, frantic moments had already blurred in his memory, but Armand vaguely recalled Dominie's savage struggle when he had tried to shift her up from beneath him. He'd wanted to assure her that he was trying to aid her. Part of him had been angry that she'd shown so little trust in him.

"This should help to warm you," she said. "Then, I hope you can squeeze into my tunic. It may not cover much of you, but at least it's dry."

"I can't take your tunic!" He couldn't stand to be any deeper in debt to her. "It's my own fault my clothes are too wet to wear. You should not suffer for my mistake, after you warned me."

She dealt him a light cuff on the head with the woolen hose. "Don't talk daft! I have my smock and these to cover my legs. Boots for my feet and a cloak to wrap around me. I can spare the tunic to keep you from freezing. You won't be of any use that way."

"I reckon not." Armand pulled a wry face.

In a way, the confirmation that Dominie was only protecting his usefulness made her offer of the tunic easier to accept. In another way, one Armand loathed to admit, the knowledge rankled.

Once Dominie had rubbed his back, shoulders and arms until they tingled, she let the hose slide down his chest, onto his lap. "You can finish the rest yourself."

Turning her back on him, she sifted through his mound of wet clothes, wringing each garment with ruthless force for every drop of water it would yield.

The setting sun shot its rays through the bleached linen of her smock, outlining the willowy curves of her body. Armand knew he should look the other way, as she'd had the courtesy to do for him.

His eyes obeyed, but with great reluctance.

When she had throttled as much moisture from his clothes as she could, Dominie tossed her tunic, her cap and his sandals toward Armand. Then she dropped to the grass and began to pull on her hose.

"Once we're dressed, we must make haste for the woods." She glanced up at the sky. "I fear it will be a clear night, like last, and cold."

Armand could not gainsay her. He shivered with a foretaste of the night's chill. The tunic that had hung so loose on Dominie's slender frame clung to him like the skin of a molting snake, barely covering his backside.

He thrust his feet into the sandals and jammed the cap over his wet hair.

"Let us be on our way then." He tossed the other shank of her hose toward Dominie. "The walk may warm us a little."

As she glanced up at him, Dominie parted her lips to speak. Instead of words, a wild hoot of laughter burst out of her.

An angry blush prickled up Armand's neck to suffuse

his face. "Oh, give over, wench! It was you who bade me put this thing on, remember? Did you do it just to make a fool of me?"

Dominie shook her head vigorously and tried to answer. But she could only laugh harder, in great, frenzied heaves.

Though Armand had never been much given to mirth, least of all at his own expense, the sound of her laughter reached deep inside of him…and tickled.

He tried to scowl, but the corners of his mouth began to dance and a grudging chuckle sputtered out of him. The harder he fought to contain it, the more boisterous it grew, until he had to gasp for air, as though he were drowning all over again.

In a good way this time.

When Dominie appeared to be mastering her runaway mirth, some mad impulse made Armand cut a little caper to set her howling afresh.

"Enough!" she gasped at last. "If there is anyone within earshot who wishes us harm, we are done for."

Her warning sobered Armand. But he could not bring himself to repent their outlandish fit of laughter. It had softened something hard and unyielding within him.

"Never fear." He gave a final chuckle. "One look at me and our enemies would fall down laughing. Then you could disarm them with ease."

While Dominie pulled on her hose and boots, he approached her and offered his hand to help her up from the ground. A fleeting shadow of suspicion crossed her face. Armand feared she might refuse.

Before he could withdraw the offer, however, she grasped his hand and hoisted herself to her feet. "Lend me your staff, will you?"

"Aye." Armand picked it up and held it out to her. "What for?"

"Watch and see."

She took the slender pole and stretched his damp garments over it. Then she picked up one end, bidding him to heft the other. "This way neither of us will have to tote a wet bundle, and the clothes can start to dry while we walk."

"Clever." Armand nodded in approval. "Were you always so resourceful, lass?"

It was not how he'd remembered her.

Had the innocent, virtuous paragon he'd held in honor all these years ever existed? Armand wondered. Or had he conjured her up out of his own longing and remorse?

Dominie started walking toward the woods. "For as long as I can remember, I've had a practical bent." She shrugged. "And responsibility breeds enterprise."

Armand hastened to match his stride with hers, and to hoist his staff high enough that none of the garments dragged along the ground.

"It has been hard for you, hasn't it?" He fought a compulsion to add, "Since Lincoln?" Instead, he asked, "Even before this threat from St. Maur?"

A moment of pensive silence followed, when the only sounds he heard were the muted swish of their feet through the grass and the gurgle of the brook behind them.

"What do you suppose?" She tried to sound indifferent, but Armand could not mistake a tightness in her voice, bitter, yet plaintive. "A woman of my years in charge of two large estates? From the first, my mother relied on me."

Armand nodded, though, in truth, it surprised him to discover that Blanchefleur De Montford was still alive. He remembered her as a pious, fretful creature of faded beauty. The kind of woman his imaginary Dominie might have become after years of breeding and bearing, with only three surviving children to show for it.

"Sometimes," said the real Dominie with a sigh, "I find it hard to believe she's my mother, we are so little alike."

"You are your father's daughter," Armand agreed, as a vivid image of Baldwin De Montford rose in his mind, blessedly untainted by bitterness or remorse. "I have no doubt you rose to the challenge."

From his earliest memory, his foster father's shock of red hair and crackling voice had reminded Armand of a firebrand. Lord Baldwin had possessed a temperament to match—one that could warm and light up the lives of all around him. Or flair and scorch anyone within range. Over the years, Armand had felt both the warmth of Baldwin's pleasure and the heat of his wrath.

Amidst the madness of battle, with one senseless stroke of his sword, Armand Flambard had extinguished that bright flame. And plunged his own soul into a darkness he could never escape.

Or could he?

Perhaps, without realizing it, Dominie had offered him a chance to earn the absolution that had eluded him ever since the battle of Lincoln.

A cool breeze played over Armand's bare legs with an ominous whisper.

A chance for absolution? He shivered and the fine hairs on his legs bristled. Aye, he might get one, if he and Dominie did not freeze to death before morning.

The lengthening shadows of the trees stretched out like cool fingers to wrap around Dominie and Armand as they reached the eaves of Thetford Forest. There had been frost last night, and the coming one boded no better.

Dominie had endured it, but then she had been warmed from a day's brisk walking, not chilled to the bone from two sojourns in the brook. Besides, she had been well-clothed for sleeping out-of-doors. Tonight there would be two of them sharing garments that had barely sustained one.

Vexation with Armand rose in the back of her throat like bile, but Dominie swallowed it. She must be practical. Railing at him might ease her wrought-up feelings a little, but it would not keep the two of them warm until morning.

To accomplish that, she could think of only one plan. And she would need his cooperation to bring it about. Considering the man's exasperating high principles, he would probably deem it a choice between freezing on earth or burning in hell for eternity.

She glanced up at the trees, trying to get her bearings. "I hope I can find the burrow I made for myself last night. Let us pray no animals have disturbed it since then."

"Burrow?" Armand sounded a little winded from their walk.

Dominie could hardly fault him. Her arms ached from bearing half the weight of his waterlogged garments. But she forgot her discomfort as soon as she spied a pair of towering oaks.

"This way." She nodded toward the tall trees and began to pick her way through the underbrush toward them. "I dug out a little more earth to deepen a hollow near the base of one of those oaks. Then I lined it with moss and a layer of dry leaves to make myself a snug sleeping place."

"No wonder you smell like the forest," murmured Armand, more to himself than to her, or so it sounded.

"Smell like what?" Glancing back over her shoulder, Dominie fixed him with a glare.

"Your…clothes," he sputtered. "They smell like…the forest. Like earth, and bark, and cedar."

"If it's not to your liking, I can always take back my tunic," she snapped, anticipating the squabble they would have when she told Armand he would have to share the burrow with her tonight.

"Did I say it was not to my liking?"

His reply flustered Dominie. She pretended not to heed it. "I vow, this pole grows heavier with every step we take. Let's set it down and find some stout tree limbs to hang your clothes from."

"You'll get no protest from me." Armand sounded almost cheerful, as he let his end of the staff drop.

Both his action and tone caught Dominie off balance. Staggering under the full weight of his wet garments, she lurched backward. She might have fallen, if Armand had not swooped forward to catch her in his arms.

"I'm sorry!" he cried.

Sorry for tripping her up? Dominie wondered. Or for laying hands upon her to break her fall?

Some streak of foolish weakness made her linger in his embrace, so strong, safe and snug. That same part of her had yearned to cast all the burdens of Harwood and Wakeland upon his stout shoulders, but she must resist the urge. All too soon he would be gone again, leaving her to resume her obligations.

And, if she was not careful, to nurse a heart broken once more.

"We mustn't waste time." She wrenched herself out of his arms and rose to stand on her own two feet.

As she must continue to do.

She plucked Armand's undergown from the bed of moss and fern onto which his clothes had dropped. Spying a low-slung branch on a nearby beech tree, she hurried over to hang the garment from it. The tight buds of spring foliage at the tips of the branches were beginning to unfurl. Soon Thetford Forest would be cloaked in fresh greenery.

From up in the higher boughs of the tree, a large crow peered down at Dominie and gave a rasping caw of disapproval. She glared back at the bird.

Behind her, she heard the rustle of Armand's footsteps through the bracken, as he sought a likely branch on which to hang his robe or his cloak.

She must not delay, Dominie warned herself. The day was not getting any longer or any warmer.

Drawing a deep breath, she thrust her shoulders back and her chin out. Then she spun around and marched over to confront Armand. "Let's get busy, shall we?"

He glanced down at her as he reached to hook his cloak over the stub of a broken elm branch. One corner of his mouth lifted. "I thought we were."

She resisted his disarming hint of a grin. A scowl or a shocked glare would soon replace it, once he found out what the night held in store for him.

"There's still much to do." She nodded toward the two lofty oaks, several yards distant. "Enlarge the hollow. Gather more moss and cedar boughs."

"Very well." Armand stooped to retrieve his staff. "Show me the spot. I can dig while you gather."

"Do you understand what I'm telling you?" Dominie braced for the fight.

It was one thing to throw a man of Armand's size off balance and hold him against his will for a moment or two, as she had done back at the abbey. She could not pin him to the ground for an entire night. And she did not want to dwell on the thought of trying.

"If we are to keep from freezing tonight, you and I will have to lie down in that burrow…together. Then cover ourselves with my cloak and a blanket of cedar boughs."

Armand's only reply was a wordless shrug.

"Did you hit your head on a rock when you fell into the brook?" Dominie demanded. "Or did your ears get so full of water that you cannot hear properly?"

"Neither." He pulled off the cap she'd lent him and plowed his fingers through his damp hair. "I heard you well enough, and understood your words. Let us set to work, then, while we still have light."

Without a murmur? What was he playing at? "Do you not think it ungallant? Immodest? Sinful?"

Armand gave a rueful chuckle that trailed off into an even more rueful sigh. "If I had not squandered such words back at the brook, we might have a choice in the matter now. There will be nothing sinful in our sleeping close, provided I take no liberties with you. And you have my word, I will not."

"We dare not draw attention to ourselves by lighting a fire." Dominie countered a suggestion Armand hadn't even made.

He headed in the direction of the oak trees. "Did *your* ears take on water?" he asked as he brushed past her. "Or did I not make myself clear? I said yes, Dominie! I wish there were some other way, but since there is not, even I can bow to necessity in a pinch."

Before she could master her tongue to reply, he spun about to face her. "You sounded as though you were spoiling for a quarrel. I'm sorry to disappoint you, but I have digging to do before night falls."

"I was not spoiling for a quarrel!" Dominie stalked off through the underbrush in search of more moss. "I was surprised to find you showing a crumb of sense, that's all.''

Was that all? she asked herself, not certain she would like the answer. Or had she wanted to fortify her defenses by quarreling with Armand before spending the night in the perilous warmth of his arms?

Chapter Five

He'd sworn he would take no liberties with Dominie tonight, and he would not.

Saints help him, though. For he would have to wrestle every minute with temptation!

A drop of moisture trickled down the back of Armand's neck as he worked to dig away more earth from the base of the towering oak, enlarging the hollow in which he and Dominie would soon lie down together. He could not be certain whether it was water dripping from his damp hair, or a bead of sweat brought on by his exertions...and his sinful thoughts.

If this was a true foretaste of the heat he would feel tonight, when Dominie nestled in his arms for hour after aching hour, then there was scant danger of them freezing—no matter how thick the frost!

"Watch out." Dominie stooped beside him to line the newly dug edges of the shallow hole with strips of moss.

Was he simply bowing to necessity? Armand wondered as he watched her deft, purposeful movements and admired the way wisps of her damp hair curled into a soft, coppery-gold halo. Or was he seizing on a handy excuse to hold her in his arms, as he'd wanted to do from the moment he set eyes on her again?

Watch out! Dominie's offhand words of warning echoed in his thoughts. He would have to take care that the forced intimacy of the coming night did not seduce him to forget who he was, what he'd done and what he must do to atone.

"Should I widen it more?" he asked. "There's not much room on either side before we run into those big roots."

Dominie shrugged as she patted down the last patch of moss. "We'll have to huddle close for warmth, anyway. But you may need to make it longer. Shall we try it out while we still have some light?"

"I suppose we could." Armand forced the words out of a mouth gone dry.

"Right, then." Dominie slapped her hands together to dislodge some of the dirt that clung to them. "You first, on your back. I'll fit myself around you."

"Do you really think anyone would notice if we made a fire?" he asked, suddenly overcome with reluctance.

"Perhaps not," replied Dominie, "but I don't want to risk it, all the same. Besides, I didn't bring a tinderbox."

She gestured toward the moss-lined hollow with an open palm, the way a servant might usher a guest into his master's great hall. "Well, go on. Even if you don't need to do any more digging, we'll have to cut cedar branches before night falls."

"Very well, then." Armand pushed past his hesitation.

Gripping the hem of the tunic so it wouldn't ride up over his loins, he settled himself into their burrow. The cushion of moss felt cool, but soft beneath him. As the night wore on, it would provide a valuable buffer between their bodies and the cold earth. He would never have thought of it.

With her lower lip thrust out and her brow puckered, Dominie slid her gaze over him from head to heels, kindling a muted heat in his flesh as it went.

At last she nodded. "It looks like we should fit."

As she settled herself beside him, Armand sensed the defensive tightness in her body. But he could also feel her welcome warmth. When, after a brief, tantalizing moment of contact, she scrambled up again, it was all he could do to keep from gathering her back into his arms.

"It will do in a pinch," she said. "Come, the cedar's over this way."

Armand forced himself to get up and follow her, as reluctantly as he'd sometimes risen from a warm bed for the nocturn Mass in winter. Could it be just last night he'd gone to sleep in the cosy *dortoir* at Breckland, certain he would never set eyes on Dominie De Montford again?

Though part of him would give anything to turn back time and revert to the predictable tranquility of Breckland, a defiant spark rallied to the challenge she represented.

By the time he reached the small clump of cedar, she had broken off several boughs with their soft needles and sharp, spicy aroma. Armand set to work beside her, taking care that his eyes should not stray too often in her direction.

"That should be plenty," said Dominie, after they had toiled in silence for a short while. "We only want to keep warm, not stifle ourselves."

She gathered up an armful of boughs from the ground, leaving the rest for Armand to collect. "Do you want to eat before we bed down? Prior Gerard gave me bread, cheese and dried meat."

"I can wait until morning to break my fast." Armand followed her back to the oak trees, the pungent tang of cedar tickling his nose. "It is well Prior Gerard trusted *you* with our provisions. If I had been carrying the food it would all be cold soup by now."

He made a face just thinking of the unappetizing mess.

If Dominie felt any temptation to gloat, she resisted. "I had a better meal at Breckland than I've eaten in a great while. I need nothing more until tomorrow, either."

"Then, I suppose, there's nothing to do but—"

Dominie interrupted him. "There is *one* thing, unless you fancy holding it all night."

"Practical, as always," muttered Armand, caught between exasperation and admiration.

He dropped his armful of cedar boughs beside their sleeping hollow, then strode in the opposite direction from Dominie to a clump of tall bushes, where he relieved himself.

By the time he started back, full darkness had fallen. For a moment, Armand wasn't certain he could find his way.

"Dominie?" he called.

"Over here."

He groped toward the sound of her voice.

Fortunately for him, she kept talking. "We didn't finish a moment to soon, did we?" Her breath hissed through her teeth. "Come along. If I'm minding the cold, you must be near freezing."

As he drew close to her, Armand slowed his step, not wanting to blunder into her. Which was foolishness, of course, for he'd soon be pressed against her for a whole night—with almost nothing between them.

Nothing but a barrier of bitterness and regrets on both sides, as impenetrable as the stone walls of any keep. It would pain him to be so close to her in body, yet so far removed from her in heart.

What was the man waiting for? Dominie could hear him close at hand. Why didn't he just stretch out beside her and be done with it? No doubt he wanted to delay that moment for as long as possible. She, on the other hand, was anxious to get it over with.

That was the way she'd always approached any distasteful task, and there had been more than a few of those during her tenure as mistress of Harwood and Wakeland. The sooner a body got on with such chores, the sooner they'd be over and done. After the first few unbearably awkward moments lying in Armand's arms, it wouldn't be so bad. Would it?

If she didn't stop thinking such things, she might never find out.

She reached into the darkness, toward the sound of Armand's breathing. Her searching hand found some part of his tunic. "Down you go. It's not getting any warmer while we balk."

Armand gave a low rolling growl as he pushed past her, jerking the garment from her hand. "I wasn't *balking!*"

Under cover of darkness, Dominie allowed herself a smile at his annoyance. While Armand settled himself, with a maximum of noise and thrashing about, she unfastened her cloak.

"Are you ready for me?" She struggled to keep her question innocent-sounding.

"Aye," he snapped.

Dominie thought she heard him mutter, "Vixen!" under his breath.

For some reason, his ill humor amused her more than

it offended. All the same, she decided not to press her luck by reminding him whose fault it was that they must spend the night huddled together for warmth.

"Here I come, then."

A chill ran up her back and between her shoulder blades when she pulled off her cloak. The tips of her breasts tingled and thrust out hard against the linen of her shift. Would Armand feel them poking into his side, through the wool of his tunic? If he did, would he know it was naught but the cold that made her body behave so?

Or would he flatter himself that he had not lost the power to rouse her? That notion galled Dominie, because…perhaps…it might be true.

As she lay down beside him, she was sorely tempted to blunder against a certain tender portion of Armand's body, to see if she still had the power to rouse *him*. At least then they would be evenly matched.

Something restrained her, though.

It might have been the fear that he would stalk off and leave her to freeze. Or possibly a qualm that she might find him quite indifferent to her nearness, after all.

She spread her cloak over them and bade Armand pile the cedar boughs on top of it. Then, after a good deal of wordless shifting to find the least uncomfortable position for both of them, they lapsed into a kind of self-conscious, vigilant stillness not at all compatible with sleep.

If this awkward situation had not yielded its promised warmth, Dominie might have taken her chances with the frost. But each inch of contact between her body and Armand's *did* kindle the warmth she craved. She could no more have parted from it than a drowning man could have let go a thorny branch that was keeping him afloat in a flood.

Had Armand Flambard been cold as stone, Dominie

wondered if his touch might still have fed some gnawing hunger within her. A hunger to know, on the most intimate level, that the man she'd once loved and mourned was truly alive.

''Dominie?'' he whispered, his breath warm in her hair. ''Are you awake?''

''Aye.'' Did he honestly suppose she could sleep? ''What do you want?''

''A while ago, you asked why I refused to aid the folk of Harwood and Wakeland against Eudo St. Maur. I never gave you a reason.''

''Perhaps not.'' Her body tensed. ''But you rebuked me for begging your help. You said I had no right, because my father had gained your old estates by breaking his oath.''

''Yes, but—''

''Then, later, you claimed there was no one to whom you would rather have entrusted Harwood. I do not understand. Which is it, Armand?''

''Both…and neither.'' He sounded as if he did not altogether understand. ''And something else besides, more than either of those.''

''And what might that be, pray?''

''I made a vow…after Lincoln…never to commit violence against another man, so long as I lived.''

''You vowed what?'' Dominie balled the hand that lay over his chest into a tight fist and gave him a token thump to relieve her feelings.

It didn't work. ''Why did you wait until now to tell me this? What earthly good is a champion who has sworn never to fight?''

''I *tried* to tell you!'' Armand spoke in a forceful tone, through clenched teeth. ''You wouldn't listen. You were

too busy with your schemes to put me in the abbot's bad
graces.''

Dominie longed to counter his accusation with a pithy
counterblow. But how could she? What the man said was
true, curse him!

She hadn't listened. She'd been too anxious to get her
own way, by fair means or foul. Too eager to vent five
years of pent-up spite. Trying too hard to ignore old,
tender feelings that threatened to ambush her at every
turn.

''I pinned all my hopes on you, damn it!'' The words
were more a condemnation of her own folly than of him.
''The moment I heard you might be alive, I thought it was
a miracle, an answer to all my prayers. Then when I saw
you in the flesh, with my own eyes…''

She should have known it was too good to be true.
Another harsh lesson the past five years had taught her
was to mistrust the appearance of good fortune. Clearly
she had not paid close enough attention.

Tears of desperation prickled behind her eyes, but she
refused to let them fall. Especially not on Armand Flambard's warm, broad shoulder. She had let him see her
naked body without a qualm. Any hint of shame she might
have felt had been eased by his extravagant embarrass-
ment. But damned if she would give him a glimpse of her
naked heart!

She could never have survived the past five years as
mistress of Wakeland and Harwood if she had not learned
to put on a capable face and hide her vulnerability.
Clenching her eyes tight, she swallowed the warm brine
that trickled down the back of her throat.

''I know you must think ill of me, for what I did today
at the abbey. I am not proud of it. I was desperate. You
cannot imagine what it's been like, trying to muddle along

with so many men called up to fight. The levies of crops to feed the army. Poor harvests. Trying to keep peace among our vassals, and prevent the reeves from stealing us blind. And that was before the menace from St. Maur.''

She didn't want to tell Armand any of it. Even if she succeeded in making him pity her, it would not be enough to make him break his foolish vow. Yet the solid warmth of his shoulder invited her to unburden herself. At the moment, she was too tired and too wrought up to resist.

''There have been days I would have given my own life to have Father or Denys ride through the gates of Wakeland and say the news of their deaths was all a mistake. The way it turned out to be with you.''

Perhaps her plight did move Armand, a little. Carefully, so as not to disturb the cloak that covered them, he raised his hand and passed it over her damp hair in a soothing caress.

''Though I vowed never to take arms against another man, I could still train your vassals to fight, organize some system of defense for Harwood and Wakeland.''

''You could?'' Dominie tilted her face toward his, though all she could see by the light of the newly risen moon was his crisp profile. She knew when he turned toward her, for she could feel the warm whisper of his breath against her face. ''You would?''

''Short of raising a sword myself, I will do everything in my power to keep your people and your harvest safe from St. Maur.''

A sweet, strange expectancy seemed to quiver in the brief space that separated her lips from his.

Armand Flambard was *not* going to kiss her, Dominie chided herself. Though they had been sweethearts once, that was five long years ago. Too much had happened in the meantime.

They were two different people now. The ardent young man and the demure young lady were as dead as her father and her elder brother. Armand had his heart and soul set on the celibate life of a Benedictine. She had a duty to her vassals to marry a warrior, capable of protecting them.

Any small amount of fancy she'd ever possessed had been beaten out of her by the burdens of her new role. She knew no kiss could restore her and Armand to what they'd once been, and yet...

In spite of everything, Dominie found herself wanting to believe in magic or miracles. For a few stolen moments in the darkness and the cold, she wanted to pretend the past five years away and once again share with Armand the kind of kiss they'd exchanged in happier days.

Through a gap in the branches overhead, the plump, pale face of the full moon stared down at Armand and Dominie, huddled in their forest burrow. From her lofty perch in the night sky, was she laughing at the folly of men and women?

Armand could imagine few tortures more exquisite than for a man of good character to lie all night with a desirable woman in his arms. A desirable woman who made no secret of loathing him. His body didn't care about that, though. It wanted her just the same. And it was making him pay dearly for denying its desire.

He lay on his back, with Dominie's head resting in the hollow of his shoulder, his arm crooked around her. She was tucked at his side with her left arm and leg spread across him. Arranged that way, her cloak covered most of them. Parts of Armand were still cold, while other parts were warmer than he could bear.

Was she aware of the effect she had on him? he wondered. Did she relish his discomfort and the grave temptation she held for him?

Dominie's breath had warmed and moistened a spot on the tunic a little way above his heart. When Armand turned his face toward her, a stray tendril of her hair whispered against his cheek in a provocative caress. Her scent, which he swore he could not discern from the smells of the forest, still beguiled him with every breath.

How he wanted to kiss her! And to do so much more.

Armand wished he'd let their talk wait until morning, when he could have kept a safe distance. Before he'd spoken, he had ached for her, yes. But ached for her only as a warm, feminine body pressed against his, with the recent sight of her naked form seared into his memory goading him further.

Their talk had brought her identity alive for him. She was not just any woman. She was Dominie. *His* Dominie.

Not the bashful, virtuous maiden of his distorted memories, yet all the more alluring for that difference.

What had she endured all these years, on his account? A fresh load of guilt settled on top of the heavy one he'd grown accustomed to carrying. For the first time, Armand asked himself whether he should have let his vow of allegiance to the empress take precedence over his betrothal pledge to Dominie, or his unspoken pact of loyalty to her father.

Since Lincoln, his only shield against despair had been the unshakable certainty that he'd done right. That he'd had no choice but to pursue the path where his ideals had led, no matter what the cost. Dominie had shaken that comforting certainty to the core by making him realize he was not the only one to pay a price for his actions.

He owed her a debt far beyond any he'd reckoned before. If, by some miracle, he could save Harwood and

Wakeland from Eudo St. Maur, single-handedly without ever lifting his sword, it would still not begin to compensate her.

Slowly, he let his hand trail down her hair to cup her cheek. "I'm sorry."

"Sorry?" Her voice sounded high and breathless. "You said so already."

"I know." Armand raised and tilted his head ever so slightly toward her. "I said I was sorry my actions had caused you grief. But it's more than that. It's everything. I am sorry for everything."

That was as close to a confession as he dared come, now. Though the ideal of truth demanded that he make a clean breast of it all, how much more might that cost Dominie?

Hardly daring to breathe, Armand brought his lips closer to hers. He put his desire under the tightest possible rein. It would not be that kind of kiss, rather a token of his service to her. If she showed the most subtle sign of reluctance, he would stop, though the effort might tear him in two.

Dominie did not say a word to prevent him. Nor did she turn her face away. Nor raise her hand. But when his lips finally found hers, with a tentative, whisper-light touch, he felt them tremble beneath his.

From somewhere, he summoned the control to draw back, though he could hardly bear it.

"Don't stop!" For a moment Armand could not be certain whether the fierce whisper came from Dominie or from his own banked desire.

"You went away without a parting kiss." She passed her hand over his chest and up his neck. "I claim payment, now. It may help to keep us warm."

He should have known she would have some practical reason. Armand wished he'd had the wit to suggest it.

"It has worked before." He gave a shaky chuckle. "Do you remember our last Twelfth Night, when we slipped away from the feast in the great hall of Wakeland?"

"That was a far colder night than this."

"Aye, but we were both better clad." The memory of it alone warmed Armand.

Fueled by the certainty that Dominie wanted this as much as he did, for whatever reason, Armand kissed her with some of his old confidence and energy. He almost fancied he could taste the special Yuletide draft of mulled ale and roasted apples on her lips.

He remembered how he had longed for spring, and their wedding. How he had burned to bring her to his bed. Now he burned again, but without the promise of eventual fulfillment.

And to think he'd found fault with her, only half a day ago, for standing too close to him. Only permissible if she had some claim upon him, indeed! Dominie De Montford had succeeded in making him acknowledge her claim upon him, but it was not this kind of claim. Nor could it ever be.

Only the fear that he might lose control and humiliate himself gave Armand the willpower to draw back from her again. This time with the firm intention to keep his proper distance.

"There, now." He tried, with little success, to tame the raw, panting edge of his breath. "We have sealed our old parting with a kiss. I fear if we kindle much more heat, the cedar boughs above us might burst into flame."

"It is never wise to meddle with fire." Dominie bowed her head until her brow rested against his chin. "I pray we've warmed ourselves enough to get some sleep. We have a long walk ahead of us tomorrow.''

''Will we have any more brooks to ford?''

''None as wide and deep as the one we came through today.''

''Good.'' Armand pretended to shiver. ''I doubt I could undertake another one so soon.''

They fell silent again, but it seemed to Armand that their talk and their kiss had eased some of the tension between them. His eyelids and his limbs felt heavy and his mind began to drift on the deep, lazy waves of his breathing.

Dominie's breath came in the same slow gusts as she lay beside him, her limbs loose.

It felt strangely familiar to have her sleep in his arms— as though she had nestled beside him, in spirit, every night in the *dortoir* at Breckland. Armand was too near sleep for that idea to scandalize him as it should have.

But he could not forget Dominie's words. *It is never wise to meddle with fire.*

Whatever the provocation, he must resist the urge, in future. For he sensed how badly they both could be burned.

Chapter Six

Had all that talk in the night with Armand been real? Dominie wondered as she reluctantly came awake. Or had it only been a wishful dream?

For a time, she lay still, watching him, sating her gaze upon every rugged ridge of his features, much the way she'd sated her hunger on the filling meal she'd been given at the abbey.

It could not have been a dream, she decided at last. For she never would have imagined that foolhardy vow of his to forswear violence. No wonder he'd taken refuge in an abbey! The man was not fit to survive in her world, let alone claim any place in her life.

But when she remembered some of the things he'd said, and the mellow murmur of his voice in the darkness, Dominie could not help but wish it had turned out differently for them both.

What had made him like this? she asked herself. So crammed full of honor and ideals that he had no room left for workaday virtues like discretion, or common sense? It was not the way she remembered Armand from their youth, when she had believed him to be little short of perfection.

He had always been one to fight fair and open. Of course, his skill had been such that he'd never needed to resort to such devious moves as she'd used on him in the abbey cloisters.

Last night she had begun to regret what she'd done. In the cold light of morning, she glimpsed her actions through Armand's eyes and felt sick with shame.

She had not given him a fair hearing. She had not respected his right to refuse her. She had gone about securing his help by whatever means necessary, justifying herself in the name of her vassals. How much of it had been sheer spite? her long-denied conscience demanded.

Five years ago, Armand had left her, when she'd desperately wanted him to stay. She'd been powerless to prevent it then. This time, she'd been determined to fetch him back, willing or no, whether or not he was capable of doing what she needed.

Had she also been determined to make Armand pay for every ill that had befallen her family since he'd left? Somewhere in her heart, if she still had such an organ, did she not blame him for all of it? From the poor harvests, to her father's death, to Eudo St. Maur's reign of terror?

After all she had done to provoke him, Armand had begged *her* pardon. He had held her in his arms through the night and given her a kiss that had felt both more innocent and more perilous than any they had shared in the past.

It was all Dominie could do to keep from rushing down to the brook and washing herself in its pure, cold water until her skin turned blue!

At the very least, she could not bear to lie beside Armand until he woke. What if he opened his eyes upon a new day, only to look at her with disgust? She needed a little time alone to reconstruct her defenses.

With utmost stealth, she edged away from him, careful not to disturb her cloak or the blanket of boughs that covered them.

He stirred once, muttering some half-swallowed words she could not understand. Dominie froze, waiting for his breath to settle back into the heavy rhythm of deep sleep. Once it had, she continued to make her way out of their snug burrow, wishing a curse of dumbness upon the song-birds that trilled their blithe daybreak music from nearby trees.

As she picked her way through the underbrush, Dom-inie wrapped her arms around herself, rubbing her hands rapidly over her arms. Her linen smock had not grown any thicker during the night, and a bracing spring breeze had risen with the April sun.

What a miserable time to get an attack of scruples! Perhaps she should crawl back into the burrow with Ar-mand and suffer the awkwardness of his waking as her just desserts.

At that moment, a white spectral shape danced in the breeze before her. Dominie stifled a scream, scolding her-self for her foolish alarm. It was only Armand's under-gown, after all.

Dominie ran her hands over it. The cloth was still a little damp, not to mention rather stiff and very cold from the night air. So were Armand's robe and cloak when she checked them. Perhaps, if she bundled herself in all the layers, the outer ones would protect her from the wind, while she warmed and dried Armand's undergown from the inside out.

She could take a short but vigorous walk, to scout out a bit of the forest trail they would follow this morning.

By the time Armand woke, she might be able to present him with garments that would not be too uncomfortable to wear. It seemed little enough to do to make up for all the trouble she'd caused him.

Dominie clenched her lips together, to keep from gasping or squealing when the damp undergown slid over her smock. For a mercy, Armand's robe did not add to her chill when she put it on, nor his cloak.

If one of them had to fall in the brook fully clothed, Dominie almost wished it had been her. Any one of Armand's garments would have made a fair-size tent for her!

Walking briskly along a forest path wearing three tents turned out to be more of a challenge than Dominie had reckoned with. By the time she decided to head back to where she'd left Armand sleeping, his undergown had warmed to a bearable degree. Still, she looked forward to exchanging it for her less bulky tunic and cloak.

Suddenly, her foot caught on a tree root and Dominie tumbled to the ground, cursing the clumsiness of Armand's clothes and the foolish impulse that had led her to put them on in the first place. Before she could struggle to her feet, a weight landed on her back, pressing her down again.

A reedy male voice, laced with mocking malice, inquired, "Where are you bound in such a hurry this morning, Brother? And in clothes twice too big for you?"

Dominie's hackles rose, as she cursed her lack of proper caution. Having Armand nearby had given her a dangerous illusion of security. Eudo St. Maur and his pack were not the only outlaws of whom an honest traveller needed to be wary. Just the best organized and most vicious.

Fighting down a flutter of panic, Dominie plundered her

mind for a ready means of escape. Until she could think of something, she must delay.

She pitched her voice as deep as it would go. "Who are you?" It would never do to let her assailant know she was a woman. "And what do you want with me?"

"You might say I'm begging alms, Brother." The fellow pressed his foot between her shoulder blades.

Before Dominie could protest that she had nothing worth giving...or stealing, he added, "With them as don't show proper Christian charity, I help myself. At the point of my knife."

Vermin!

In the time it took him to utter his threat, Dominie had thought up and discarded several plans.

She might scream for help. But the burrow was some distance away and Armand had given every sign of being a sound sleeper. What help could he be to her if he would not stoop to violence?

She groped on the ground beneath her for a good size stick to wield as a weapon, but none came to hand.

If she had not been swathed in these cumbersome garments of Armand's, Dominie might have rolled out from beneath the thief's foot and sprinted off. But if she was lucky enough not to trip over the hem of the robe in her haste, the thief had only to bring his boot down on the billowing cloak to stop her cold.

Was it possible she could use the bulk of Armand's clothes to her advantage?

The outlaw nudged her with his foot. "I answered your questions, Brother, and right mannerly, too. But you dodged mine. Where are you bound for?"

"Breckland Abbey, a few hour's journey to the north." Dominie concentrated on deepening her voice to sound like a man's. "Do you know it, friend?"

Trying not to draw attention to what she was doing, Dominie withdrew her arms from the wide sleeves of Armand's garments.

"Aye," answered the outlaw. "A wealthy house with its holy well." He gave a harsh bark of laughter. "Not many pilgrims on the road these days, though. All afraid of the Wolf."

"Do you serve that vile enemy of the church?" While she pretended to puff up with indignation, Dominie tugged away the folds of linen and wool beneath her until Armand's clothes truly fell around her like a tent. Now, if only her head were not stuck through the ridge pole!

"Be at ease." The outlaw lightened the pressure of his foot on her back. "I do not run with the wolves. I am but a poor crow, collecting shiny things to trim my humble nest."

While he laughed at his own wit, Dominie pulled loose the tie that fastened Armand's cloak about her neck, and made ready to draw in her head, like a tortoise retreating to the safety of its shell. Not that wool and linen would offer much protection against whetted steel.

Now to wait for her chance. "Friend, I am but a poor lay brother. I carry nothing of value. Come back with me to the abbey, and I will see that you are given alms."

The outlaw answered her offer with a sound kick to her backside. "I said I'm a crow, not an ass! The minute I set foot in your precious abbey, I'd be seized and trussed up for delivery to the sheriff at Norwich."

"As you deserve!" cried Dominie in her own voice, hoping it might startle the outlaw into a vital moment of inattention.

It must have worked, for she was able to pull in her head and perform a quick roll, catching the outlaw by his foot. With a burst of strength born of desperation, she pushed it up as high as she could, to unbalance him, then kept rolling, to ram against his other leg.

Fie, but she hated being hampered by the robes winding around her, blinding her to her foe. Supposing he did fall, could she fight free of the garments to run?

She must, that's all there was to it. If he caught her now, a quick death would be mercy.

The outlaw bellowed as his feet flew out from under him.

Dominie could feel and hear his thrashing beside her, muffled somewhat by the thick carpet of dead needles, leaves and bracken on the forest floor.

She tried to throw off Armand's robes, but her rolling had twisted them around her. Somehow, she staggered upright and fumbled her way free. The chill morning air felt so blessed good on her face after being trapped inside those heavy folds of wool and linen.

She had less than no time to savor her freedom.

Perhaps the outlaw had hit his head when he fell, or got the wind knocked out of him, for he was just struggling to his feet.

He was no beauty—small, wiry and gaunt of face, with a wicked-looking scar slashed across one cheek.

Their eyes met for a fleeting instant. His fierce scowl changed to a triumphant grimace, with a glint of lewd amusement in his close-set eyes that could only mean he had recognized her as a woman.

Dominie's heart pounded like the hammer of a crazed blacksmith, and she gasped for air to feed the fire in her belly.

The outlaw's gaze fell to her feet just as she realized he was empty-handed.

His knife!

She dropped to a crouch, fumbling for the weapon as

the outlaw dived to retrieve it. Her hands closed over the hilt. As she raised the blade, he slammed into her.

The next few seconds were a tumbling, breathless blur of terror. Over and over they rolled. Branches whipped against Dominie's face. Something sharp gouged her side, beneath her ribs, when she rolled over it with the weight of the outlaw pressing down on her.

She knew it could not be his knife, for her whole ragged, desperate awareness was fixed on two urgent necessities—holding the hilt and keeping the blade pointed away from her.

Finally she and the outlaw came to rest in a tangled heap.

All her instincts urged Dominie to get up and run as fast as her feet would carry her. But her head spun and the outlaw's wiry weight pinned her to the ground. The pungent odor of his unwashed clothes and body overpowered her with every heaving breath.

A voice inside her head screamed for Armand, but Dominie could coax no sound from her throat. Not that it would have done any good. She was finished.

Her dizziness eased a little and the outlaw's face came into focus, hovering above her with a wild, mad look in his eyes. He opened his mouth to speak and a gobbet of thick bright blood gushed from his lips, landing on Dominie's cheek.

The scream she had not been able to choke out suddenly burst from her, followed by another and another. And when she tried to stop them, she could not.

Armand woke with a start, wondering where he was.

It occurred to him that he might be dreaming—must be dreaming. Why else would he be out in the woods, buried under a layer of cedar boughs, rather than back in the Spartan comfort of Breckland's *dortoir?*

As he composed himself to await a true waking, the events of the previous day flashed in his mind like a blinding fork of lightning cleaving the night sky. At the same time, a score of intense, conflicting emotions wrung his heart. The last of those was a gaping hollow, and the urgent sense of something vital missing.

Dominie? He swept aside her cloak and the blanket of foliage, searching for her. Peering about, he could see no sign of her. When he called her name, the only answer he got was the twitter of morning songbirds.

As Armand surged to his feet, the bracing chill of morning nipped his bare legs. He plucked her cloak from the ground and shook it free of dead leaves. Then he wrapped it around his lower limbs.

Where could Dominie have gone? And why? The lass would soon perish with no warmer covering than her smock.

That thought reminded Armand of his own clothes. After peering around for a moment to orient himself, he strode away from the two tall oaks to the place he recalled leaving his garments to dry. They were gone, but the tree branches still hung low from bearing their sodden weight through the night. Dominie must have taken his clothes, confound her!

His cloak and undergown he would not begrudge her—they'd have been a fair trade for her own cloak and tunic. But had it been necessary to take his robe, as well?

Armand bit back a curse.

He could guess, now, where she had gone, and why. Having listened to him at last, long enough to understand that he'd forsworn violence, she must have decided he would be no use to her, after all.

She'd stolen away, leaving him behind like a cumbersome piece of baggage she no longer needed. Filching his clothes to warm her journey back home.

Striking the nearest tree with the palm of his hand, Armand let out a grunt of vexation. Part of him wanted to oblige her, by hastening back to Breckland and telling Abbot Wilfrid she no longer required his services. It was true enough to pass muster even with his rigorous conscience.

His conscience. Armand heaved a sigh as he recalled some of the things Dominie had told him last night. Just because she no longer wanted his help did not release him from the abbot's charge, nor from the demands of his guilt-riddled soul. In spite of the vow he had made after Lincoln, he must find some means to aid her and her vassals in resisting Eudo St. Maur.

Suddenly, from off in the distance, came a faint but terrified cry.

"Dominie!" Armand shouted.

He began to run in the direction of the noise, but the cloak he'd wrapped around his waist checked his stride and threatened to trip him. Whipping it off, he charged through an opening between some trees, with it fluttering in his hand.

He roared Dominie's name again, and paused for a moment to listen. Though no answer came, he thought he could hear muffled noises coming from far ahead, along a rough footpath.

Armand set off running again, following the track. A sick sense of dread churned deep in his belly. A moment later, a patch of rusty black and bleached white caught his eye among the forest greens and browns.

As he rushed toward it, puzzled to discover his clothes

but no sign of Dominie, an anguished scream broke from the bracken nearby to echo in the branches overhead.

Armand's gaze flew across the flattened underbrush to the writhing form of a dark-clad man sprawled facedown. Dominie lay pinned beneath him, screaming as she struggled to push the man off her.

White-hot rage exploded inside Armand with a force that shook him from heels to crown. He plunged into the brush and seized the man by the hair, wresting him off of Dominie and hurling him back toward a clump of moss-crusted rocks.

One of the first lessons of warfare Armand had learned from Baldwin De Montford was never to turn his back on an enemy. He transgressed it now without a second's hesitation.

His only thought was for Dominie. He must discover in what ways and how badly she'd been injured. Then he must comfort and tend her. Woe to any man wicked or foolish enough to interfere.

Her screams had subsided to choked sobs when Armand tried to gather her into his arms. Her face was streaked with blood and the front of her looked drenched in gore. If that filthy beast had defiled her...

The thought of it alone took Armand by the throat and throttled him. Would a hundred vows sworn in the very presence of God be enough to stay his hand?

Fortunately his warrior's reflexes did not desert him altogether. When Dominie lashed out at him, Armand recoiled, even before he saw the bloody knife in her hand.

"Dominie!" He caught her wrist, squeezing hard to make her drop it. "It's Armand. You're safe now. Be still!"

Her death grip on the knife hilt slackened. The weapon fell to the ground at Armand's feet.

Dominie's vacant, shifting gaze slowed, and seemed to focus on his face. "Armand?"

"Armand," he repeated softly, drawing her tight to his heart and pressing his cheek against the crown of her head.

He glanced back to where he had hurled her assailant. The crumpled figure had not so much as twitched. "That man, did he harm you, love? Did he…force himself on you?"

"He…no, I'm…not harmed." She clung to him as if she wanted to burrow into his heart, gasping out the words that left Armand dizzy with relief. "He tripped me. He tried to rob me."

She was trembling all over, as violently as any victim of the palsy. Armand realized his knees were quaking, too. Slowly, he sank to the ground with Dominie cradled in his arms as he stroked her hair and her back.

Nearby lay her cloak. Armand could not recall dropping it. Now he reached for the garment, wrapping it around her.

She began to weep harder, in great shuddering sobs.

"Hush," he crooned. "All's well now. I'm here. I won't let any more harm come to you."

How could he stop it, though? The question struck new fear into Armand. What protection could he offer Dominie when he had vowed never again to fight, not even in her defense?

He had been prepared to give his own life rather than ever take another one. But could he let those dearest to him meet harm because his hands were bound by shackles of his own making?

"H-he *would* have c-cut me." Dominie retched the words between sobs. "Would have k-killed me. But I k-killed him."

She pulled away from Armand and began to retch more than words. Having eaten nothing that morning to break her fast, she had little to spew from her belly.

"It's all right." Armand gathered her back into his embrace when the dry heaves had left her spent. "You have nothing to reproach yourself for. I have fought and killed men with far less cause than you had, just now."

Over and over, he grazed his cheek against her hair. "If it eases you to talk, I will understand."

He wasn't certain she would accept his offer, but almost at once, she began to speak. "I only wanted to run away."

In jumbled, halting words, she told him what had happened that morning. When Armand heard that she'd taken a walk wearing his clothes in order to warm them, he quailed with shame. When he heard how she had tripped the outlaw, a glow of pride warmed him in spite of the early morning chill. No question she was Baldwin De Montford's daughter!

As she talked, he held her in a firm, close embrace, to give her at least an illusion of safety. He petted and caressed her, soothed her when she wept, and assured her that no one could blame her for what she'd done.

"Who knows how many innocent folk that creature may have killed already? Or how many more he might have killed if you had not slain him today?"

That thought seemed to comfort her. At last she grew quiet and ceased to tremble.

"We should not linger here," Armand said gently. "In case this outlaw has comrades who might come looking for him."

"I do not think so." Dominie told him what the thief had said about being a crow in search of shiny trinkets.

"Just the same." Armand released her from his embrace with aching reluctance. "I will not rest easy until we are behind good stout walls at Harwood or Wakeland. Can you bide here while I do…what needs doing?''

''Don't fret over me.'' Dominie squared her shoulders and inhaled a deep breath. ''I can do what I must.''

Armand remembered hearing those words from her just yesterday—when she had offered to wed him and restore his estates, in return for his help against Eudo St. Maur.

Then, he had thought her so changed from the girl he remembered, in all the worst ways. Now he understood that her pose of hardihood was one she'd had to adopt when she suddenly found herself responsible for two large estates during perilous times.

A flicker of admiration for her kindled in his heart, even as it ached with the knowledge that he had been responsible for thrusting those duties upon her slender shoulders.

With the knuckle of his forefinger, he brushed back a strand of her hair that had fallen over her brow. ''Of course you can. I won't be long, I promise.''

Slowly, he let the back of his finger slide down the soft contour of her cheek, until it reached her chin, which he tilted up. All his bones seemed to move and melt with the urge to kiss her. He had just enough power of will to turn away from Dominie before that desire overcame him.

With the need for haste pressing, and no good digging tools at hand, Armand knew it was no use trying to bury the bandit. Instead, he dragged the corpse to a hollow, where he laid it out.

Before he set about covering it with fallen tree trunks and branches, he paused for a moment to whisper a prayer. He opened his eyes to find Dominie looking at him askance.

Armand scowled. ''This rogue is bound for hell, no doubt. But that is all the more reason to say a blessing over him. We'll never know what lured him or pushed him into a life of thievery. We dare not grudge him Our Lord's mercy. We may have need of it ourselves one day, perhaps with no better claim than this man.''

His explanation received no answer.

It was futile trying to justify himself, Armand decided. How could Dominie understand? She probably thought he betrayed her by showing such misplaced compassion for her enemy.

By the time he got the body covered as decently as possible, Armand no longer felt the morning cold.

He gathered up his robes and cloak from where they lay. ''I need to change back into my own clothes. I should go back and retrieve my staff and your scrip, too. Will you be all right by yourself for a short while? I promise I won't be long.''

She did not appear to heed him as she sat there with her knees tucked up and her arms clasped tightly around them. Her eyes had an empty look.

But when he finished speaking, she nodded.

''Good lass.'' He patted her shoulder, then hurried back to their sleeping place almost as quickly as he'd run from it.

Armand was just pulling on his robe when he heard the bark of a dog and the sound of voices approaching the forest. He froze for a moment, the threat of danger tightening his throat. Then he sprang into action.

Gathering up Dominie's tunic and scrip, along with his cloak and staff, Armand fled down the path. He had never been as frightened on his own account as he was now... for her.

Chapter Seven

The muted pounding of feet on the path made Dominie tremble and her heart flutter like a bird struggling to take flight on broken wings.

She tried to get up and run, but her legs would not support her. She had just enough strength in her hands to draw the hood of her cloak over her head and curl herself up small and tight. With luck, she might be taken for a tree stump.

The footfalls drew closer and closer. Suddenly they stopped.

Armand's voice sounded nearby, hushed but urgent. "Dominie? Where are you? We must get away!"

She tried to call out to him, but her voice seemed stuck in her throat. Lifting her hand, she pushed back her hood and saw him standing nearby.

He saw her, too, for he swooped toward her, his robes billowing around him. "Dear heaven, lass, you gave me a wicked fright! I thought some ill had befallen you."

Throwing down everything he carried, he began to remove her cloak with firm, but gentle hands.

Some strange compulsion made Dominie resist, pulling

the garment tighter around her. It felt as if Armand was stripping away her only source of comfort and protection.

"Did you not hear what I said?" He knelt in front of her, nudging up her chin with the crook of his forefinger to make her look him in the eye. "We have to get as far away from here as we can. I heard people coming this way. They may mean us no harm, but after what just happened, I don't want to risk it."

Dominie gazed into his steadfast blue eyes, savoring the illusion of safety she found there.

"Let's get your tunic back on you," Armand coaxed, "then we can be on our way."

The calming tone of his voice and his unwavering gaze worked a kind of enchantment on her. Some of the tightness went out of Dominie's limbs. She loosened her desperate grip on the cloak so Armand could ease it off her shoulders.

"Good lass." He scooped her tunic from the ground. "Now, slip this over your head and you'll soon be—"

As Armand's gaze trailed down to the front of her smock, his speech halted abruptly, as if invisible hands had throttled him.

Dominie let go of her legs, which fell slack, exposing great livid bloodstains smeared over the bleached linen. She gagged on the bile that flooded the back of her throat.

"Get it off!" Armand tugged at the smock. His touch no longer gentle or hesitant, he looked ready to tear the garment from her body.

Dominie would not have minded if he had. As desperately as she had clung to her cloak, she now desperately longed to rid herself of this too-vivid reminder of what had happened here. And what she had done.

As best as she was able, she cooperated with Armand

to get herself out of the smock. And when she sat before him, naked from the thighs up, she felt curiously indifferent, as though her body belonged to someone else.

"You can have my undergown," Armand offered. "It feels quite warm now."

Dominie shook her head as she reached for her tunic.

"No time." She heaved out the words, hoping they would be sufficient to convince him.

In truth, she feared the generous folds of his undergown would remind her too much of the attack, and of the helpless terror that had gripped her when she'd become tangled up in them.

Armand made no reply, but lifted the tunic and held it so she could wriggle into it. Then he secured her scrip back around her waist and fastened her cloak over her shoulders.

Off in the distance a hound bayed.

"Let's go!" Armand leaped to his feet and hoisted Dominie up after him.

She only managed a few unsteady steps before her knees gave way.

Armand cast an anxious glance in the direction from which the barking had come.

"Leave me." Dominie sank to the ground, cursing her useless limbs. "I'll hide behind a tree and cover myself with leaves. Once I get some strength back in my legs, I'll catch up with you."

His brow furrowed for a moment as he considered their options, then Armand shook his head. "I cannot leave you."

Grasping her under the arms, he lofted her over his shoulder.

"What are you doing, Flambard?"

"Can you not tell?" He retrieved his staff and lurched down the path, carrying her. "I am taking you away from here. Let me know when you think your legs might hold you again."

A catch in his breath told her he hoped it would not be too long.

Luckily, it wasn't.

The discomfort and indignity of being slung over a man's shoulder and toted through the forest shook Dominie from the worst of her horrified bemusement.

They had not gone far before she tapped Armand on the back. "Put me down before you stumble and break a limb. I think my legs will bear me now."

"Very well." He could not disguise his breathlessness as he staggered to a halt and lifted her down.

"I'll lend you my staff," he offered. "On the condition that you promise not to smite me on the head with it the next time I offend you."

She rewarded his feeble jest with a faltering smile. "We have a bargain, Flambard."

At first, Dominie leaned heavily on the staff, concentrating all her will upon taking her next step. But each tottering stride grew more certain until at last they emerged from Thetford Forest onto a green ridge warmed by bright spring sunshine.

Dominie felt as though she'd just woken from a terrifying nightmare.

"I want to thank you." She blurted out the words that had been in her thoughts for a while, grateful that her voice did not break.

When Armand raised his brows, she added, "For the way you took care of me after…well, after."

"You're welcome, of course," he replied. "But I didn't

do much. If I hadn't been there, I'm not sure it would have made any difference in the end."

Because he hadn't been there to deal with the outlaw? That had been the least of her troubles.

Armand shaded his eyes with his hand and peered down onto the rolling patchwork of fallow fields, grazing land, small copses and hedgerows that covered the western corner of Suffolk.

"Once you realized you had no one but yourself to rely on, I expect you would have picked yourself up, done what needed doing and soldiered on."

He shifted his gaze from the countryside, to fix it on her. "Just as you did after Lincoln when you got the news about your father and Denys. Just as you did when your tenant warned you that St. Maur had set his greedy sights on Harwood and Wakeland. Abbot Wilfrid said you are a remarkable woman, and he was right."

Dominie sensed the glow of admiration in Armand's eyes and in his voice, as plainly as she could see the sun's light and feel its warmth. But she did not feel very worthy of admiration just then.

"You held me while I bawled and puked like a babe." She wanted to hate him for seeing her that way, so weak and distraught—the way she had hated him for breaking their betrothal and forsaking her without a word.

He had made it more difficult than ever to hate him. And far more difficult to scorn his lofty ideals. Even his vow to forswear violence, which might cost her people dearly.

Now that her hands had run slick and red with the blood of an enemy whose death she'd caused, she could begin to understand. She had not intended to kill the bandit, only to keep him from harming her. Though his gruesome death had shaken her, she could not pretend such a rogue was any great loss to the world.

What if, like Armand, she had hoisted her sword in battle, with every intention of destroying the enemy? Then, in the course of one bloody day, what if she had killed several men whose only crime was their allegiance to a different lord? Men who might have once been her neighbors, perhaps even friends?

Entering an abbey and forswearing violence was a more temperate response than many she could imagine, especially for a man of honor and impossibly high ideals.

Lost in thought, Dominie did not notice Armand edging closer to her with each step, until he reached out and touched her arm. ''I'm glad you wept.''

She flinched back from his touch. ''What?''

Armand caught her hand in his and slowed his stride. ''I'm glad you wept. I would never forgive myself if the burdens you've borne these past years had made you so unfeeling that you could spill a man's blood without a care.''

''Why should you blame yourself?''

''Because those burdens should have fallen on me. But I was not there.''

A new thought struck Dominie. ''If you had declared for King Stephen, as my father tried to persuade you, you might have perished at Lincoln, too. All those responsibilities would still have fallen on me. And you would not be here now.''

Armand made an effort to smile that was almost painful to behold. ''So you'd rather have a live traitor than a dead hero? Your practical nature baffles me.''

Wrenching her hand from his grasp, Dominie began to walk faster. Since this morning, and even before—from the moment she'd laid eyes on him again—she'd begun to feel like a stranger to herself. All her feelings were too raw, too near the surface. Apt to break through the brittle crust of her composure without warning.

Not even in exchange for Eudo St. Maur's head on a platter would she permit Armand to see her weep twice in one day.

"I thought you'd be pleased—" she flung the words at him "—to hear that I'd loosened my hold on the bitterness I bore against you for so many years."

"I am." Armand hurried to catch up with her. His hand landed on her shoulder, spinning her around to face him. "I am, Dominie! I marvel that you are able to."

"Marvel or baffle, which is it?" She thrust Armand's staff back into his hand. Now that she had found her legs again, she seemed to need it less than he did.

"Both, if you must know." His gaze roved over her face, as if searching for a resemblance to someone he'd once known. "You have changed so much in the time we've been apart. Or perhaps I never knew you as I once thought I did."

Dominie's gaze faltered before his. "Changed for better or worse?"

She did not want to care about his opinion.

"That is not for me to judge." He raised one large hand to rest on her shoulder in a comradely manner. "Though I begin to think I may enjoy the challenge of becoming acquainted with the new Dominie, in spite of myself."

The simple, chaste gesture pried something loose inside of her, as she had untied the tight, slippery knot of his belt after they'd emerged from their baptism in the brook.

"You don't have to stay." The words burst out of her with a bewildering mixture of eagerness and reluctance.

Armand's high brow furrowed. "Stay?"

"At Wakeland, once we reach there." Dominie spoke quickly, before the warm pressure of his hand tempted her to recant. "Nor Harwood neither. You said yourself they are no longer yours to defend. I should not have compelled you to come with me against your will."

Where was the flush of relief she had expected to see on Armand's face when she released him from his obligation? Instead, his brow creased and the corners of his eyes tightened in a look she could not interpret.

Was he troubled, perhaps? Or torn?

"*You* did not compel me, remember? Abbot Wilfrid did that."

"At my urging." Why was Armand making this more difficult for her? "And perhaps to test your obedience."

Armand lifted his hand from her shoulder, as if it had suddenly grown hot to the touch. "I think Father Abbot wants to test me in many ways. If I have true courage of my convictions, I should welcome the ordeal."

The notion that he would regard the time he spent with her as an *ordeal* stung Dominie. It strengthened her resolve to set him at liberty.

"If I release you from your obligation, no doubt the abbot can find other ordeals to test you."

"Tell the truth." The barest hint of a smile raised one corner of Armand's mouth. Though with his brow still furrowed, he looked more pensive than merry. "You've decided I'll be more trouble than help to you—a champion hamstrung by his foolish vow."

"That is part of it." She lowered her gaze. "But not all."

How she hated admitting her faults. But Armand deserved to know the truth. "I saw, today, how swiftly death can come and with how little warning. It made me examine my actions and my motives in all of this. I find I cannot be proud of either. I have made practical needs an excuse for too many misdeeds.''

Let him take satisfaction in knowing he'd been right about her.

Did he dare put *his* deeds and motives to such ruthless scrutiny? Armand wondered. Might he discover that his lofty ideals were no more than a bold, comely front behind which to hide guilt and uncertainty? Perhaps even a touch of cowardice? And if he did discover such shameful weaknesses of character, would he have the fortitude to make a clean breast of them, as Dominie had just done?

''Do you *want* me to return to Breckland once I have seen you safely home?'' he asked.

Not that she couldn't do without his protection, if she had to.

Dominie had been staring at the ground. Now she lifted her gaze to look him in the eye. ''I want you free to go or stay as you wish. Reluctant service can be worse than none at all, and you have already done me better service than I deserve.''

Her offer tempted him for more reasons than he could count, including a few he dared not acknowledge. What help he could give her might not signify in the least against so vicious a foe as Eudo St. Maur. And even if Armand's efforts could turn the tide, it would still not be enough to repay her all he owed.

But how could he go back to the abbey, say prayers, plow fields, tend fences, with his fragile peace poisoned by the knowledge that he had forsaken her when she'd needed him…for a second time?

''My service may be of little use.'' Armand gulped a quick breath, as though he were about to plunge into dangerous waters. ''But there can be no question of your deserving it. I offer it to you now, as I should have done when you first spoke to me at the abbey—without reservation.''

Dominie did not speak for a moment. Armand feared she might refuse him, after all.

Then a smile lit her face. It seemed to illuminate something inside him as well.

''I accept your help.'' She held out her hand. ''With thanks.''

Armand reached to clasp her fingers in his. But at the last moment, some impulse, as baffling as it was powerful, made him raise her hand to his lips instead.

Though she might deny it, he knew Dominie could still use someone to lean on at times. Someone with strong arms and a stout heart to steady and comfort her when she needed it. But with the discretion to know when she was ready to stand on her own again.

And the confidence in himself to let her be as weak or as strong as she needed to be.

If only he had not forfeited his right to be that someone.

The rest of Armand and Dominie's journey to Wakeland turned out to be as uneventful as the beginning had been fraught with danger. They were giving the Fenlands a wide enough berth that there was little to fear from the Wolf or his pack. In the company of a tall, strong-looking man, Dominie had no need to travel in stealth.

As they walked, Armand questioned her about what changes the past five years had wrought on their estates. The more he heard, the more his admiration for her increased.

And the closer they came to the country where he'd been bred and raised, the lighter his step grew and the more avidly his gaze sought familiar landmarks. The cords of his soul seemed to resonate with deep, mellow music of wistful sweetness.

They took shelter for the night in a shepherd's hut that had been abandoned because the pasture was too distant and vulnerable in such lawless times. They shared a frugal meal of bread and dried meat from Dominie's scrip. Then they slept between fleeces that were old and none too clean, but so blessed warm that Armand did not grudge their pungent odor.

Murmuring his prayers, he drifted into a sleep more deep and peaceful than any he'd enjoyed during his years at the abbey.

The next morning, he woke to the firm touch of Dominie's hand on his shoulder and the sound of his name murmured by her husky voice. "Come, Armand, it's past time to rise and be on our way. I am anxious to reach home before sunset."

He opened his eyes slowly, to savor his first sight of her for the day.

She did not bear much resemblance to the ethereal creature of his old dreams. Wisps of straw stuck out from her hair. Tawny freckles dappled her nose. And there were fine lines of worry etched around her eyes that he had not noticed before. In spite of those things, or perhaps because of them, her ripe autumnal beauty moved him in a way it never had before.

Their gazes locked and a look of dangerous intimacy passed between them. Dominie must have sensed it, too, for she snatched her hand from his shoulder and spoke in a breathless rush.

"Heaven alone knows what a muddle I will find after being gone for six whole days. Gavin will have fallen from the battlements or lamed one of the horses. Mother will have had a sick spell, the ale will have soured or my reeve will have run off with the rents.''

Armand sat up and stretched. ''We must make haste then, while there may still be hope of finding castle walls standing.''

''Mock me, will you?'' She planted her hands on her hips. ''You'll see for yourself how it is, when we get there.''

A new thought occurred to Armand and the question was out of his mouth before he had time to think better of it. ''Why did you never seek a husband to lift the load from your shoulders, or at least share the burden?''

Would he truly have wanted that? Armand asked himself the instant the question left his lips. If Dominie had wed, it would have meant another man as master of his estates, holder of his titles. Yet that did not trouble him as much as the thought of her in another man's bed.

Perhaps Dominie did not recognize the significance of his question, for she tossed off a careless reply as she stooped to retrieve her scrip. ''Good men are scarce in time of war, and they have more urgent matters to occupy them than courting.''

''Surely you've had offers, though.'' No doubt. A beauty like her with such a fine dowry. The thought made Armand's insides clench.

Dominie cocked her head and pulled a wry face. ''Of the few who were at hand, most would have been no great help to me. One or two who seemed capable, I judged a little *too* ambitious. I feared they might not be satisfied with my dowry lands, but might be tempted to wrest Wakeland from young Gavin, as well.''

Were those the only reasons Dominie had refrained from taking a husband? She'd seemed willing enough to offer *him* her hand and lands in exchange for his help.

Caution warned Armand not to venture any further down that path.

"Gavin." He seized upon a safe subject. "I'll hardly recognize him, I suppose. He was just a wee fellow when I…the last time I saw him."

Rising reluctantly from his soft but smelly bed of fleeces, Armand fastened his cloak, hefted his staff and followed Dominie out of the shepherd's hut. The Suffolk countryside was swathed in a silvery mist.

"Gavin recollects you well enough." Dominie gave a rueful chuckle as she set off westward, toward Cambridgeshire. "It's a wonder the young rascal has lived to grow up, after some of the devilment he's gotten up to. Pretending to be a great warrior like father and Denys…and you."

"The great warrior who's forsworn violence." Armand could not keep the self-mocking bitterness from his voice. "I fear I'll be a great disappointment to him."

Almost as great a disappointment as he had been to Gavin's sister.

"Nonsense." Dominie spoke in a brisk tone as she picked her way over a patch of uneven ground. "Gavin will be beside himself to have another *man* about. Besides, I see no reason to tell him or anyone else about your vow."

Was she ashamed of him as well as disappointed?

"I refuse to lie to everyone!"

Dominie heaved a sigh. "I'm not asking you to lie, Armand. I'd just like you not to proclaim the truth at the top of your lungs to everyone you meet. Would that be such a sin?"

She sounded so vexingly sensible.

"I know you think I'm a fool." Armand pushed a damp lock of hair off his brow. "I cannot blame you. I often think myself a fool. A clever man would not see so much of life in black and white, as I do. A clever man would not come over all bewildered when he encounters a patch of gray…or, heaven forbid, red.''

The next thing he knew, Dominie had planted herself in front of him and was glaring up at him. ''You are *not* a fool, Armand Flambard!'' She shook her head. ''Though heaven knows, you see the world in a vastly different light than most folk. Perhaps an abbey is the best place for you when all's said and done.''

Armand could not gainsay her. Nor should he want to. He had told himself the same thing many times over the years. Somehow, hearing the words from Dominie's lips made him flinch.

Chapter Eight

"Home at last," said Dominie when she spied Wakeland Castle off in the distance, perched atop its high motte. She jogged the reins of her gentle hackney gelding. "It feels like a month since I left for Breckland."

Armand nodded as he rode along beside her on a roan mare. "A good deal has happened since then. To me it seems at least a week since we left the abbey. We are ending our journey in finer state than we began it."

Glancing down at her gown and kirtle, Dominie smiled to herself. She no longer looked anything like the "lad" who had first accosted Armand in the abbey fields.

Not long after midday, she and Armand had reached the most easterly of the De Montford manors. There they had eaten their first hot meal in two days. After washing herself and combing her hair, Dominie had changed into garments more suited to a well-dowered maiden.

She'd found herself strangely reluctant to part with her tunic. Without her linen shift beneath it, the rough wool had rasped against her skin as she and Armand had walked. It had provided a subtle but necessary penance that had somehow soothed her spirit, allowing her to carry on when guilt and revulsion over killing the bandit threatened to paralyze her.

When she'd emerged from their hostess's solar, groomed and garbed, Dominie had seen a reluctant flicker of admiration in Armand's gaze, which he'd quickly suppressed. Later, when he'd lifted her onto her saddle, she'd felt an expectant tension in his touch, unlike the way he'd handled her during the previous two days.

Now, on the western horizon behind Wakeland Castle, the spring sun was setting, tinting the evening sky in a soft palette of rose and lavender hues.

Dominie and Armand had spoken little during their ride. The few times they had exchanged words, Armand had addressed her with more careful courtesy, which made her feel a growing distance between them. Though she knew she should welcome it, she could not help missing the quarrelsome candor they had shared until now.

She cleared her throat to draw his attention. "Before we reach Wakeland, I have a favor to ask of you."

"You know I will do whatever I can to oblige you." As Armand spoke, he did not glance her way, but kept his eyes fixed on the castle ahead.

"When we arrive," said Dominie, "there are bound to be questions about our journey from Breckland."

"Aye?" That one word carried more than its weight in wariness.

Dominie could not keep her own tone from growing sharper. "When I left, I did not tell anyone where I was bound. They would have only tried to dissuade me. Nor did I want to raise false hopes, in case it turned out not to be you Father Clement had seen when he accompanied my mother to Breckland. The Wakeland folk likely thought I'd gone to Harwood to check on their spring plowing and sowing."

Armand did not appear surprised that she had misled her family and servants. "What has that to do with the favor you ask?"

"My mother is apt to have a swooning fit if she hears about our dunk in the brook or my...brush with that bandit."

The danger was only part of it. Dominie could imagine the flutter that would ensue if her mother learned how she and Armand had spent that first night huddled together in Thetford Forest.

Before Armand could raise his usual objection, she assured him, "I'm not asking you to lie. Just keep silent on the subject and let me speak for both of us if an awkward question is put to you."

When he hesitated to give her an answer, she added, "You don't want to upset my mother, do you?"

"Of course not!"

"Good. Then that's settled."

He grumbled something under his breath, which Dominie did not ask him to repeat. Privately, she congratulated herself that she was learning how to work around Armand Flambard's troublesome rectitude.

They rode the rest of the way in silence, hers a trifle smug and his a trifle sullen.

When they reached the bailey gate, the guard called down, "Who goes there?"

"It is your mistress, Will, son of Edgar," Dominie snapped. "If you cannot see that, then perhaps your eyes are no longer sharp enough for gatekeeping."

"I—I could see it were *you,* Lady Dominie," the guard stammered. "But who is the holy man come with you?"

Before Dominie could reply, Armand spoke. His voice rang with an eager note she had not heard in years. "I can excuse you for not recognizing me, Master Will.

Many springs have come and gone since you once humored my whim to stand watch with you on this gate.''

"M-my lord Flambard? Is that you come back to Wakeland?'' The guard's questions echoed with wonder and a subtle shade of fear. ''What, risen from the dead?''

Armand threw back his head and gave a rolling, robust laugh that made Dominie's heart ache as it revived a host of old sweet memories. ''Never fear, Will, I am no ghost.''

Dominie raised her voice, so it might carry into the bailey and the encouraging news might spread. ''I can vouch that Lord Flambard is alive and hale as ever. He has come to lead us in our fight against the Wolf of the Fens.''

"Those are good tidings indeed, my lady!'' cried the gatekeeper. ''The folk of Harwood will rejoice to hear it.''

"So they may,'' Dominie answered. ''If you do not make haste to let us in, I may take his lordship on to Harwood, where we might receive a more mannerly welcome.''

"Your pardons, my lady and my lord!'' The flustered gatekeeper scrambled to admit them. ''I was that amazed, I forgot myself. I only do as you bid me when I keep an extra cautious watch on who I let within these walls.''

"So you do, Master Will.'' Dominie smiled at the gatekeeper as she rode into the bailey, to let the poor fellow see she did not hold his prudence against him. ''Now that Lord Flambard has come to help us marshal our defenses, I pray the day may soon arrive when you will not need to be so vigilant.''

By the time Armand had dismounted and lifted Dominie down from her horse, a small crowd of folk, who should rightly have been eating their evening meal, had gathered in the bailey. Dominie's spirits rose when she saw how they whispered feverishly to one another and stared at Armand with a mixture of fond recognition and bashful awe. When he greeted one or two of them by name, the favored ones beamed with pride.

Father Clement elbowed his way through the small crowd of castle folk.

"So my old eyes did not deceive me, after all." The priest clasped Armand's hand. "After Lady Dominie left, I feared she might have gone to Breckland to see for herself. I have hardly slept a wink since then for worry I might have sent her on a wishful goose chase."

Before Armand could reply, Dominie dismissed the crowd with a flick of her hand and a stern look, which she then turned on Father Clement. "You said nothing of this to my mother, I hope."

"Never fear, my child," replied the priest. "I have more wit than that. Lady Blanchefleur believes you went to Harwood, though she has been watching anxiously for your return this past day or two. Word reached us in the great hall that you had arrived with a guest. Your mother bade me come fetch you both to dine. There will be much rejoicing once the identity of our guest is known to all."

"If our reception in the bailey is a token, I believe you may be right, Father." Dominie clasped Armand by the elbow and together they followed Father Clement up the long, steep drawbridge to the keep itself.

Good news flew ahead of them on swift wings. When they entered the great hall, a deafening series of cheers went up. Gavin pelted across the chamber to greet them, while Dominie's mother watched from the high table, her eyes round with wonder.

The boy skidded to a halt in front of Armand, staring up at him as if trying to reconcile the habit-clad stranger with the hero he dimly remembered. "So it is true, Dominie. You found Armand Flambard and brought him back. I wish you'd taken me along with you.''

As if she'd needed more trouble, with her mischievous little brother in tow! Dominie had to bite her tongue to stifle those words lest they alarm her mother.

Armand ruffled her brother's tangle of red-brown curls. ''Your sister could hardly take you along, sir. She needed to leave a capable warrior in charge of Wakeland in her absence.''

Gavin puffed up proudly, as though he believed it. ''You must be hungry after your journey. Come, we've set places for you.''

As they walked toward the high table, rushes crackling beneath their feet, Dominie cast a sidelong glance at Armand. He was staring after Gavin with such a forlorn look…as if his heart were breaking.

She leaned toward him and whispered, ''What's the matter? Are you ill?''

Armand shook his head and made an effort to appear cheerful. Dominie was not fooled. Nor would she be put off.

''What is it then?''

For an instant, she doubted he would tell her. Then, just as they reached the high table, he murmured, ''The boy looks so much like Denys when he and I were that age.''

His voice fairly ached with longing.

Could it be that Armand, too, wished they could turn back time to the days when life had been safer and simpler? Days when the Flambards and the De Montfords had been each other's closest allies? Days when a secure, happy future had stretched before the two of them?

The great hall of Wakeland looked exactly as Armand remembered it, with its high ceiling supported by stout oak beams, and huge stone hearths on either side. Windows with slats of polished horn let in the light. Two long trestle tables stretched down each side of the hall, with a third at the far end, upon a raised platform, where the family sat with honored guests.

It sounded the same, too, with the rustle of reeds underfoot, the clatter of wooden serving plates on the tables and the confusing chorus of many people talking at once. Even the smells were familiar—roasted meat, hot bread, the odor of bodies in various stages of cleanliness. And beneath it all, the subtle sweetness of lavender, Lady Blanchfleur's favorite strewing herb.

Armand recognized so many faces turned toward him, lit with homely smiles of welcome. The quiet but powerful joy of homecoming wrapped around him; warm as the roaring hearth fires during Yuletide. Nourishing as a trencher loaded with braised beef. Sweet as the modest fragrance of dried flowers rising from the hall floor. It seemed to restore a vital part of him that had been missing for far too long.

Then young Gavin had come forward to greet them.

His resemblance to his dead brother had shaken Armand, making him realize that Wakeland *had* changed in his absence. What was missing from it could never be restored.

As they reached the high table, Lady Blanchefleur rose from her chair and opened her arms to Armand. "Dear boy, it is a tonic to my heart to see you again in this hall!"

Armand stooped to receive her motherly embrace. "It is good to be back at Wakeland again, my lady. So much is as I remembered it."

"You are changed enough for all of us." Dominie's mother shook her head, as if ruing some of what the years had wrought. "But come, sit here by me and eat. You must be hungry from your journey. Whence came you?"

As he lowered himself onto the chair beside her, Armand shifted a furtive glance toward Dominie, who had taken a seat to the left of her mother. Was there any harm in him answering that question?

When Dominie did not jump in to reply on his behalf, Armand went ahead. "From Breckland Abbey in Norfolk, my lady."

"Breckland?" Lady Blanchefleur cried. "Why, I just returned from the abbey a fortnight ago! To think I did not see you. But then, I should hardly have recognized you."

While Armand broke his bread and took a joint of fowl from the platter set before him, she chattered on. "I thought you had made your full growth when last I saw you, but I vow you have grown taller yet. And lost flesh, too, poor fellow, though you are still comely enough to suit most women."

Abruptly, she turned to Dominie. "Is he not, Daughter?"

An instant of awkward silence greeted her question.

Resisting the urge to glance at Dominie's face, Armand took a bite of his bread and chewed as if his life depended on it.

"He looks as well as he ever did," replied Dominie at last, in a rather sullen tone.

Lady Blanchefleur paid no heed to her answer, but plucked at the sleeve of Armand's habit. "And what is this? You have not taken vows, I hope?"

Before Armand could swallow his bread to clear the way for his reply, Dominie spoke up again. "What is wrong with the man joining the Benedictines if he wishes, Mother? I thought you valued piety."

"So I do, my dear. Though I hope a body may serve Our Lord as well out in the world as in the cloister. Some folk are meant for that sort of life and others aren't. Armand Flambard is—"

Just then, he could not bear to hear what sort of life Lady Blanchefleur thought he was meant for. "I am only a lay brother at Breckland, my lady."

For some reason, he could not bring himself to add that he meant to take full vows as soon as Abbot Wilfrid would permit him.

"Mother…" Dominie sounded eager to distract her from the subject. "Armand has come to aid us in our defense against Eudo St. Maur."

"He has?" Lady Blanchefleur turned to her daughter, then back to Armand. "You have?"

"Aye, my lady. To help in any way I can."

Her lower lip trembled and tears misted her wide brown eyes as she crossed herself. "Then my prayers have truly been answered. Thanks be to Our Lord!"

How much would her prayers have availed, Armand wondered, if her daughter had not taken the initiative to seek him out and recruit him by whatever means necessary? Perhaps the invisible power of those prayers had kept them from drowning or freezing when they'd fallen in the brook, he decided. Perhaps it had protected Dominie from the bandit who'd accosted her in Thetford Forest.

He recalled the abbot's wise words about what could be accomplished when a man and woman of great ability worked together. Might it also be so, when bold deeds were hallowed by faith and prayer?

Lady Blanchefleur whispered a brief prayer of thanksgiving, then looked Armand over again. "A Benedictine habit is no fit attire for a warrior. Once we have eaten, you must come along to my solar. I still have a few clothes that belonged to my dear Baldwin, God rest his soul. They might hang a trifle loose on you, but otherwise should be a perfect fit.''

Armand felt as if all the air had been knocked out of him. ''A-are you certain Lord Baldwin would have wanted that, my lady? Five years ago, we parted with ill feelings between us.''

''Nonsense!'' For a woman who often seemed quite helpless, Lady Blanchefleur was not without a will. ''If he'd lived, I am certain the two of you would have reconciled by and by. Why, he thought as much of you as he did of our own children. Such ties stretch further than you suppose before they break altogether.''

Perhaps, but he had trespassed miles beyond that point.

Dominie leaned forward to look past her mother at him. ''She is right, Armand. The men may balk at taking orders from a commander in a monk's habit.''

He'd probably stand a better chance against Eudo St. Maur than against the De Montford women if they united in opposing him.

''But,'' Dominie added, ''I hope Harwood and Wakeland have not fallen so far in fortune that we cannot afford better than castoffs to dress our champion. I will order new garments made for you.''

She probably couldn't stand the thought of her father's clothes warming the body of a traitor. Whatever her reasons, Armand was grateful Dominie had spared him the ordeal of walking in the garments of the man he'd once loved…then killed.

''Do not trouble yourself over new clothes for me. I have come to work, not to attend court. If *my* father's old armor is still to be found at Harwood, that will fit me well enough.''

Besides, he did not want Dominie put to the expense of new clothes he would wear only a few months, until the harvest was safely in.

"Yes!" cried Dominie. "There is a great chest full of your father's clothes and armor. Even his sword."

The last word had scarcely left her mouth when she winced.

Armand felt compelled to reassure her...and perhaps himself. "It is fitting I should carry my father's sword." As long as he did not draw it in violence against another man. "It may remind me of my father's high principles and the ideals he tried to instill in me."

His gaze caught and held Dominie's as he spoke. A wordless awareness passed between them, as if everyone else in the great hall of Wakeland might hear their words, but only the two of them truly understood what they were saying.

Dominie's mother certainly didn't, for she nodded, an emphatic endorsement of Armand's suggestion. "A splendid idea, my dear boy. Have you been to Harwood yet?"

"No, my lady."

"We will go in a day or two, Mother, once Armand has rested from his journey."

"I wish I felt well enough to accompany you. Think what rejoicing there will be at Harwood to have a Flambard in residence once more."

An eager expectancy quickened in Armand's chest when he looked ahead to his return to Harwood.

He had been fostered at Wakeland and grown to manhood here. In many ways, it felt like the home of his heart. But Harwood had been built by his great-grandsire not long after the Conquest. And it had been Armand's for the short interval between his father's death and the forfeiture of his estates.

Even though it belonged to Dominie now, and her future husband would eventually be master there, Armand longed to pretend for the next few months that he was still its lord.

The next days passed swiftly for Dominie, as she and Armand conferred with the De Montford tenants and laid plans for the busy months ahead.

Though he still wore his Benedictine habit, Armand rapidly slipped back into his role as a leader. With every suggestion he put forward and every decision he made, he seemed to stand a little straighter. His voice grew more resonant, his manner more assured. In spite of her attempts to suppress it, Dominie felt some of her girlhood admiration for him rekindling.

The previous day, he had summoned a council of tenants and chief castle officers—the marshal, the steward and the reeve. Unrolling a large parchment map of East Anglia, he had used a nub of charcoal to mark St. Maur's stronghold in the Fens, sites of raids by the outlaws and De Montford manors most vulnerable to attack.

As she'd watched the other men's faces, Dominie had seen signs of growing confidence and determination. Perhaps her reckless scheme to locate Armand Flambard and win his help had been the right course, after all.

Now they rode toward Harwood with a small retinue, including young Gavin, who'd insisted on leading the procession.

Dominie caught Armand's eye, lowering her voice so her brother might not hear. ''Are you certain it was wise to let Gavin come along?''

Her mother had not been in favor of the idea, and had only relented when Armand made a special appeal to her, thereby winning Gavin's adoration for life.

"The lad's growing." Armand's gaze strayed toward Gavin and a smile of fond forbearance hovered on his lips. "Before you know it, he will hold the De Montford lands in his own right. He has much to learn before then."

"If he does not come to grief in the learning," Dominie grumbled. "I have never known anyone with his penchant for misadventure. The instant he conceives of some new and daring exploit, he undertakes it without a moment's pause to weigh the risks."

Armand laughed. "Have you never glanced in that silver mirror of your mother's? There are many who might call your recent journey to Breckland *misadventure,* if they knew the right of it."

"That was altogether different!" Dominie sputtered. "I was mindful of the dangers and took care to avoid them."

"As the lad will learn, given a chance." Armand shaded his eyes and peered into the distance, most likely hoping for his first glimpse of Harwood. "Perhaps you were too young to remember some of the trouble Denys and I got into when we were Gavin's age. I would say boldness runs in the De Montford blood. With a little seasoning of caution, it is not an ill trait for a nobleman."

"Provided he lives long enough to cultivate it." Dominie watched the young rascal putting more and more distance between himself and the rest of the party.

"I won't let any harm come to your brother," said Armand, in a tone that suggested Dominie might mistrust him. "Mark me, if you and your mother try to coddle him too much, he may run into worse danger just to prove his hardihood."

Armand's advice sounded like good sense. Still, it rubbed Dominie the wrong way. "I did not fetch you all the way from Breckland to instruct me how to raise my brother, Flambard."

"Perhaps not. But since you did fetch me, I feel it my duty to give you good value for all your trouble." Armand shot her a teasing look that held a little boldness of its own.

Boldness that might bring her to grief if she did not exercise proper caution. She must bear in mind that Armand Flambard would be gone once the crops were safely in. He would not stay to harvest any of the tender feelings he chanced to sow in her heart.

Perhaps some sign of her thoughts revealed itself on Dominie's face, for Armand suddenly urged his mount to quicken its speed, outpacing hers.

"What are you doing?" Dominie called after him.

He glanced back, the wind whipping his rich brown hair, and Dominie was struck anew by his handsome looks.

"I'm going to catch up with Gavin and see that he comes to no harm."

Could that be another reason he had allowed her brother to accompany them? Dominie wondered. To provide a buffer between the two of them, in case she tried to get too close?

Well, he needn't bother!

Boldness might run in the De Montford blood, but her people were not fools. They learned from their wounds, and she had suffered deep ones on Armand Flambard's account.

She watched as he caught up with Gavin and began to engage the boy in talk. Little by little, Armand slowed his horse, compelling Gavin to curb his speed so they could remain together. The rest of the party had caught up with them by the time they reached Harwood.

The guard in the watchtower called down his usual challenge.

Before either Dominie or Armand could answer, Gavin cried, "Throw open the gates! Armand Flambard has returned to Harwood to rally your people against the Wolf of the Fens!"

Armand glanced back at Dominie with a slightly sheepish grin. Hard as he might try to hide it, she sensed his excitement in this homecoming.

She waited for the cry of disbelief and the shout of joy that had first greeted them at Wakeland.

Instead, the gatekeeper's reply bristled with dismissive scorn. "Aye, we heard he'd come."

None of the others in the party might have noticed, but Dominie saw Armand Flambard's proud head bow beneath the unspoken rebuke. She did not want to feel a crumb of pity for him.

But her heart would not be denied.

Chapter Nine

What ailed the people of Harwood? Armand had never seen such a sullen, grim-faced lot.

After the jubilant welcome he'd received at Wakeland, he had anticipated an even warmer one here. After all, most folk on these manors had been born Flambard vassals, like their parents. Since their lands lay nearer the Fens, they would bear the brunt of any assault by Eudo St. Maur. By rights that should have made them all the more anxious for whatever aid they could get.

But they had made him feel about as welcome as a leper, from the castellan, Wat FitzJohn, down to the lowliest stable boy. Armand had told himself to pay no heed, but that was not as easy to do as it sounded. Not with two dozen pairs of eyes trained on him as if eager to catch a stumble or a word misspoken. Two dozen lips curled to varying degrees. Two dozen noses wrinkled as if they smelled something foul. In spite of his best efforts, Armand felt his hackles rise.

They all ranged around one of the trestle tables in the great hall, arms crossed in front of them, directing dubious gazes at the map Armand had brought with him from Wakeland.

"There is much to be done before harvest tide," he warned them, "if we hope to keep the fruit of our labors for ourselves rather than filling the bellies of Eudo St. Maur's outlaw band."

A restive murmur rippled among his listeners.

Armand rounded on the castellan. "If you have aught to say to me, spit it out, man, before it gags you!"

The man's scowl deepened. "*Whose* labors would those be, again, my lord Flambard?"

"Ours," Armand repeated. Seeing many brows raised, he amended, "That is…yours. Theirs."

Before he got thoroughly rattled, Dominie spoke up. "I did not fetch my lord Flambard all this way to quibble over words, Wat FitzJohn. If you have any wit, you will heed him."

Her forceful gaze picked out each man in turn, making most of them squirm. "The same goes for all of you."

When she had her servants and vassals all thoroughly cowed, she nodded to Armand. "Pray continue, my lord."

Armand pressed his lips together to keep them from twitching. It appeared he was not the only man over whom Dominie De Montford rode roughshod when she felt it necessary. To look at her now, he could scarcely believe she was the same lass who had trembled and wept in his arms after slaying the ruffian who'd attacked her in Thetford Forest.

He offered her a curt nod of gratitude for her support, then pointed to the map. "Regardless of whose labor it is, *our* chief task will be to protect the harvest on the outlying manors."

"How can anyone protect 'em?" asked a stocky men with grizzled hair as he stepped forward. "The Wolf and his pack know where to find us right enough, but we have no way to guess where or when they may strike."

"A fair question, Harold Bybrook." Armand recognized the man as one of his father's favorite tenants, who held a large manor on the northern boundary of the Flambard estates.

The De Montford estates, he reminded himself, trying to stifle a pang of betrayal that wrung his heart whenever he thought of it.

Master Bybrook's truculent appearance softened a little when Armand called him by name. Had he thought himself forgotten by the man who'd once been his lord? Had they all?

Armand ran his finger over the map, along the boundary between farmland and the Anglian Fens. "St. Maur and his pack cannot strike from just anywhere along this line. There are only so many dry paths through that swampy terrain. Fewer still that horses may tread."

"That's so." Harold Bybrook gave a ponderous nod, as he glanced around at some of the men nearest him. "It still makes too many ways he can come at me for my peace of mind."

"And mine," Armand replied. "But it is a place to start, at least. We need to scout those routes our enemy is most likely to take, so we can mount watches and lay traps."

A few of the men Armand recognized as living nearest the Fens appeared to approve his suggestions. Some of the others, however, muttered among themselves, glancing toward him now and then with scowls.

Finally, one stepped forward, nudged by his neighbors. "Why have we been called here, I want to know? I have plowing and sowing to oversee, fences that need tending and the like. All this talk of watch-guarding and traps and defending is all well and good, but it has naught to do with me…with any of us."

A low grumble of agreement rose from those near the speaker, emboldening him to wax even more brazen. "The De Montfords are our lords. We pay our rents and work our time on their demesne. In exchange, they're meant to let us work our own strips and to protect us from the likes of the Wolf. Must we now see to our own defense on top of all else we have to do?"

Armand glanced at Dominie to find her fair face pale as whey and her eyes blazing green fury.

"I have heard about as much as from you as I can stomach, Roald Fowler." She looked ready to flay a good wide strip off him with her tongue.

Catching her eye, Armand shook his head. "I believe I can answer your questions, Master Fowler. But not here." He strode toward the door of the great hall. "We ride."

When they lingered behind, whispering to one another, he bellowed, "Now!" in a voice that echoed in the high vaulted beams of the ceiling.

That brought them scurrying after him, with Dominie driving out the last stragglers.

A short time later, when he helped her mount, she leaned close to him and whispered, "What are you about now, Flambard? Are you certain this is a good idea?"

Her scent made him dizzy.

"You needn't come if you'd rather not." He didn't need the distraction. Besides that, he wanted to reestablish his authority with his vassals...*her* vassals...on his own terms.

For all that, Armand could not contain a perverse glimmer of satisfaction when Dominie replied, "Of course I'm coming."

"Then you'll soon see what I'm about." He gazed up at her, his hands still clasped around her slender waist. It took an effort of will for him to pry them off. "As for whether it is a good idea, I cannot be certain. I only know it must be done."

"I hope you're right." Dominie sounded skeptical.

Armand could feel hostile gazes directed his way as the bailey echoed with the nickers and whinnies of horses, the rattle of harnesses, the muted clatter of hooves on the hard-packed earth, and the grunts of men hoisting themselves into saddles.

"So do I, lass." He ran his hand over the smooth, firm flank of Dominie's horse. "So do I."

Where in heaven's name was Armand taking them? Dominie asked herself with mounting alarm as their party rode farther and farther from the relative safety of Harwood.

A raw spring wind fluttered the horses' manes and their hooves beat a brisk rhythm over the Icknield Way, an old royal road that had fallen into disuse since Eudo St. Maur had occupied the Fens. Surely a large troop of armed horsemen would be safe enough…provided they did not tarry too long.

Glancing around at those tenants and vassals riding nearest her, Dominie could see the grim set of their features and the way their eyes trained on Armand's back. If looks were arrows, he'd have been a dead man.

For all their sakes, she hoped he had a good reason for whatever he was doing.

Just then, Armand reined in his steed and raised his hand for the others to halt. He waited in silence as they curbed their mounts and the last few stragglers caught up.

"Well?" came a gruff demand.

Dominie could not see who had spoken.

Armand gave no sign he'd heard. Slowly turning in his saddle, he pointed to the northwest and spoke one word.

"Behold!"

A few questioning grunts gave way to gasps of horror as the party looked where Armand had bidden them. Dominie guessed the men had been so busy staring daggers at him that they had not noticed the countryside around them until that moment.

Now she understood why Armand had brought them here.

The road had climbed a crest of rising land, providing a wide view of the devastation that had been wrought. For as far as Dominie could see, no living thing stirred. Fields that should have been plowed and sown lay barren. Snug thatched cottages had been reduced to blackened rubble. The bleached bones of some large animal, a horse, perhaps, or an ox, lay in the middle of an empty field where the beast had fallen.

And what had become of the people who'd once tilled this land? The thought made Dominie's throat tighten.

Armand let the appalling sight sink in. Then he raised his voice once more. "No lord, alone, can protect you and your families from *that*. If you would keep the Wolf and his pack from devouring everything you have spent your lives building, the old ways will not suffice."

He paused, perhaps waiting for one of them to challenge what he had said. But no one spoke. Dominie suspected the nightmare scene before them had robbed her vassals of words.

Armand nodded, as if satisfied that he had finally gained their attention. "Every man, woman and child in Harwood and Wakeland will have to pitch in and labor as they have never labored before if your lands are not to look like these when next spring comes."

His face took on a grave, troubled expression. "Even then it may not be enough."

Dominie had to remind herself that it would not matter to him. Succeed or fail, he would be back in the peaceful cloisters of Breckland.

"It *will* be enough!" she cried, startling her horse, which tossed its mane and whinnied. "It *must!*"

"Aye!"

"So it will!"

A chorus of support swelled from men who were shocked and frightened, but also angry and resolved.

Armand's gaze roved from one to another, seeking, meeting and challenging them.

"Go home now," he said at last. "Tell your families what you have seen, or not, as you deem fit. Think upon what we must do between now and harvest, and upon what part you can play. Come back to Harwood tomorrow prepared to listen and to contribute. We cannot afford to waste much time in talk, but neither do we dare go forward without a sound plan."

A murmur of grudging agreement ran through the party. Some turned their mounts back toward Harwood, perhaps too sickened to bear the sight of St. Maur's devastation a moment longer.

But they stopped and looked toward Armand when he gestured for their attention.

"One more thing we cannot afford, good men, is to waste our time and our energy fighting among ourselves, when we need every scrap of it and more to deal with our common enemy. If any man among you is not prepared to submit to my leadership, let him declare it openly when we meet tomorrow. After that, be warned, I will not forbear underhanded dealing from any of you."

For a moment after Armand fell silent, the men did not

stir. Even their horses stood quiet, as if bound by the spell of his authority. Dominie found herself caught up in it, too.

Here was the Armand Flambard of whom she'd gone in search. The Armand Flambard she remembered from their youth. Not some prickly, prudish monk-to-be.

But a man. A leader. A lord, in the very best sense of that word.

She had done right to recruit him from Breckland, even against his will. In her extravagant fancies, she had pictured Armand besting Eudo St. Maur and his rabble single-handed. But this was better. It was real. It was possible.

He would show the folk of Harwood how to defend themselves, and he would inspire them with the confidence to take their own part against any who assailed them. Then he could return to Breckland Abbey with a clean conscience.

Though Dominie pulled her cloak tighter around her, a chill snaked its way up her backbone just the same. For the spring wind was only partly to blame.

It was bad enough that Armand Flambard meant to desert her again. Would he twist the knife by making her admire and care for him again before he went away?

"You certainly put the fear of God into my vassals, Flambard," said Dominie the next day, after their second meeting had drawn to a close. "I've never seen them so quiet and biddable."

Her words should have sounded like praise to Armand, but they did not.

She'd been subdued ever since they had returned from yesterday's ride. Had she been shaken by the harsh reminder of what might happen to Harwood if they failed to rout Eudo St. Maur? If so, Armand was sorry, but he had tried to warn her. She'd insisted on accompanying the men.

Somehow, he doubted that was the cause. More likely Dominie had been afflicted with the same thinly veiled antagonism that plagued her vassals. The kind she had bristled with when they'd first set out from Breckland. He'd thought the shared perils of their journey had broken through it. Or perhaps he'd fooled himself into believing so.

"Remember what it says in the book of Proverbs." He tried to banter her out of her ill-humor. "'The fear of the Lord is the beginning of wisdom.'" At least he'd hoped it would be so for the men of Harwood.

Dominie did not look amused. "Spoken like a true Benedictine."

That might be. Armand didn't feel much like one, though, wearing a fine robe that had belonged to his late father, with a sword girded around his waist. His old life had the power to seduce him, if he let it.

That fear sharpened his tone. "You make it sound a crime to be a holy brother."

"So it is in your case!" Her palm slammed against the table with such force it made Armand start. "A crime of waste. I've watched you from the moment we reached Wakeland. Yesterday, especially. It's plain you were put on this earth to be a leader of men, just as a hawk was meant to fly and a fish to swim."

Why must she say such things? He had felt it himself, every time he'd given an order, and with every part of their plan that had unfolded. Like a caged bird taking to the sky, or a fish wriggling through a hole in the net to hurl itself back into the welcoming sea.

He had refused to let himself acknowledge it, but Dominie's indignant challenge made that impossible.

"I made a vow," he reminded her…and himself. "And even if I hadn't, what is there for me in the world?"

He made a sweeping gesture that took in the great hall, almost identical to the one at Wakeland. "All this is yours now. As are those stubborn vassals."

"So they are." Dominie's eyes flashed with a warning a wiser man might have heeded. "But only after you turned your back on them. Do you blame my family for taking what King Stephen offered us after you abandoned it?"

Was *that* the answer to his question about what ailed the people of Harwood? Did they resent him for standing by his oath to the empress?

"I cannot deny it cut me to the heart when I heard the king had given Harwood to your family. I felt the De Montfords had betrayed me somehow. As though a lifetime of devotion had been spurned for gain. Can you understand *that?*"

"Better than you might think." With each word, Dominie took a step closer to him until they stood toe-to-toe. "At least I could understand betrayal for gain. If you had broken our betrothal to wed an heiress with thousands of acres as her dowry, I could have pictured myself measured on a merchant's scale, and felt as if I were worth *something,* if not enough."

"Never!" The very notion made Armand bilious. "I would not have given you up for a king's ransom. Nor a thousand times a thousand acres!"

He glanced down to find his hands curled around her upper arms. The urge to prove his words by kissing her was almost more than he could resist.

"Yet you gave me up for *nothing.*" Dominie did not shake off his hold as he'd expected—and half hoped. Instead, she gazed up at him with eyes full of bewildered bitterness. "A word. An ill-made promise."

"Can you not see?" He tried to let go of her, but he could not. "That promise was worth more to me than any amount of property or gold."

Armand might have borne the breach between him and his foster family more easily if they had declared for Stephen of Blois on some point of principle. That Stephen would make a better sovereign, perhaps, or that a woman had no right to rule England.

But Lord Baldwin had never claimed any great partiality for the king. Indeed, he had often said he would switch his support back to the empress without a qualm, if ever she gained power in the east of England. How could a man live with himself, Armand wondered, if he put his allegiance on auction to the highest bidder?

"No." Dominie spoke in a whisper, but her voice was as unyielding as stone. "I cannot see how a word that is gone the instant it leaves my lips, or a thought that has no form at all, can have more value than things of substance—food I can eat, land I can till, coin I can spend."

He felt the hurt that radiated from her, and it tempered his resentment.

"'Do not lay up for yourself treasure on earth,'" he reminded her in a gentle voice, "'which moth and rust can destroy or thieves break in and steal.'"

His kindly meant words seemed to provoke her worse than his earlier anger.

"More monk's mouthings!" she cried as she wrenched herself from his grasp, then strode toward the staircase that led to her solar. "Perhaps it is a good thing events fell out as they did."

"Do not say so!" Armand would have done or given almost anything to have made it all come out differently.

Anything but his honor.

"Why not say it?" Dominie spun around to face him again. "It is true, and truth seems to be one of those ideals you cherish above all. If this war had not prevented us from wedding, you and I might have driven each other mad with our quarreling." Her voice broke, then recovered. "For we are as different as can be and neither of us can see the other's side."

Her indictment struck him a harder blow than it would have if she'd spoken those words in any other place but here—the heart of the home he had once hoped to share with her.

"Perhaps I cannot see the world as you do," he admitted. "But I see now that the manner of my going caused you pain. That grieves me more than you will ever reckon."

"Do not fret yourself. That was long in the past." Though Dominie tried to appear indifferent, a suspicious glitter in her eyes betrayed her true feelings.

Perhaps she was right. Perhaps the time for explanations and apologies was too long past. They would not change anything.

Except, perhaps, the way she regarded herself.

Had that been the true reason she'd never wed another man? Because she believed he had weighed her in the balance and found her worthless?

He could not let her continue to think so, no matter how it would grieve him to acknowledge what he had lost. No matter the danger in revealing the depth of his old feelings for her.

Feelings that five years had not altered nearly as much as he'd tried to pretend they had.

"Though you may not value the things I do," he said as he walked slowly toward her, "or ever understand *why*

I value them so highly, can you at least accept that I do treasure them? And that, in my own eyes, I did not cast you away easily?''

She retreated a little from his approach, into a shadow-wrapped alcove that led to the stairs.

"I wish I could believe that, Armand." Her murmured words ached with longing for his assurance.

Armand sensed that nothing he could say would convince or comfort her. He took another step toward her, not quite knowing what he meant to do.

Perhaps Dominie understood better than he did, for she did not retreat this time. Instead, she moved toward him, almost reluctantly. As if drawn against her will by something within him that called to her.

Then, suddenly, she was in his arms, her head tilted to accept his kiss.

His lips closed over hers. Softly at first, with no more pressure than a cool breeze on a fevered brow.

Then the fever swept through him—a raging sickness for which there could be only one remedy.

He pulled her closer, tasting her more deeply, tormenting himself with the truth of what he had lost forever.

"I promise you," he assured her in a fierce whisper, "your pain was no more than my own in having to make the choice I did."

She had melted into his embrace, supple and receptive. Now Dominie tensed, as if her flesh had suddenly frozen. She pushed him away with such savage force, he staggered backward.

"At least you had a choice!" She hurled the words at him, then turned and fled up the stairs, leaving Armand's composure and convictions in tatters.

Something urged him to follow her and thrash this matter out. Clearly, neither of them would have any peace while it hung between them, unresolved.

But this was not the proper time or place, his well-honed sense of caution warned him. If he were to go to her private quarters now, with feelings running so high between them, he was not certain he could trust himself to behave with honor.

Chapter Ten

What might have happened if Armand had followed her up to the privacy of her solar that day?

Too often in the past weeks, Dominie had fretted about that question. And too often she had lapsed into foolish, wanton fancies, imagining the answer.

In an effort to banish both from her thoughts, she'd thrown herself into the exhausting, multifarious task of preparing the De Montford estates to meet the threat that lurked in the Fenlands. Scouting possible routes of approach with tenants who knew the area well. Debating the merits of different alarm signals—horns, flares, riders. Even hefting a shovel to help dig pits where provisions might be hidden from marauders.

Her labors helped occupy her thoughts during the day, while bringing sleep swiftly at night, before she could succumb to fruitless fancies.

Now, as she rode toward Wakeland in the golden sunshine of May, with nothing else to occupy her mind, they threatened to return and bedevil her.

On either side of the narrow road, a gentle breeze wafted through thriving grain that seemed to grow measurably taller from one day to the next. Dominie inhaled a deep breath, savoring the fresh, sweet fragrance of flourishing life. It nurtured a bud of hope that had begun to take root in her heart.

Off in the fields, older children roved among the tall rows of oats, rye and wheat with long hoes, rooting out weeds wherever they found them. One boy raised his hand in a sweeping wave that caught Dominie's eye. As she slowed her horse, he shouldered his hoe and ran toward her.

"Mind the grain, Gavin!" she called to her brother. "You mustn't trample it."

Heeding her warning for once, the lad slowed his pace and picked his way to the edge of the field with more care.

"Where are you off to?" He gazed up at her, raising his arm to shade his eyes from the sun.

"Wakeland, to visit Mother and to see how everyone is getting along there. Do you want to come?" Dominie patted her mount's flank. "You can ride pillion."

Her brother's boisterous company on the ride might help to keep thoughts of Armand at bay.

For a moment Gavin looked tempted by her invitation, then he shook his head. "Armand promised if I helped with the weeding, he'd let me take part in the fighting practice after noon. He says I'm getting to be a fine shot with the short bow."

An indulgent smile tugged at the corner of Dominie's lips. Ever since Armand's return, Gavin had stuck to the poor man like a burr.

"As you will, then. I'll tell Mother you're well and fetch you back some clean linen. Do take care where you aim that bow after this," she pleaded. "Poor Wat might have been badly hurt if Armand had not pushed him out of the way at the last instant."

Gavin scowled at the ground, scuffing the grass with his foot. "Wat FitzJohn ought to pay better mind where he goes. He's so busy grumbling about everything that he takes no notice what is going on about him."

"You're a fine one to talk about people minding where they go. Behave yourself while I'm gone and don't pester the life out of Armand." Dominie jogged the reins and her horse set off again. "If all's well at Wakeland, I should be back the day after tomorrow."

His brief scolding over, Gavin brightened again. "God go with you, Dominie!" he called after her. "I'll keep Armand such good company he'll hardly even miss you."

Her brother's carefree assurance troubled Dominie vaguely as she continued her ride to Wakeland. Gavin or no Gavin, Armand Flambard was not likely to miss her. Was he?

The two of them had kept so busy in the past month that many days they saw one another only at the evening meal. And then their talk was about practical matters such as the encouraging growth of the crops and the favorable farming weather that felt like a special blessing from heaven. They kept each other informed of progress in their ongoing efforts to improve defenses and protect the harvest once it was reaped.

Never in her life had Dominie been so indifferent to practical matters! She found herself both hoping and fearing their conversation might stray into sensitive territory, as it had on the eve he'd kissed her.

It had come as a mixed revelation that Armand had not given her up without a struggle, after all. His words alone would not have been enough to convince Dominie. But in the passionate remorse of his kiss and the raw anguish of his tone, she had sensed the bitter truth.

In some ways this new insight made their old parting

harder to reconcile. If only he had given her some sign at the time, perhaps she could have persuaded him to follow his heart rather than his high-flown principles. And yet, knowing she had once meant so much to him restored a vital confidence in herself that Dominie had not missed until she'd suddenly regained it.

No amount of talking could change the past, her practical nature insisted. Nor could it alter the future. So many barriers loomed between her and Armand. One might be crumbling, but others remained as stout and impregnable as ever.

"I promised Dominie I'd keep you close company while she's gone." Gavin De Montford fixed Armand with a worshipful gaze that never failed to disturb his unwilling hero.

"That was good of you." Armand stifled a passing wish that the boy had accompanied his sister back to Wakeland for a visit.

Not that he disliked young Gavin—quite the contrary. But the vivid reminder of his happy, lost youth and the boy's undeserved admiration chafed at his tenuous peace of mind almost as much as Dominie's constant nearness.

"I've spent the whole morning battling weeds, as you bade me." Gavin held up his dirt-encrusted hoe as proof. "Now will you teach me some sword craft?"

Armand glanced around the bit of flat meadow outside Harwood's bailey. During this month's lull between harrowing and hay-making, he had summoned together Dominie's able-bodied male vassals to teach them some fighting skills they could use in defense of their homes and families.

His conscience protested that training other men to fight was little better than hoisting a sword himself. Worse, perhaps, since it multiplied the violence many fold. But prayers alone would not stop Eudo St. Maur, he reminded himself. If they had, abbeys and churches on the fringe of the Fens would not have suffered so cruelly.

"I'd rather you perfected your bowmanship before you move on to swordplay." Armand steeled himself against the boy's pleading gaze.

An archer could fire from a distance, behind cover. Armand could not bear the thought of Gavin making any closer acquaintance with danger.

"*If* an attack comes..." How desperately Armand prayed it would not! "...I hope we will be able to drive the marauders off with as little bloodshed on our side as possible."

"I'll make them rue the day they menaced *my* lands!" Gavin dropped his hoe in favor of an imaginary sword, cleaving the air with energetic strokes.

Armand stooped to pick up the hoe before the lad hurt himself by treading on it. "Don't be too eager to spill another man's blood, Gavin."

He pointed to a large canvas sack stuffed with straw, which several men were striking with swords and staves. "They aren't like that, your enemies. They will have faces and names and kin, just like you. And they will have reasons for assailing you as compelling as yours for combating them."

Gavin's phantom sword drooped as he mulled over this new and questionable notion.

It seemed to spawn another idea in his young mind. He fixed Armand with a troubled gaze. "You were once our enemy, weren't you?"

Armand replied with a rueful nod. "Sadly, true. Though not by any desire of my own."

"Then why have you come to our aid now?" Gavin

appeared as distressed to ask the question as Armand was to hear it. "And how do we know we can trust you?"

As Armand struggled to frame an explanation that would make sense to the lad, a deeper voice rang out behind him. "Pray answer the young master, why don't you, my lord? 'Tis a question I have asked myself more than once since you returned to Harwood unlooked for."

Turning to face Wat FitzJohn, Armand battled to keep his rising temper in check. The man vexed him in a way no Benedictine should allow himself to be vexed. Was it the fellow's barely concealed insolence? Or could it be the familiar way he looked at Dominie and addressed her?

"If the question has been on your mind, why did you not ask it aloud, as the boy has, Master FitzJohn?" Before the castellan could do more than glower, Armand swept his hand toward the vassals practicing combat skills. "Is there aught I am doing that would make you think I could be in league with Eudo St. Maur?"

"Perhaps my doubts are unfounded," FitzJohn admitted in a grudging growl, "but these are perilous times for a man to be blindly trusting."

"So they are."

These folk had every right to regard him with suspicion, Armand reminded himself. He had abandoned Harwood to danger. He had deprived Wakeland of a capable lord. All for what? A word that was gone the instant it left his lips, or a thought, which had no form at all?

"Believe me or not." He looked from Gavin to Fitz-John and back again. "I owe allegiance to a higher power now. I came back to help you."

"Aye, my lord." The castellan did not sound convinced as he stalked off.

Gavin made a face at the man's back that would have

done credit to some of the leering gargoyles that adorned the cathedral in Cambridge.

"Now, now." Armand tried not to chuckle. "You voiced the same doubts he did."

"It wasn't the same at all." Gavin reached to take his hoe back from Armand. "I do not believe you could mean us any harm. He does."

"Pay him no mind." How Armand wished he could heed his own advice. "Time will prove him wrong. Come, let's find you a bow and quiver."

As he strode toward a part of the field where a number of men were shooting arrows at another straw-stuffed sack, Gavin hurried to fall in step with him.

"You never did tell me *why* you came back to help us," said the boy. "But I can guess."

Armand slanted a glance toward him. "There wasn't much need to ask then, was there?"

Gavin's golden-brown eyes danced with secret glee. "It's Dominie, isn't it? You came because she asked you."

He was mighty tempted to deny it. After all, he had left Breckland at the abbot's bidding, not Dominie's. And he did not want to encourage Gavin in impossible hopes the boy had no business entertaining.

But neither could Armand lie outright. He *was* there because of Dominie. For all she had once meant to him and for all he owed her.

He gave a brief nod in answer.

"I *knew* it!" Gavin thrust his hoe skyward and kicked his heels together. Then he lowered his voice. "Are the two of you going to get married, as you were supposed to?"

"No!" A vision of Dominie with a wedding wreath in her hair stirred in Armand's fancy, taunting him. "Once the harvest has been safely gathered, I will return to the abbey and become a monk. And your sister will find herself the kind of husband she needs.''

A man with estates to add to hers. A man whose practical nature would accord well with hers. A man who had not broken her heart once already. A man who had not given her beloved father his death blow.

''But you love her, don't you?'' Gavin's brow furrowed in puzzlement. ''She's agreeable enough, though she is a girl. I know she can sometimes order a body to death, but that's just her way of taking care of us, Mother says.''

Armand could not stand to hear another word. ''There is nothing *wrong* with your sister, boy! She's the fairest lass I've ever laid eyes on. She's clever and brave and able.'' His tongue ran away with him. ''Why, she's like a cup of mulled wine on a cold winter night. She…''

He bit down on his voluble tongue so hard he drew blood.

''Well,'' said Gavin, looking rather taken aback by Armand's passionate outburst, ''that's fine then. So you do love her.''

Before Armand could find a way to deny it, Gavin prattled on. ''Dominie's never been able to oust you from her heart. That's what I heard Mother tell one of her ladies a while ago. And that was back when we all thought you were dead. Fancy how much better she likes you now that she knows you're alive.''

''Enough of this!'' cried Armand, with such force he made the boy jump. ''You came to practice with the bow? Then do it, or go back to something useful like your weeding. I have too much work to do to stand around talking foolishness with you.''

''I…beg your pardon for speaking out of turn.'' The boy's chastened look reproached Armand. ''It's just that it has been so good to have you back among us. There is a different feeling in the air and among the people. Dominie most of all. If you stay, perhaps we can keep that feeling.''

Armand shook his head. ''It is I who should beg your pardon, Gavin, for being so testy. Someday you will think back on this and understand. There is more to marriage than a man and a woman having a liking for one another.''

No matter what wishful opinions her brother might harbor, Dominie no longer cared for him. She had told him so, frank and plain. If she seemed altered to Gavin, in a good way, it must be because Armand had succeeded in lightening her burden. Or because she believed her estates might be ready to withstand an attack from Eudo St. Maur.

Solid, practical reasons, not some intangible fancy, like love. And that was well, for if she did not love him, she would not be hurt when he went away again.

Armand wished he could claim that protection for his own heart.

''How have you been feeling, Mother?'' Dominie stooped to drop a kiss on her mother's soft, pale cheek. ''Any weak spells lately?''

Blanchefleur De Montford looked up from her needlework with a smile. ''Nary a one since I returned from Breckland. Their holy well is truly blessed.''

Father Clement had been reading to her mother from his breviary when Dominie entered the solar. Now he nodded his agreement. ''Our visit there was doubly blessed. Gaining healing for my lady and restoring Lord Flambard to us.''

''How is dear Armand?'' Dominie's mother gestured for her to take a seat, then called for wine and cheese.

"And Gavin? I miss him so, but I know he needs a man in his life again. And I trust Armand to see that he does not come to harm."

"Gavin is well. He sends you his love. He has little time for mischief these days. Armand is keeping us all busy."

Dominie launched into an eager account of their activities and plans. Watches mounted on the approaches from the Fens. A system of signals that would summon help from all the neighboring manors in the event of an attack. Precautions to limit the amount of provisions the brigands could plunder from any one manor or village.

"Fancy that!" Her mother's eyes grew round with wonder. "Young Armand learned well from your dear father, God rest his soul."

"It is not all Armand's planning." Dominie took the cup of wine offered by one of her mother's ladies. "I had a say in it, as did many of my vassals. Come to think on it, the notion of digging pits to hide foodstuffs came from a serf woman."

For all she had adored her father, Dominie harbored no illusions that he would have sought advice or solicited cooperation from his vassals. Perhaps the vow that limited Armand's ability to lead the fighting had been a blessing in disguise.

"This is good cheese," she said, after she had taken a bite.

Her mother nodded. "The goats and cows are giving rich milk this year, for the pasturage is so good. The women can hardly keep up with butter and cheese making."

Father Clement glanced heavenward. "Another boon for which to give thanks." He rose from his chair. "Now that Lady Dominie has arrived, I will see to my other duties and leave the two of you to talk in private.''

After an exchange of parting pleasantries, the priest withdrew.

Dominie glanced at the swath of soft green wool on her mother's lap. It reminded her of the moss in Thetford Forest. ''What is that you're working on? It looks pretty.''

''It's a new gown for you, of course.'' Lady Blanchefleur held up the garment, of a simple but flattering design.

The sleeves flared out from the elbow and there was a band of delicate embroidery, in shades of gold and darker green, at the neck.

''You see?'' said Dominie's mother, looking quite proud of herself. ''I haven't had time to be ill. I want this ready for you to wear at our Lammastide feast.''

''You need not work yourself so hard. Lammastide is two months off yet. Besides, I don't need a new gown. I have a number that are still good and serviceable.''

''But not pretty.'' A coy smile arched her mother's tiny, primrose mouth as she picked up her needle again. ''You don't want Armand to go away again, do you?''

Dominie found herself far from eager to answer that question. Even in the privacy of her own heart.

She countered her mother's troubling question with one of her own. ''What does that have to do with new gowns and Lammastide?''

Lady Blanchefleur gave a tinkling laugh, as though she had never heard so ridiculous a question. ''Why, everything, my sweet, if you want to coax Armand to offer for your hand!''

''Who says I want that?'' Dominie bolted the last of her wine. ''If Armand desired me for a wife, he had his chance.''

Somehow, she could not summon up her old bitterness to its usual intensity.

"Can you not forgive him, after all this time?" Clucking her tongue, Lady Blanchefleur made a dainty stitch with her gold thread. "That may be a measure of how much you cared for him once."

"And what if I did?" Dominie leaped from her chair, which was beginning to feel like a torturer's rack with herself a victim from whom painful confessions were being wrung. "As you say, time has passed. Time in which he entered an abbey and set his heart on becoming a monk. Wouldn't you think it wicked to seduce a man away from the church?"

"So I would!" Lady Blanchefleur looked shocked at the very suggestion. "*If* that were where he belonged. After working alongside Armand Flambard these past weeks, can you truly tell me he belongs in an abbey?"

How could she say so, no matter how far she was prepared to bend the truth? She had told Armand he would be wasted in an abbey, and she believed it. Besides, could a man destined for celibacy kiss a woman the way he had kissed her that day at Harwood or that night in Thetford Forest?

"It does not matter what *I* think." Dominie fixed her mother with a severe look. "Nor what you think. Armand has made up his mind that an abbey is the place for him. I doubt a green gown will change his mind, no matter how fine your embroidery."

"Not the gown by itself, perhaps," agreed her mother, still intent on her needlework. "But the gown with you in it, perhaps your hair dressed in a different style, might make him reconsider. When a man becomes occupied with work and warfare, he sometimes cannot see what is right under his nose, poor creature. But let him take a little ease at a feast, drink and dance. Then a lady he has taken for granted may suddenly catch his eye if she goes to a little effort.''

Fie, but her dear, pious mother was as persuasive as the serpent in Eden!

"But, Mother..."

Lady Blanchefleur looked up from her embroidery, fixing Dominie with a gaze that was almost forceful. "We need Armand Flambard, my sweet. Me, Gavin, Harwood and Wakeland. You most of all. You are changed since he returned. You were like a young tree caught in the grip of an early frost. Now you have begun to bloom again."

When her own heart had tempted and taunted her with such thoughts, Dominie had been able to smother them under a thick blanket of work and practical matters. Her mother was proving much more difficult to silence. Especially since some foolish, fanciful part of Dominie longed to heed and believe.

"As much as you need Armand," said Lady Blanchefleur in a persuasive murmur, "I believe he needs you even more."

"If Armand needs me, he knows where to find me." He could have found her in the solar of Harwood that day she'd fled from him, if only he'd bothered to follow.

Her mother gave a little shrug. "But does he know he is allowed to look?"

"What does that mean?" Dominie snapped.

Since her father and Denys had left Wakeland to fight for King Stephen, she had become accustomed to her mother turning to her for assistance, support and advice, almost as if their roles had been reversed. Dominie felt strange, and somehow vulnerable, being on the receiving end of her mother's counsel.

"Don't be cross with me, my sweet. I only want to see

the two of you happy after all this time. What I meant was that Armand may not feel he has the right to vie for you again, after having given you up once.''

That simple notion tumbled Dominie's whole world onto its head.

With halting steps she approached her mother's chair and sank to the floor at her feet. Then she did something she had not done since she was a young child—rested her head against her mother's knee.

''But what if I try and he still doesn't want me? I don't know if I could bear that again.''

Her mother's delicate fingers caressed her hair. ''It will take courage, my sweet, but you have never lacked for that. You are so like your dear father. I don't believe you can bear *not* to fight for what you want.''

Chapter Eleven

Dominie's vassals had learned to fight, Armand acknowledged, leaning on the handle of his scythe and wiping the sweat from his brow with his forearm. Now he must keep his part of their compact, by pitching in with the field work. With St. Barnabas Day past and the weather favorable, the folk of Harwood and Wakeland were busy making hay.

To Armand's mind, the vassals had the better part of the bargain. Learning to wield a weapon was not half the labor of plying a sharp, curved blade through thick swaths of green hay.

"A drink?" offered a familiar woman's voice from behind him.

He turned toward Dominie. "You must have read my mind, lass."

"It is not difficult to guess that when a man rests at his work on a hot day, he may be ready for some refreshment."

She lofted a teasing smile in his direction as she poured a generous measure of ale from a clay pitcher into a cup, then handed it to him. If he hadn't know better, he might have called her smile flirtatious. But that was nonsense, surely.

"The sun has baked you good and brown." Dominie's husky voice bubbled with laughter as she ran her finger down Armand's bare back from his shoulder to his waist.

A great mouthful of ale spewed out of his mouth in a fine spray.

Dominie paid no heed to his reaction, but went on bantering as if nothing had happened. "Remember when we fell in the brook coming from Breckland? You were white as a fish's belly then."

A beguiling memory took shape in Armand's mind, of Dominie as she had emerged from the brook with her clothes held over her head. That and the unexpectedly intimate touch of her fingertip against his hot, bare skin roused him to a painful pitch.

"Blue as the sky, more like," he muttered.

"Aye, that, too." Dominie gave a deep, delicious chuckle as though they were sharing some private lovers' jest. "'Tis a wonder we ever warmed up after that."

Not *such* a wonder. Armand would have defied any man to hold Dominie in his arms for a night without kindling a fire in his flesh.

The memory of it heated him almost as much as the hay cutting had. He took a long, thirsty swig of his ale, then handed the mug back to Dominie.

"Thank you for the drink. Now I had better get back to work before your vassals accuse me of shirking my duties."

All traces of mischievous merriment left her face. Her eyes gleamed with the lost admiration of their younger years. "There is nary a soul on these estates who does not know how hard you have labored these past weeks on our behalf. I marvel at all you have accomplished."

"I promised I would do my best for you."

That was what it had been, he suddenly realized. *For her.* Showing her, in a hundred small, practical ways, how much he regretted what his decision five years ago had cost her. Diverting the forbidden feelings that had begun to surge in his heart into more prudent channels.

"So you did." She set the mug and pitcher on the ground, among the freshly mown hay. "And so you have."

Reaching up, she rested one cool, slender hand against Armand's cheek in the most tender caress. Her vibrant hazel gaze ranged over his face in the softest, sweetest benediction he could imagine.

Around them, the scythes of the other mowers sliced through the tall hay with a sharp, rhythmic hiss, while the drone of bees hummed a promise of sweet honey. The wholesome fragrance of clover infused the summer air. And one sinner's heart swelled to bursting with a tantalizing foretaste of heaven.

"This is where you belong, Armand Flambard. Don't you feel it...in your flesh?"

The provocative music of Dominie's voice and the shimmer of heat in her gaze promised something even sweeter than honey. Warm, delicious fruit, ripe and succulent.

And altogether forbidden.

"I feel it," he whispered. "I taste it with my heart."

For one blissful, stolen moment, Armand leaned into her caress, nuzzling his whisker-stubbled cheek against the smooth palm of her hand and the sensitive tips of her fingers.

Then, with aching reluctance, he drew away. "For all that, I know it cannot be."

Her gaze faltered a little as she lowered her hand. Just then, his indomitable Dominie looked uncertain.

But why? He had only told her a truth her practical nature must recognize.

Then her moment of hesitation passed, as Armand had known it must. She did not square her shoulders, tilt her chin or give any of the usual signs of this change. But Armand hadn't watched her so avidly these past weeks without learning much about her.

"Know? Cannot?" A challenge rang in her voice. "Those words betoken more certainty than most men presume when they look to the future in such uncertain times."

What was she trying to tell him? Did she not sense how desperately he wanted to doubt his fate?

"I am only trying to be practical about my prospects." He stooped to retrieve his scythe. "Does that not please you?"

She considered his words for a moment. "It is not impractical to be hopeful."

"Hope for what?"

Armand turned away from her and proceeded to take out his longing and frustration on the hay. Given enough time and effort, he *could* hew it all down. Unlike the forest of thorns that stood between him and Dominie, which seemed to throw up two tough, twisted spines for every one he rooted out.

The exertion of mowing left him little breath to speak, but Armand managed something between a gasp and a grunt, intoned to the swing of his scythe. "We both know I couldn't stay here if I wanted to."

"Do you want to?"

Dominie's question so unnerved him he might have

slashed his own foot off, if he hadn't checked the scythe's wild swing at the last instant.

He didn't dare answer her question. It would make him sound too pitiful. "We have a crop of hay to get in before the weather breaks or Eudo St. Maur decides to attack. Hay that will feed your breeding stock through the winter. This is not the time for riddles and daydreams!"

The minute the words were out of his mouth in that harsh tone, Armand regretted them. Dominie had given him this rare opportunity to reclaim his soul from perdition. She had made him see why his old vassals resented his sudden return, yet she had backed him staunchly when they had balked at his plans.

If she'd tempted him, just now, with bittersweet glimpses of a desperately desired future he could never claim, she meant him no harm. Likely she was inspired by misplaced feelings of gratitude, or a sweet, false sense of the past revived.

All the same, Armand curbed his urge to offer her an apology, or even to glance back so he could watch her stalk off in anger. He would not be doing her a service by letting her entertain impossible fancies. Besides, the sight of her firmly rounded backside, swaying as she walked away, might tempt him to entertain a few of his own.

That man! Dominie was sorely tempted to baptize him with the remaining ale. And maybe break his crown by smashing the pitcher over his head for good measure!

She marched out of the hay meadow muttering curses under her breath.

Her mother was a ninny for making her think Armand Flambard could want her again! And Dominie was a bigger ninny, for letting herself be persuaded of something she should have had sense enough to doubt.

"Dominie!" Gavin's voice rang out behind her.

She turned, and before she had time to govern her tongue she snapped, "What do you want now?"

Her brother, who had been running toward her, skidded to a halt. "Only to know if I can go swim in the millpond with the other boys. We've finished turning all the hay that was cut yesterday, and it was hot work." Before she could answer, he asked, "Is that why you're cross—because it's hot?"

"I am not cross," Dominie insisted. "Not with you, anyway. You may swim with the boys, but not too much acting the fool or one of you is apt to drown."

Gavin ignored the permission he'd been granted. "Who are you cross with? FitzJohn? Armand?"

Her face must have betrayed the answer.

"Why?" asked Gavin. "What's he done?"

"Nothing." Dominie spun away and continued her walk toward the castle. "Armand has done nothing wrong. Your hero is a paragon. Now, go swim and leave me be."

Heedless as ever, Gavin fell into step beside her. "I'm sure Armand didn't mean to displease you. He likes you very much. That's why he came back and why he's worked so hard."

Against her will, Dominie's footsteps slowed. "H-he told you that?"

"He did!" Gavin's words tumbled out, all eager, as if he had been waiting for an excuse to tell her. "He said you're beautiful and clever...and something about mulled wine."

Dominie's cheeks blazed. She refused to glance at her

brother, in case her feelings should betray themselves. "Why did he tell you all this, pray?"

"Because I asked him if the two of you were going to get married, now that he'd come back."

"Gavin!" She fought the urge to box her brother's ears. "You didn't!"

"Why not? What was wrong with my asking? I am Lord of Wakeland and you are my sister. I have a right to know."

"Worry about getting a wife for yourself when you're grown, stripling, and stay out of my affairs!" Hard as she tried, she could not prevent herself from adding, "What did Armand say when you asked if he and I would wed?"

"He got cross, too. He said he would have to go away once the harvest is in, and that you would have to wed the kind of man you need. What does that mean, Dominie? Is Armand not the right kind of man for you? He's no longer our enemy, if that is what troubles you."

Why could Armand Flambard not see what was obvious even to a child like Gavin? "Did he say anything else?"

"Only that there was more to marriage than a man and woman liking one another." Gavin sounded perplexed by the notion. "He said I'd understand better when I get older."

Dominie almost dropped her ale pitcher when she heard her own opinion about marriage attributed to Armand. Had his sojourn into real life beyond the abbey walls taught him a little practical wisdom at last?

Slowing her steps, she turned to look at her brother. "Armand is right. You will understand when you are older. I'm sorry I spoke to you so sharply just now. You know my temper—hot to blaze, quick to cool."

"So you aren't angry with Armand anymore?" Gavin's step took on a bounce. "You won't send him away?"

Dominie glanced back toward the hay meadow. If Armand had learned some sense about marriage, perhaps there was a chance for them. Mother had been right about her being compelled to fight for what she wanted. The events of this war for the English throne had shown her that one lost battle did not mean total defeat. Only the necessity to retrench and try again.

A better time, a better place and the result might be a stunning victory.

When she finally answered her brother, it was as much to herself as to him she spoke. "If Armand Flambard goes away, it will be his decision, not mine."

Gavin gave a little cheer, then raced away to join the other boys. Sounds of laughter, shouting and splashing water drifted on the still, warm air.

They gave Dominie an idea.

By the time the day's mowing was over, Armand could scarcely lift his arms or stagger the short distance to Harwood's bailey. Though weary in body, he savored a singular contentment of spirit over a productive day's work done. He began to understand Baldwin De Montford's preoccupation with such commonplace matters in a way he never had before.

One certain benefit of such a strenuous day's work would be a deep, dreamless night's sleep. At least so long as he did not dwell on the memory of Dominie's fingertip, tracing a provocative path down his sweat-slick back. Or the fond caress of her hand against his cheek.

Come to think on it...perhaps he would not sleep so peacefully, after all.

Trudging through the bailey gate, Armand stopped by the smithy to leave his scythe for honing. Then he made his way to the stables, where he knew he could find water.

Two evenings before, he had joined the other men and boys in the millpond, but his presence had seemed to subdue their merriment. The next night he had washed himself off in the horse trough before entering the castle.

He was just about to plunge his head into the water when Dominie called softly from nearby, "Have Harwood's fortunes fallen so low?"

Armand straightened and glanced toward the sound of her voice. He could not decide whether he was more surprised by her affable tone or by the fact that she was speaking to him at all.

Before he could ask what she meant about Harwood's fortunes, Dominie supplied the answer. "Can we afford no better than a horse trough for our lord to wash himself after a hard day's labor?"

Her tone was more than affable. It lured Armand even as it made him uneasy. Had she not heard what he'd said to her out in the hay meadow? Or *how* he'd said it?

"I am no longer Lord of Harwood, Dominie." He heaved an impatient sigh. "You are mistress of these lands. Remember?"

Another troubling thought occurred to him. He made himself say it aloud, the better to remember it. "At least until you choose a husband. Then they will become his."

"This estate may be mine by royal writ." Dominie sauntered toward him, one thick auburn braid falling over the shoulder of her linen undergown. "But Harwood is yours by right of birth and by right of the heart. I have seen it more clearly with each passing day. I believe you have, too."

So Armand had, though he wished otherwise. To acknowledge the fact would only make it more difficult for him to give it up when the time came.

"Right of the heart?" He plowed one aching hand

through his damp hair. "That doesn't sound like a very practical notion."

"Perhaps not." She hoisted her shoulders and raised her palms in puzzlement. "I only know what I know."

She took another step toward him. "I beg your pardon for broaching all this to you a while ago, when you were in the middle of your work. You were right to chide me. It was neither the time nor the place for such talk."

The minx! She knew as well as he that had only been an excuse. For the things she wanted to say, there could be no *right* time or place.

Armand gestured around the stable yard. "Do you think this is any better?"

Her lips twitched in an impudent grin. "At least I'll have your full attention with no fear that you might cut a foot off. Come." Her hand darted out to catch his.

"Can you not let me wash first, at least?"

"Of course." Contrary to her words, she towed him away from the horse trough, to a quiet nook beside the stable.

There sat a low three-legged stool, several buckets of water and a shallow wooden tub with some coarse linen towels draped over the edge.

"What is all this?" Armand gently detached his hand from Dominie's.

"Can you not tell? This is what I was talking about. A better place than a horse trough for you to wash. *And* a better place for us to talk."

"Thank you for going to so much bother." Armand sank onto the stool. "But this is not a good place for us to talk."

"And why not, may I ask?" Dominie planted her hands on her hips. Fine hips there were, too. Not too narrow, not too broad. Just an inviting armful for a man.

Armand shook his head hard to dislodge that improper thought from his mind. "Don't play daft! You know very well why."

With a lazy, swaying gait, she walked toward the buckets. Hearing a soft splash, Armand glanced back, just as a cool, wet cloth was swiped across his shoulders. After a hot, wearying day, the refreshing sensation robbed him of words.

Dominie seemed to have enough for both of them. "Because it is too intimate, you mean?"

Hovering behind him, she guided the wet cloth over his shoulder and across his bare chest.

Her lips grazed his ear. "We have been rather intimate in the past, remember?"

If only he could forget.

"Are you trying to seduce me?" He reached up and closed his hand over her wrist. "Whatever for? To prove you can?" He gave a harsh growl of bitter laughter. "Well, be content. You would find it no challenge."

"You want me, then?" Her voice lost its sultry edge. It sounded innocent and uncertain. "The way you once did? To be together, man and woman?"

"Oh, yes." Might as well not leave her in any doubt. Besides, he was too tired to battle his desire.

He tilted his head to rub his cheek against her upper arm. "Worse than ever I did when we were young. And you need not work so hard at it, either. I want you almost as badly when I see you eating our evening meal, or going about the business of the estate. Or kneeling in prayer, heaven help me."

"I'm so glad!" Dominie threw her other arm around his neck in a swift, ardent embrace.

The delicious swell of her bosom pressed against Armand's back, and her soft cheek against his rough one.

"I want you like that, too. When I saw you in the hay meadow without a shirt, I couldn't keep from touching you."

"It's nothing to be glad about. Can you not see?" Wresting himself out of her embrace, Armand jumped up from the stool. "That kind of wanting is for marriage. Not for a man who means to be a monk and a woman who had best keep her virginity for the man she'll wed."

"Why can I not wed *you?*" Dominie rose from her crouching posture behind the stool and fixed him with a far too compelling look. "That way we can be together and you can stay at Harwood, where you belong."

When she had first offered to wed him, on that cool spring day in the cloisters of Breckland, the notion had tempted Armand. Now, after three months pretending to be master of Harwood and being near Dominie, it threatened to tear him in half.

"Why can you not wed me?" Armand stalked to the tub. "Sooth, woman, I could list the reasons until I run out of breath without naming them all."

He untied his garters, then pulled off his hose. Wearing only his linen breeches, he sank down into the tub. "Come, then. Pour some water over me and let us thrash this thing out. I can see you will give me no peace until we do."

"Are you apt to find peace by acting contrary to your own desires?" Dominie tossed the washcloth to Armand and moved the towels to the ground. Then she hefted one of the buckets and slowly tipped it over his head.

"What do you think I've been doing for the past five years?" he sputtered as the water sluiced through his hair and down his face.

"You didn't look very peaceful to me at that abbey." Dominie let the water flow faster. "Besides, things are different now than when you went away before. We need you here. Ask my mother—she'll tell you.''

"Your mother?'' The cascade of water over his hot, aching flesh felt too good. Armand scrubbed himself with the washcloth.

"She thinks we ought to get married.'' Having emptied the bucket over him, Dominie set it down. "So does Gavin, in case he hasn't told you.''

"He has.''

Was it possible he could repay Dominie and her family by taking her as his wife? By looking after them the way Lord Baldwin would have if he'd lived? Armand would have given almost anything to believe it. But what kind of penance was that—to do the thing he so desperately desired?

"More water?'' she asked.

Armand bowed his head. "If you please.''

She hoisted a second bucket and began to pour the water over him. "You belong here, we need you and we desire one another—what better reasons can there be to wed? You told Gavin there is more to marriage than… love.''

He should have known she'd have practical grounds for this sudden urge to wed him.

"Come, then,'' she said. "Tell me some of these many reasons why we cannot wed.''

"Very well.'' If one of *her* grounds had been love, his counterarguments would not carry so much weight. "You said yourself we do not see the world in the same way. We would likely drive each other mad with our quarreling.''

Dominie dismissed his point with a chuckle. "What man and woman *are* alike? It would be a dull life if we were. Besides, we have not quarreled too often or too heatedly these past weeks. More and more, I come to understand these ideals of yours, and respect them…in their proper place.''

The gentle fun she poked at him was even harder to resist than her physical allure, if that were possible.

As Dominie drained the last drops from the second bucket, Armand shook the water from his hair, like a hunting hound coming in out of the rain.

''I will concede you that one.'' He reached for a towel and began to dry himself. ''But there are plenty of others. Good, practical ones, too.''

Dominie set down the empty bucket. ''I'm listening.''

''I own nothing in the world,'' Armand reminded her as he rose from the tub. ''You have a substantial estate as your dowry. You could make an advantageous marriage. Into the court, perhaps, where you would have a life of ease.''

''Court? Ease?'' Dominie's nose wrinkled. ''Fish with better bait, Flambard! I am content with what I have here. And more than willing to share it with a landless husband, if he can help me manage it, as you have done.''

The wench would soon persuade him, if he wasn't careful. It did not help his cause that a weak part of him sorely wanted to be persuaded.

Armand grabbed the coarse linen towel from the ground and wrapped it around his waist to cover his wet breeches. ''Do not forget my vow to abstain from violence. I have been fortunate so far, but such good fortune cannot last. Even if Eudo St. Maur were rooted out of the Fens tomorrow, there are many other dangers in the world. You deserve a husband who can protect you…and your children, not one who is bound hand and foot.''

''If my father had returned from Lincoln broken in body, unable to defend our family, should we have turned him out?'' Dominie shook her head. "Even I am not so ruthless. Men-at-arms can be had for a price. You have proved you can lead men even without wielding a sword. That is a rare gift, one that should not be buried in an abbey.''

Her words reminded him of the parable of the talents. Was he like the foolish servant who buried his coin in the ground rather than risk using it to make more?

While he mulled the question over in his mind, Dominie drew nearer. ''Perhaps all these reasons of yours are only excuses, Armand, because you do not find me pleasing. Because you do not want me for a wife.''

She was as ripe and bursting with life as the summer fields. To turn his back on her would have been as grave a failing as leaving perfect, golden grain to rot, unreaped. Armand tried to restrain his hands, but they seemed to have a will of their own.

''I find you far too pleasing.'' He pulled her toward him, burying his face in her hair and letting his hands rove over her body, praising her beauty with his touch.

Dominie did not accept his attentions passively, but nuzzled his bare chest with her cheek and explored his body with her hands. ''I have waited for you, Armand Flambard. Even when I did not know you were still alive. You have made me wait too long.''

He knew her responses did not fully satisfy his reservations. Nor had he told her his most compelling reason why it would be impossible for them to wed.

But her obvious desire for him took Armand hostage, the way she had pinned him to the cloisters pillar that spring day at Breckland. He had never wanted anything in the world as much as he wanted her at that moment.

Slowly, he sank to his knees, clinging to Dominie, drizzling kisses down her face and neck as he descended.

Until his cheek came to rest against the sweet bounty of her bosom. She ran her hands through his wet hair, pressing him closer.

Then, with the sobering shock of a wave of icy water on hot flesh, a great commotion in the ward broke out—the clatter of horses' hooves and voices raised in alarm.

Among the clamor, Armand heard someone call, "St. Maur!" and "Attack!"

He and Dominie detached from their embrace with a reluctance on his part as painful as any battle wound. As she rushed toward the disturbance, Armand staggered to his feet and followed, chiding himself for being caught unaware.

In the ward he saw several people being helped down from horses. Most of the folk had smudges of soot on their faces. Some were bleeding.

"What is wrong?" Dominie ran to meet them. "Who are you and where have you come from? Are we under attack?"

One of the men, who looked vaguely familiar to Armand, gave a weary shake of his head. "Not yet, my lady. We have come from Cambridge. The Wolf and his pack have looted and burned it!"

Chapter Twelve

When the first flurry of noise and activity penetrated the sweet madness of her embrace with Armand, Dominie had barely been able to curb a shriek of frustration.

After much hesitation and many second thoughts, she'd finally decided what she wanted, then made up her mind to fight for it. Armand had mounted a worthy resistance. Enough to make his eventual surrender all the more satisfying. What a dizzying sense of power it had given her, to drive such a mighty man to his knees under the force of his banked passion for her.

The wild ardor of his touch and the frenzy of his kisses had struck tinder to the fuel of her secret desire for him. A desire that had first sprouted in an innocent way during their youth, then been brutally harrowed by his desertion, to lie fallow for the past five years. Ever since that day at Breckland, it had begun to flourish again, all the more lush for its long slumber.

Then, when she'd finally begun to reap its bountiful harvest, danger threatened to ravage everything she held dear. If Eudo St. Maur had ridden into Harwood just then, Dominie would have assailed the scoundrel with her bare hands!

She peered into the soot-smudged face of the man who had reported Cambridge looted and burning. "Godwin Smith, is that you?"

"Aye, Lady Dominie." The brawny, flaxen-haired man dropped to one knee before her.

The second son of Harwood's blacksmith, he had left home three years ago to ply his trade in King Stephen's city. Now and then, he'd come from Cambridge to visit his family on feast days.

"Folks is fleeing the city in all directions, my lady." The man's blue eyes had a vacant look, as though he were not seeing the bailey of Harwood, but the flames of burning Cambridge. "I didn't know where else to come."

"You were right to come home to us, Master Godwin." Dominie beckoned for him to rise. "We owe you thanks for bringing us these grievous tidings so swiftly."

From behind her, Armand's hand came to rest on her shoulder. Godwin Smith and the other Cambridge folk stared past her with curious looks. Armand gave no sign of heeding them.

People from the village and the castle began crowding into the bailey, some still wet from their swim.

"Edwin, Harry, James!" Armand's deep voice rang out over the clamor of the bailey. "Take horses and set watch on the roads from the east! Will Brewster, go gather the women and children from the village and bring them into the shelter of the bailey."

Several other men he bid carry the news to the manors and to Wakeland.

"Me, Armand!" Gavin came pelting up, wearing nothing but his breeches. "What can I do? Shall I fetch my bow and go to defend the east road?"

"You'll fetch your *clothes!*" Dominie prepared to swoop down on her brother and grab him by the ear.

Before she could take a step, Armand's powerful hand tugged her back.

"Gavin, just the man I need." Armand pointed toward the castle. "Hie you to the watchtower as fast as you can and keep a lookout to the east. If you see a force of men advancing from that direction, get word to me at once!"

Dominie barely curbed her urge to spin about and throw her arms around Armand's neck. He would put her brother in the safest spot on the whole estate, all the while convincing Gavin he was doing a vital task.

The boy's jaw fell slack and his eyes grew so wide Dominie feared they might never return to their proper shape. Armand had gone on to give his next order when he noticed Gavin still gaping. "Now!" he shouted. "There is no time to lose."

Gavin came back to earth with a start. "As you bid." He scrambled toward the castle, then paused a moment to call back, "You can count on me, Armand!"

"I am. Do not fail me."

As the boy dashed off, Armand cried, "Once all the riders have departed and the villagers are safely within, close and bar the gate."

Men rushed to obey him as eagerly as Gavin had. No one seemed to notice that he was practically naked, for he wore his air of authority like a suit of armor.

Despite the peril of their situation, a comforting sense of security enfolded Dominie, as strong as Armand's embrace…but much more safe.

Immediate matters of defense attended to, Armand now looked over the refugees from Cambridge. "These people need food and drink, and their hurts tended."

Before he could ask or command, Dominie turned toward him. "I will see to them. And to the villagers."

"I know you will." He flashed her a brief, grim smile,

his eyes shining with absolute confidence in her, as if her presence gave *him* the same sense of security his gave her.

Dominie recalled what Abbot Wilfrid had said about how much a man and woman of great ability could accomplish together. At the moment, she felt as if they could move mountains.

Perhaps even snare a rogue wolf.

Armand glanced down at himself, as if he had also forgotten his state of undress. "I must go find some clothes. Then I would speak to Godwin Smith about St. Maur's attack."

As he strode toward the castle, Dominie stood for a moment, watching him go. Then she took a deep breath, preparing to do what needed to be done, grateful that Armand had lifted the worst of the burden from her shoulders.

"Come up to the great hall." She beckoned to the Cambridge people. "We will tend to you there."

Some of the villagers had begun crowding into the bailey. Dominie called out to a pair of older women who had some skill in healing and who had no children to mind. "Mother Alfreda, Mother Margaret, will you come and help me tend to these poor souls?"

While Godwin Smith led the Cambridge people up the motte drawbridge, Dominie raised her voice to carry above the growing din in the bailey. "Seek a place to settle yourselves until we find out what is what. Keep the children away from the gate and the stables. Any who can lend a hand in the castle kitchen would be a boon to us all."

For the next several hours, she had no time to think of Armand or desire or marriage or anything but tackling her next task.

As she washed and bound wounds and applied a salve of herbs and goose grease to burns, she listened to the Cambridge people tell of a day that had begun like any other, only to end in flames, terror and flight.

More than ever, their tales convinced her that she and Armand should wed. And the sooner the better. In these erratic, dangerous times there could be no certainty beyond the present hour. A body needed to wrest from life what small pleasures could be found. After what had happened today, surely Armand would see it, too.

That green gown her mother was embroidering would make fine wedding garb.

As the midsummer moon rose over the still, watchful countryside of East Anglia, Armand Flambard looked westward from the watchtower of Harwood. He expelled a sigh as his tightly clenched muscles relaxed for the first time in hours. He was finally convinced that Eudo St. Maur and his bandit horde were not about to come swarming toward Harwood at any moment.

Armand glanced at young Gavin, still clad only in his breeches. "You did your part well, lad. I doubt we will be molested before dawn. A night attack always favors the defenders if they are forewarned, as we are. St. Maur may be wicked, but he is no fool. Go get yourself dressed and fed before your sister chides me for mistreating you."

Though Gavin's stomach squealed with hunger, he did not seem in any hurry to depart. "Do you think they'll attack tomorrow, Armand?"

"I doubt it."

He prayed the attack on Cambridge had temporarily sated St. Maur's craving for violence. Though Armand grew daily more confident of their ability to fend off an attack, the survival of Harwood depended on them reaping the summer's harvest first. While the grain stood in the field, it was vulnerable to fire, theft or the swarming of many feet.

As much to himself as to the boy, Armand added, "We have nothing worth taking yet. By the time St. Maur judges that we do, I hope we'll have secured most of it beyond his reach."

Gavin's shoulders sagged a little. Perhaps he foolishly regretted this lost opportunity to do battle.

If it were up to Armand, the boy never would.

Gavin started down the steep, winding steps to the great hall. "Have you eaten yet?" he asked.

"Not yet. I'll be down in a while. For now I'd rather taste the cool night air." If only it did not carry the faint but ominous reek of smoke.

"Good night, then."

"Good night, Gavin. Rest well. There will be plenty for all of us to do in the days ahead."

The boy had descended several steps when another thought occurred to Armand. "A few acres of grain is worth more than any battlefield, you know. It is there we will wage our greatest campaign against the Wolf of the Fens."

Gavin yawned and continued on his way. "I'd still rather shoot arrows than hoe or make hay."

The news came as no surprise to Armand. At Gavin's age, he would never have stooped to farmwork himself. He'd had no room in his life for anything but riding, hunting and learning war craft.

Shaking his head over his youthful folly, Armand leaned against the half wall of the tower and stared out into the night.

Had anyone cleared away the tub and buckets from beyond the stables? It seemed like weeks since he had bathed, rather than hours. The arrival of the refugees from Cambridge had shattered something fragile and precious. They had made him remember why any notion of wedding Dominie was dangerous folly.

Somehow, he must find the strength of will to steel himself against her seductive persuasion. Or perhaps he should nip her efforts in the bud, by convincing her to give up any thought of him as a husband.

Behind him, Armand heard soft footsteps on the stairs. "Go eat your supper, Gavin, then get to bed," he murmured.

"Good advice, Flambard," replied Dominie. "Perhaps you should heed it yourself."

The savory aroma of onions reminded Armand how long it had been since he'd last eaten.

Dominie climbed the last few steps. "I saved you some food from supper." She thrust a wooden bowl toward him. "Here, eat it while it's hot."

"Thank you." Armand spooned a portion of thick stew into his mouth, relishing the mingled tastes of rabbit, beans, vegetables and herbs. "You've been most attentive today. Bringing me ale in the fields, preparing my bath, now fetching me supper."

Having Dominie anticipate his needs and see to his comfort nourished a different kind of hunger within him. It enticed Armand as powerfully as did his desire for her.

Perhaps that desire called to hers, for she moved toward him until they were standing side by side, looking out over the battlements, her hip pressed against his thigh.

"If you take me to wife, I would attend your *every* need, my lord."

Her words and her nearness roused Armand to an aching pitch akin to ravenous hunger or parched thirst. But this was one craving he dared not allow her to satisfy.

He stepped away from her, breaking the contact between them. "Don't." The word heaved out of him with a weary, troubled sigh. "Please. Not now."

It felt as if he were begging a strong opponent for mercy. Though the notion galled Armand, he had no choice.

"What is wrong with now?" Rather than pursuing him, Dominie took a step away.

Not that it helped a great deal. She was still within arm's reach, inviting him with a silent, invisible summons more potent than words.

"It is quiet here." Her tone had a ragged edge of frustration. "And private."

Armand wolfed down his rabbit stew, as if it might magically fortify his faltering resolve. Everything that made Harwood's watchtower a favorable battlefield for her placed him at a perilous disadvantage. But he must not tell her so.

She stood silent while he finished eating, her comely, resolute profile a shadow in the moonlight. Then, in a husky murmur that slid over his skin like a touch, she said, "You were magnificent today."

Fortunately, Armand had consumed all of his supper, even licked the spoon clean. If he had still been eating, her praise might have made him choke.

"I only did what was needed. As you have done these past five years better than I, for you were not trained to it as I was."

"That was more than training, Armand. You must see. It was the exercise of a gift."

He clutched his bowl in one hand and his spoon in the other, as though they were a sword and shield. "I only hope that gift and all our precautions will be enough to foil the Wolf and his pack. Hearing the Cambridge folk tell of their ordeal has shaken my faith.''

''Well, I have faith enough in you for both of us, Armand Flambard. Faith that you are a fine leader and faith that you will make a fine husband.''

Tell her the truth! Armand's conscience exhorted him. Knowing that he had killed her father would surely put a stop to all her talk of marriage.

''Dominie…''

''Yes?'' She turned toward him.

He could not do it. The knowledge would hurt her too much. Gavin and her mother, as well. It would reopen old wounds that had almost healed. Though he despised himself for betraying his ideal of truth, that scorn was a price he would willingly pay to protect those dearest to him.

Abbot Wilfrid's words broke over his turbulent thoughts like a benediction.

How much easier life would be for us poor sinful creatures if all our choices were between right and wrong. Too often we must hoe a stony path between two vastly different rights. Or commit some small evil to avoid a great one.

The cost of such ambiguity was the peace of mind that came with certainty…and perhaps self-righteousness. Had he known true peace at the abbey? Dominie had claimed not. Now Armand began to question it himself.

What if he let her decide? She seemed so sure of where he belonged and what they should do. Of one thing Armand had no doubt—she could not make a worse muddle of matters between them than he had.

The choice he was about to offer her would either drive her away forever, or give them a chance to recapture something he had lost and bitterly mourned.

* * *

Was the man never going to speak? Every silent moment that passed made Dominie more anxious.

Had she pushed him too far with her talk of marriage? Might he risk the abbot's displeasure by returning to Breckland at once? She desperately prayed not.

At last Armand began to speak. "When I gave up my lands…and you, to honor my vow of allegiance to the empress, you said I did not give you a choice. That is true."

Was that all? Dominie leaned against the battlements as her legs grew weak with relief. "Don't fret about it, Armand. That is all in the past. I should not have brooded on it so long and let myself grow bitter. Yesterday is gone. Tomorrow may never come for us. It is today that matters."

Armand stooped to set his bowl and spoon on the floor of the watchtower. When he straightened up again, he caught her hand and threaded his fingers through hers. "A very practical outlook."

He spoke in a caressing tone, as if it were rare praise, rather than second cousin to mortal sin.

"Yesterday may be gone," he continued, "but we can learn from its mistakes and try to atone for them. Five years ago I did not give you a choice, because I wanted to protect you. If you had chosen me over your family, I feared you might reproach yourself."

The significance of his words jolted Dominie. She had blamed him for abandoning her without a word. But what if he *had* entreated her to come away with him? How would she have chosen, and how would she have lived with that wrenching choice?

"If you had come with me—" Armand did not sound as though he'd deemed that likely. If only he'd known!

"—how would we have lived, with my lands gone? I could not have asked you to make such a sacrifice."

Back at Breckland, Armand had said as much to Abbot Wilfrid. But Dominie had been too consumed with resentment to believe him. Slowly, as spring had thawed and blossomed into summer, she'd grown willing to forget the past.

Now she found herself ready to forgive…and needing to be forgiven.

Armand had once cared for her enough to let her hate him rather than present her with a choice that might have broken her heart. Was that the kind of love he had once insisted should hallow a marriage? A love she had dismissed as foolish fancy?

"Though it was done with the kindest intent," said Armand, "I see now that I erred."

"You did?"

"Indeed." He reached up with his free hand, playing it gently over her hair. "I should have trusted in your fortitude and your good sense. If I had left the decision to you, it might not have changed what happened, but at least my going would not have made you doubt yourself."

Slowly his hand strayed down the side of her face to cup her cheek. "Who knows but that you might have been able to find some way out of my deadlock, since you see all those subtle shades between black and white."

Dominie wished she could be as sure of her judgment as he sounded. "Do not disparage yourself." She tilted her face to drop a soft kiss on his hand, at the base of his thumb. "You stand for good values—truth, honor, fairness, peace. And you do stand for them, in fair weather or foul, no matter what the cost. Our country would not be so torn by strife now if more men on both sides shared your integrity."

"Do not praise me too much." He stroked the pad of his thumb over her cheekbone. "I am not the same man you admired when you were a girl."

"I know that. It vexed me at first. I wanted to find you exactly as I'd remembered you. I did not want you to have changed, even though I had. What a fool I was."

"I can match you folly for folly and then some," Armand admitted. "I wanted you to have remained as you had been, but I did not remember you truly. I wonder if I made up that other Dominie because she would be easier to resist than the real one."

The caress of Armand's hand and voice coaxed forth a feeling of sweet delight in Dominie that had long since become a stranger to her heart. By rights she should have been giving rein to her desire and exploiting his to make certain he would stay at Harwood. But she could not bring herself to intrude on the chaste intimacy of the moment.

He turned his hand to graze her cheek with the backs of his fingers, continuing down her neck, over her shoulder and down her arm.

"This time, I will place the choice in your hands," he said, as he clasped both of hers in his. "I promise you, I will not take offense, whatever you decide."

"I know my choice already." If he had not held her hands so firmly, she would have thrown her arms around him.

"So you think," said Armand. "But heed. If I stay, if we wed, I will be back in the world, and the allegiances of the world will have claim on me again."

"What are you saying, Armand?" If he had threatened to hurl her from the watchtower, Dominie could not have been more dismayed. "After all your vow to the empress has cost you, have you not learned?"

"A moment ago, you did not deem my ideals so foolish." He released her hands almost reluctantly. "Nor my willingness to sacrifice for them."

"That is different!"

"How? Because it is in the past? Because it cost you nothing?"

"Cost me nothing—how can you say so? Your decision to support the empress cost me more than it did you. Every day for five years, too."

"So it did. Pardon me for suggesting otherwise. The cost to you was hardest for me to bear. Especially because it was not of your choosing."

What kind of choice was he giving her now?

"Please try to understand, even if you cannot support me. If I give and take my allegiance as it suits me, it will lose all value. *I* will lose all value."

She had been so close to regaining most of what she had lost five years ago. So maddeningly close to securing the man she desired with every womanly fiber of her being. Now to be thwarted at the last instant...

And yet part of her did understand, against her will and against her better judgment. Armand Flambard untrue to his ideals would not be Armand Flambard as she knew and admired...and cared for him.

If she tried to speak now, with all the volatile, contradictory emotions churning within her, she was apt to scream or rail or blaspheme. So she locked her lips and clasped her arms tight around her body.

Faced with her bristling silence, Armand seized the chance to speak his piece. "King Stephen will not want Harwood held by one who opposes him. I wonder that you did not take that into account when you first offered to barter your hand for my help against St. Maur."

"I did!" The words burst out of Dominie. "But I thought his Grace would be too much occupied with other matters to mind the affairs of one estate. In the end, I believe the Angevins will have the throne, through Maud's son, Henry. If we could only bide quietly until then, your service to the empress might win us favor.''

Armand did not reply at once. Could it be that her words stirred some long-suppressed sense of expedience in him?

''Is that why you wanted to marry me?'' he asked at last, in a wounded tone. ''To have wagers placed on both sides of the table so you cannot lose?''

Of course not! At least not of late. But with any shared future for them looking sadly doomed, she could not bring herself to tell Armand her true reasons.

''You make it sound like a crime,'' she replied. ''It is not. The crime is that this war ever came upon us in the first place. How we survive and protect those who rely on us is not for others to judge. Least of all those who take no account of how their noble actions will bring ill fortune on others.''

''You are right in saying it is not for me to judge. In the end, your way may bring the least harm on the fewest people. A part of me wishes I could embrace it, but I cannot.''

He sounded so bereft. Dominie's arms ached to reach for him, but she dared not let them.

''But come,'' he said. ''The hour grows late. We have both had a long day and who knows what ill fortune tomorrow may visit on us. Let us have this out, then make peace with our choices. Will you wed me at the risk of King Stephen stripping you of Harwood?''

''Why ask? You know I cannot. What would become of my mother and Gavin, my vassals and tenants? I cannot forsake them.''

''No, you cannot. Nor would you if the empress offered

me a magnificent estate in the West Country in place of this one.''

''Not even then.''

From out of the darkness where Armand stood came the last sound Dominie had expected to hear—a soft chuckle that trailed off in a sigh. ''That is not such a practical outlook, after all. You told me once that you have no ideals, that you care for nothing you cannot eat, drink, wear or spend.''

''Aye, what of it?''

Armand shook his head. ''It is not true. You have one ideal, perhaps two that take precedence over all others. In their defense, you would transgress against the rest without a qualm.''

She was about to bid him quit talking nonsense, when his next words froze her tongue.

''Loyalty and responsibility. To your family and your people. I place a high value on loyalty to those above me. Those to whom I have sworn my word. You hold fast to the loyalty of those who depend upon *you*. That is all the more selfless, for I might hope to profit from my allegiance.''

''Don't flatter me to soften the blow!'' She backed away from Armand, even though he had made no move to approach her. ''We cannot be together.''

''By your choice.''

Dominie turned away, though the friendly darkness masked her tears. ''Don't taunt me!'' She started down the stairs, clinging to the wall so she would not fall and break her neck. ''You know I have no choice.''

Armand's parting words followed her. ''Neither did I.''

Chapter Thirteen

The folk of Harwood went about their work the next days with breath held and one ear ever alert for the sound of an alarm. But none came.

A few more refugees straggled in from Cambridge on foot. They reported that St. Maur's men had retreated back to the Fens once they had looted all they could carry, and set fire to the rest. There was talk of King Stephen coming, but no one put much store in his ability to restrain the monster he had let loose upon them.

No attack came the next day, either, nor the day after that. The haycocks dried and presently were loaded in carts and taken to a special stone enclosure Armand had ordered built onto the bailey.

There had been some resistance to his plan of storing the bulk of the harvest at Harwood. Even after four score years of just rule by the Flambards and the De Montfords, a residue of suspicion toward the Norman lords still festered among their Saxon vassals.

Armand had given them a harsh choice. They could entrust their hay and grain to the castle from whence it would be rationed back to them, a fortnight's supply at a time. Or they could risk losing their entire crop to St.

Maur's marauders. After that, no one had elected to store all their crops on their own property.

If only the choice he'd given Dominie had turned out so well.

Their servants and vassals, even her brother, might not have noticed the change in her after the night she and Armand had talked in the watchtower. She carried on, indomitable as ever, but the sparkle had left her eyes and the vigor had gone out of her step.

Armand would have given most anything to restore them. Anything but the one most likely to work.

As Lammastide came upon them, everyone at Harwood prepared for the Loaf Mass and the long days of work ahead to harvest the wheat crop. Armand kept a wary eye on the heavens, praying the dry weather would continue. He also kept his ears peeled for any warning of an attack. So much hung on the continuation of sunshine and peace.

"Armand, have you heard?" Gavin ran toward him as he examined a stalk of ripe, golden grain with cautious satisfaction. "My mother has come from Wakeland for Lammas!"

"You bear good tidings, lad," Armand replied with false cheer.

Lady Blanchefleur had made no secret of setting her heart on him wedding her daughter. Armand pictured a Lammas celebration plagued with well-meant lectures about his unsuitability for the abbey and how much he was needed at Harwood. Blatant hints about how well he and Dominie worked together.

If her mother's presence helped brighten Dominie's mood, Armand supposed he could bear it. At least as long as her ladyship did not raise the topic of what fine children they might breed. The reminder of that sore regret would be one too many for him.

"Do you know how long your mother plans to stay?" Only long enough to attend the feast, he hoped. They would not need any distractions during the harvest itself.

Gavin seemed not to have heard his question. Instead the boy stared past Armand to the west, where a narrow road threaded its way between two broad fields of ripe grain. "I wonder what's the matter?"

Armand spun around to see a horse galloping toward the castle. His bowels clenched in his belly, even as he ran to intercept the horseman.

"What news?" he called to Lambert Miller as the wiry young man reined in his badly lathered mount. "An attack?"

"I think not, my lord. Leastways, I hope not. We stopped a lone rider headed this way under a flag of truce. He gives his name as Roger of Fordham and says he would speak with Lady Dominie."

Roger of Fordham? Armand knew the name. The man was near his age and had once held estates on the border between this county and neighboring Norfolk. Why had he come alone, under a flag of truce? And what could he want with Dominie?

"What have you done with him?"

Lambert nodded toward the Cambridge road. "He is coming, my lord. With an escort to guard him. I rode ahead to warn you. Have you any orders?"

"Aye." Armand squeezed his eyes closed, the better to concentrate. "Blindfold him, so he does not see too much of our harvest or our defenses."

"As you bid, Lord Flambard." Lambert turned his mount.

Armand called after him, "One is enough to escort a blindfolded man. Send the others back to their posts. This may be a feint to draw us away while a larger force comes behind. I will send what men I can spare to aid you.''

Dominie appeared at a dead run, holding the hem of her skirt high so as not to trip her. Armand caught a glimpse of her bare calf that made him ache to lie with her long, lithe legs wrapped around his. He checked that dangerous fancy with ruthless force.

''What's happened?'' Dominie gasped. ''I heard…a rider…''

''It does not look too threatening yet.'' Armand tried to reassure her, even while his own senses grew more alert. ''A man named Roger of Fordham is on his way to see you. He came alone, under a flag of truce.''

''Roger of Fordham?'' Dominie spoke the name in a hesitant, guarded tone, as if she feared it might burn her tongue.

''You know him?''

''I…did.'' Her answer came haltingly. ''Not long after you went away, he came courting me.''

''Indeed?'' Armand told himself it was all in the past and that he had no right to care, one way or another. That did not stop his close-trimmed nails from biting into his palms. ''What made you refuse him?''

''Why do you care?''

Did she still not understand, even after he had given her a taste of impossible choices? If she didn't, this was not the time to enlighten her.

''Because it may have some bearing on what the man wants with you now.''

She considered for a moment, then seemed to concede that he might have a point. ''My father sent him away, if you must know. Father said I should not be hasty, that you might change your mind and return to us.''

''I see.'' Armand turned and shaded his eyes, looking

westward. But that was only an excuse to avert his face from Dominie.

After all the ill-feeling that had led up to and surrounded his leaving, Baldwin De Montford had still been willing to welcome his prodigal foster son back, even allow Armand to marry his cherished daughter.

The notion baffled Armand, and moved him.

"I heard tell Roger joined Eudo St. Maur after they both lost their lands." Dominie also turned her gaze westward.

When Armand risked a quick glance at her face, he saw that her high, clear brow was furrowed.

"I wonder what he wants this time?" she whispered.

What *had* brought Roger of Fordham to Harwood? Dominie wondered as she watched the man ride up, blindfolded, his horse led by Lambert Miller. And how many other men would wear such an air of arrogant assurance in so vulnerable a position?

Had the man come to spy out their defenses? Or to demand their surrender? In either case, he would be disappointed. And once his errand was accomplished, she would treat him to a surprise that would cure his arrogance.

When the horses came to a stop in front of them, Armand growled, "What brings you here, sir? Is it true you serve the traitor, St. Maur?"

Roger of Fordham made no move to take off his blindfold, suggesting that he was content to wear the thing until invited to remove it.

He tilted his head toward the sound of Armand's voice. "I will answer no questions but from the Lady of Harwood herself."

"Speak more civilly, man." The sharp edge of Armand's voice cut the summer air. "Or you may cool your insolent heels awhile before you're brought to the lady."

Until this moment, Dominie had welcomed Armand's exercise of authority, for it had lifted responsibility from her tired shoulders. This time it rankled.

What gave him the right to meddle in matters that might affect her family and her people long after he had gone?

She drew herself to her full height and adopted a gracious but imperious tone that would have done credit to Empress Maud herself. "I see we have a guest for our Lammastide feast. Pardon our poor courtesy, my lord of Fordham, in receiving you as we have, but these are perilous times. We must exercise caution, even in greeting friends of old."

A haughty little smile arched their guest's full lips, perhaps at Armand's expense. "I will be pleased to accept your hospitality, Lady Dominie. After the feast, I would talk with you on a matter of importance to us both."

"As you wish, sir." Dominie addressed her next words to Lambert Miller. "Order our guest's mount to be stabled, then lead him to the great hall. Once there, he will be at liberty to uncover his eyes. Have him brought what food and drink he wishes, and show him every courtesy. Stay close to him to attend his bidding."

Lambert was a shrewd enough young fellow to know that would mean maintaining an armed guard on their well-treated prisoner.

Her vassal shifted an uncertain glance from Dominie to Armand and back again. Out of the corner of her eye, she saw Armand give a curt nod, endorsing her orders. Woe to him if he had dared do otherwise!

Once the two mounted men were through the bailey gate and out of earshot, however, Armand changed his tune. "What are you doing? Have you no idea how dangerous that man could be? He's probably come to spy on Harwood!''

Ever since their talk that night in the watchtower, Dominie had tried to curb her physical yearning for Armand Flambard. Thus far it had proved stubbornly resistant to her will.

Even now his nearness stirred a heightened awareness in her. One she begrudged, but could not help.

He was a fine figure of a man, his lean, muscled body tanned and hardened by the summer's toil, the candid blue of his deep-set eyes haunted by a shadow of gray. The way one lock of brown hair fell over his brow still made her breath quicken. So did his air of authority, even when she resented it.

That Armand Flambard should remain so potently attractive to her, even after he had convinced her they could never have a future together, felt like deliberate provocation.

''If Roger of Fordham has come to spy, he will not see much to his advantage in the great hall. In fact, he might gain a false impression based upon what we let him see.''

If she had expected her words to vex Armand, she would have been disappointed. Instead, his eyes glowed and a sudden smile of bewildering intensity transformed his angular face.

''Abbot Wilfrid was right about you, Dominie. You are a remarkable woman.''

A light, intoxicating feeling rose inside her, like the foam on a mug of ale, but it left a bitter aftertaste. ''Save your flattery! How am I ever to stop liking you if you say such things?''

Armand sobered. ''Must we stop liking each other?''

''Aye, if we ever hope to know a moment's contentment. When the day comes for you to leave Harwood, I want to be able to say to myself, 'Good riddance to him!' and not…'' Dominie forced her mouth shut. She'd already said more than she'd meant to.

"And not…what?" asked Armand.

And not feel like you have pulled my heart out and carried it away with you. "Why do you care? You proved your point. We can never wed while our loyalties tug us in two different directions."

Armand reached toward her, perhaps to grasp her hand. At the last instant he stopped himself. "Believe me, I take neither pleasure nor satisfaction from our dilemma."

"I know." The longing she saw in his eyes mirrored her own. If his vow bound him as unquestioningly as her obligations bound her, she might not be able to understand, but she could sympathize. "I do not mean to beshrew you, but it is hard to accept."

By an arduous exercise of will, she forced the topic to the back of her mind. Evicting it completely was beyond her power. "Let us concentrate on what we have to do now, and save our regrets for another day."

Armand began to smile again, then grew serious. "I will endeavor to be practical. I'll invite some men from the village and such Cambridge folk as remain to join in the feast."

With a nod, Dominie approved his plan. "Fit out as many as possible with weapons. I will go speak with the cook and his helpers to see how we may augment our meal. I want Roger of Fordham to leave here believing we are well-fed, well-manned, well-armed and confident to fend off any attack."

Armand agreed. "Like any wolf, St. Maur is more apt to prey upon the weak."

* * *

The people of Harwood looked anything but weak
when they marched in procession from the village church
after the traditional Mass to bless the harvest. Gavin
proudly led the way up to the castle, bearing a symbolic
sheaf of wheat, while the villagers and some folk from
the outlying manors lustily sang the harvest home.

At first the atmosphere of the feast was noticeably
strained, with many stares directed at Dominie's "guest"
and angry mutters exchanged behind raised hands.

Dominie rose from her seat and clapped loudly. "Let
us have music while we eat!"

She tried to keep from glancing at Armand, but her
gaze strayed to him just the same. And though she tried
not to let his approving look please her, it did.

A trio of pipers took up their instruments, and soon the
hall echoed with lively music. Once meat and drink were
brought, the Harwood folk forgot about Roger of Fordham, and turned their attention to merrymaking.

For the first time since Lady Blanchefleur's unheralded
arrival, Dominie was glad of her mother's talkative company. Her ladyship seemed to have heard nothing of
Roger's dubious reputation. But having known his late
mother in their youth, she chatted away at great length on
a safe subject.

Dominie found herself too anxious to enjoy the feast.
With each day that had passed since St. Maur's raid on
Cambridge, she had let herself become a little more hopeful that her estates would be spared. The advent of her
guest had shaken that fragile, unfounded optimism.

Once everyone had eaten their fill, Dominie beckoned
Wat FitzJohn and whispered in his ear, "Bid the musi-
cians take their tunes out into the ward. Urge everyone to
follow them. I need quiet to talk with my guest."

The castellan was quick to do her bidding. Soon the great hall emptied. When the serving wenches came to clear away after the meal, Dominie urged them to join the others for dancing down below.

Then she glanced toward the far end of the high table. "You may go as well, Gavin."

"I don't mind staying."

Armand shot Gavin a look. "Your sister said you may go."

The lad pushed back his stool with the sigh of one much put-upon. "Very well. I will be master of Wakeland by and by, don't forget. You had better not make any decisions that concern my estate while I'm gone."

"This has nothing to do with you." Dominie prayed she was telling the truth, for she had no idea what Roger of Fordham wished to discuss with her.

Though she had listened in on his conversation during the meal, he had vouched not the slightest hint of his intent.

Once Gavin had departed, she could bear the suspense no longer. "My lord, when you arrived, you asked to speak with me. I am prepared to hear you now."

Roger gestured to the other occupants of the high table—Armand, her mother, Wat FitzJohn, Father Clement, and Harwood's priest, Father Dunstan. "I had hoped to conduct our discussions in greater privacy, but no matter."

He rose and walked around to take up a position facing the table. "Lady Dominie De Montford of Harwood, I have come to ask the honor of your hand in marriage."

Armand's fist hit the tabletop with a resounding bang.

Dominie felt her jaw go slack. With some effort she managed to close her mouth. With greater effort, she answered. "B-but you…I… Some years ago, you bid for my hand. I declined."

The man did not seem taken aback by her reaction. If anything, he appeared to savor the sensation he had created. "So you did, my lady. But times have changed. A union between us could be of great mutual benefit."

Mutual benefit. Roger of Fordham was talking about practical matters, the kind she had once told Armand marriages should be based on. Why then did she shrink from hearing his offer?

"Pardon me, sir, but were your lands not forfeit? And have you not allied yourself with him who was Earl of Anglia?"

From her seat beside Dominie, Lady Blanchefleur gave a little gasp.

Something flickered in the depths of Roger's dark eyes that heightened Dominie's uneasiness. "I like a woman who is direct. It is true King Stephen stripped me of my lands and that I have had to join the earl in order to defend my interests."

Armand's voice rang out. "Prey upon a strife-torn land, you mean!"

Roger's lip curled. "My business is with Lady Dominie." He turned his attention back to her. "I will be plain with you, my lady. This contest for the throne cannot last forever, and I have my eye on the future. There is also an immediate necessity to consider, for us both."

"What immediate necessity?" Dominie did not like the sound of that.

"The king has turned his attention upon Cambridgeshire. He begins to cut off our routes of supply. My lord St. Maur's forays against the estates of our neighbors have been rather too thorough, I fear."

Dominie heard Armand mutter, ''When you run out of places to pillage, you'll starve.''

Roger glared at him, but otherwise ignored the bait. ''It is within my power to see that the De Montford lands remain…untroubled, in exchange for safe passage of supplies and your hand in marriage to seal the bargain.''

For a moment, Dominie could find no words to reply. With some minor differences, this was the same bargain she had offered Armand Flambard, when she'd first sought him out at the abbey. And his cooperation had by no means guaranteed the safety of Harwood and Wakeland.

Roger of Fordham was not ill-looking in a swarthy, arrogant way. He was not pockmarked. He appeared to have all his teeth. And yet the thought of wedding him made Dominie's flesh crawl.

She found her voice at last, and an excuse to avoid what she shrank from. An excuse for which she could thank Armand. ''I thank you for your offer, my lord, but I fear if we marry, King Stephen will only strip Harwood from me, as he took your estates. Then you will be in no better position, and I infinitely worse.''

For Armand, she might have done it, if times had been prosperous and peaceful and she could have been certain the king would give Harwood to a worthy lord. As matters now stood, her people needed her desperately. She could not turn her back on them to suit her heart.

The bandit baron considered Dominie's answer. ''You have a shrewd mind to equal your beauty, my lady. I believe we could be a good match. Who knows how far we might advance our fortunes if we pool our abilities.''

Had he not heard what she'd said? Dominie wondered as she absorbed his reply. She could imagine the methods such a man might use to advance their fortunes—the deceit, the treachery, the ruthlessness. She had once proudly told Armand she had not a scruple in the world. Now she looked in her soul and discovered otherwise.

After a brief pause, Roger of Fordham answered her objection. "What you say is true, my lady, but I believe there are ways around the problem." He made a dismissive gesture toward the high table. "We could swear these people to silence and keep our marriage secret until it is safe to reveal to the world."

Why had she not thought of that when Armand had given her the impossible choice? It was an altogether practical solution and not strictly dishonest. As she had often warned Armand, it was not telling a lie, simply withholding the full truth. Perhaps she was a good match for the likes of Roger of Fordham, after all. The notion sickened her.

"I may lack in land at the moment," Roger continued, "but I have put by a tidy fortune in booty that could ease our way in the years to come."

Dominie could well imagine. Church plate, consecrated for holy use, now melted down for its gold and gems. Treasure stolen from the honest townsfolk of Cambridge or the castles of her neighbors. She would sooner go naked than wear fine garments purchased with tainted coin.

She nodded to acknowledge what he had said. Beside her, she sensed Armand's taut, indignant stillness. She could guess what he thought of Roger and this marriage proposal. But he could provide her with no workable alternative.

"You have explained the benefits of accepting your offer, sir, and I do not deny they are tempting. What if I decline?"

"That would be most unwise." Though Roger did not raise his voice, the threat it held was unmistakable. "I would prefer to see Harwood and Wakeland thrive, and any surplus food you produce sold to us for a fair price."

To sustain the Wolf and his pack while they ranged farther afield to prey on smaller estates, defenseless holy houses and the like. Could she exchange the safety of her people for the misery of others?

"However," Roger continued, "if you refuse my offer, I will not be able to ensure you my protection. I cannot tell when my lord St. Maur might pay you a call, but I can assure you he will. If you believe a handful of farmers armed with hay forks and billhooks is enough to keep us from taking what we want and laying waste to the rest, you are not as clever a woman as I give you credit for being."

"Infamy!" rumbled Father Clement.

"Oh my!" Lady Blanchefleur began to fan her face with fluttering hands. "Such ugly threats. The soul of your poor mother will never rest easy while you imperil your own salvation."

"Apologies, my lady." Roger of Fordham bowed low. "I have no wish to distress you. I only desire to make your fair daughter's choice as clear as possible to her. I would sore regret to see such harm fall upon you and yours, but a man must look to his own interests in such unsettled times. And he must not shrink from doing what is distasteful to him in order to achieve his ends."

The elaborate courtesy of his words did not conceal an attitude of vicious mockery, or the reminder of his original threat.

Her mother's breath came more rapidly. "Our Lady have mercy, I feel a weak spell coming on!"

Roger of Fordham regarded Lady Blanchefleur with blatant contempt.

"If you will excuse us," said Dominie. "I must tend to my mother."

"I need an answer," Roger of Fordham demanded. "I have wasted enough time here, watching you pretend that all is well and that you are prepared to meet an attack. I am not fooled, and neither should you be if you value your future."

Armand leaped to his feet. "Mind your tongue in this hall, knave!"

Roger sneered. "Muzzle your toothless guard dog, my lady. His growling offends me."

"Please, Armand." Her gaze met his, silently begging him not to make an unpleasant situation worse. Then she turned to the elder priest. "Will you escort my mother to my solar, Father Clement, and see that she is attended?"

Dominie helped her mother up from her chair. "Please don't work yourself into a state. Go with Father Clement, take a little wine and try to rest. All will be well, you'll see."

"But how can it be well, my dear?" Lady Blanchefleur had not been this upset since the day word arrived from Lincoln that both her husband and her son had been killed in the fighting. "You must not wed such a foul viper, no matter how pretty his speech. Your father never thought well of him." She pressed her palms to her flushed cheeks. "But what will become of us if you refuse him? Oh, woe!"

Stooping to look her mother in the eye, Dominie spoke in the calmest, firmest tone she could manage while her insides were quivering and her thoughts scattering like a flock of chickens set upon by foxes. "Have faith in my judgment. I will do what is best for all of us."

And what might *that* be?

If only she knew.

Lady Blanchefleur seemed a little reassured. "You are

your father's daughter, my sweet." She took Father Clement's arm. "I pray Our Lord will give you guidance."

Guidance…or a miracle? Of late, the latter seemed to be in short supply.

While the footsteps of her mother and Father Clement retreated from the great hall, Dominie held herself still and closed her eyes. Silently she prayed as she had not done since the day Armand Flambard had first forsaken her. She hoped that this time God might heed her.

There really was no choice, was there? Often in her youth she had chafed at the fact that men had so much more power to make decisions than women did. Now she realized that choice could be as much a burden as a privilege, and that one of life's deepest regrets might be having chosen wrong.

She must agree to wed Roger of Fordham, her practical nature insisted. It was the only way to insure the safety of her lands and vassals. In an instant of aching clarity, she knew she would never care for any man as she had and did care for Armand Flambard. If the two of them could never be together, it behooved her to wed someone who would not expect a place in her heart.

Roger's voice broke the tense hush of the room. "I have been patient in waiting for your answer my lady, but I can tarry no longer. Which will it be—prosperity and power, or ruin?"

Though she opened her eyes, Dominie could not banish the image of herself teetering on a precipice above hell.

"I…" If only she did not have to speak the words that would doom her.

The loud, harsh scrape of chair legs against the heavy wood floor of the dias made her start. She turned to find Armand on his feet.

His eyes met hers as he uttered one word. "Wait!"

Chapter Fourteen

"**W**ait!" Armand might have addressed that warning to himself as much as to Dominie or to Roger of Fordham.

What was he about to do? He hardly dared let himself think, or he might balk. And what would that mean for Dominie? For the people of Harwood?

Ever since Roger of Fordham had risen to speak, Armand had been a man at war with himself. Every loathsome word out of the bandit baron's mouth had convinced Armand more thoroughly that Dominie *could not* barter her future, and perhaps her immortal soul, by wedding such a man and becoming party to his corruption.

But what could he do to stop it?

Forbid her? By what right? He was neither her father nor her brother, though he had once hoped to be nearer kin than either of those. He no longer had any authority over Harwood, except what Dominie had called "a right of the heart."

Armand doubted that gave him any say in the matter, regardless of how strongly he might feel about it. And he did feel strongly—more, perhaps, than on any other single question he had faced in his life. To watch Roger of

Fordham use Dominie and Harwood to further his selfish wickedness would feel like a spiritual violation.

But could Armand compromise his honor and his ideals to stop it?

All these conflicting thoughts surged and pitched in his mind like chaotic gray waves whipped by a moral tempest that threatened to wreck any hope of peace or certainty. Then Roger had given Dominie his mocking ultimatum, and Armand had run out of time to ponder. He must speak, he must act, though he had no idea what to say or do.

The word *wait* left his mouth, more to stall for another moment than because he had come to a decision. Then he found himself on his feet, though he did not remember rising.

All eyes in the hall were turned upon him, everyone waiting, as he had bidden them, with expressions that ranged from hope and trust to suspicion and disdain. The former disturbed him more than the latter, for they burdened him with expectations and responsibilities he feared he could not fulfill. His soul lifted a desperate, wordless prayer for guidance, though he did not feel worthy of an answer.

"Stay out of this, Flambard!" Roger growled. "It is a matter between the lady and me. You have no say in it."

Dominie raised her hand. "Let him speak. The De Montfords and the Flambards have been allies longer than anyone can remember. Though my father is not here to advise me, I know he would wish me to heed Armand's counsel."

In the gaze she turned on him, fear of what he might say battled with eagerness to hear. Or perhaps, with such a distasteful choice before her, Dominie was only eager for anything to forestall it.

"I have this to say…" Armand began, still not knowing what words would come out of his mouth.

There was no good solution to this dilemma, only a variety of evils. It was just the kind of situation from which he had tried to escape by entering the abbey. The kind of situation Abbot Wilfrid had told him he must confront.

"Lady Dominie cannot wed you, sir." *That* would be the greatest evil. Armand knew he must accept responsibility for lesser ones he might commit in an effort to prevent it. "For I have a prior right, sanctioned by her late father. I mean to claim it now…if she will give me leave."

He was not certain she would, by any means. Not after all that had happened. If she refused him and accepted Roger of Fordham's despicable offer, it would be because she considered that the lesser evil. She would *know* Roger could protect her people unlike the uncertainty he represented.

"Are you daft?" Roger demanded. "What have you to offer her? Prayers? Pious mouthings?"

Five years ago, Armand would have challenged the blackguard to personal combat for all the insults he had spewed tonight.

"Dominie will need more prayers than mine if she accepts the black bargain you offer!" he retorted.

"Enough!" Dominie pressed her fingers to her temples. "Both of you! How am I to think with the two of you bellowing at each other?"

Roger of Fordham bowed low. "Your pardon, Lady Dominie."

A subtle change in his manner told Armand the fellow was as uncertain as he how Dominie might choose. Perhaps the Wolf of the Fens was not so invincible as he pretended, if members of his pack were scurrying around behind his back, securing holes to hide in when fortune turned against him.

With a gracious nod, Dominie granted Roger her pardon. Then she made a request. "May I have a private word with my lord Flambard? I wish to understand, clearly, the terms of his proposal."

"Why did I have to tender my offer before an audience?" Roger's accustomed sneer muted to a pout. "While Flambard gets to whisper his in secret?"

Armand tried to curb his tongue, but failed. "Perhaps because I have proved the lady has nothing to fear from me."

Roger snorted. "Not even the fear that you might bed her, monk!"

If only he knew! The crude reminder of what marriage to Dominie would mean for him sent a rush of heat surging through Armand's flesh. It also made him wonder if his reasons for offering to wed her were worthy ones, after all.

Could he not stand to see Dominie tainted by Roger's corruption? Or could he not stand the thought of her in the arms of any other man?

When she heard Armand offer to marry her, Dominie wondered if she could be dreaming. Or perhaps it was more like being delivered from the clutches of a bewildering nightmare. One she had struggled for years to escape, with little success.

Would this be a true escape, though? It depended under what terms Armand wanted her. Hers or his?

If he still insisted upon honoring his ill-made vow to the empress above all else, she would be doing her people no better service to accept him than to ally herself with Roger of Fordham. Worse, in fact.

When the two men had started snarling at each other like a couple of hounds over a meaty bone, she'd wanted to grab each by the scruff of the neck and bang their heads together. It had given her a fleeting sense of power to make them both hold their tongues, but her request for a private word with Armand had started them all over again. Roger's charge that she need not fear Armand bedding her hit Dominie in a vulnerable place.

Before Armand could respond to the taunt, she grasped him by the wrist.

"Come!" She dragged him toward the alcove that led to the solar stairs. "We must talk…again."

Behind them, Roger called, "Make haste, then! I have business elsewhere and cannot tarry over foolish courtship games."

Loud enough for no ears but hers, Armand muttered, "I can imagine what kind of *business* calls that scoundrel. The business of mounting a raid on Harwood, I'll warrant."

Very likely. The notion made what little Dominie had eaten at the feast stir fitfully in her stomach. Could her collection of small, scattered manors hope to withstand such a raid when a city like Cambridge had fallen prey to one?

Even with Armand Flambard in command?

Since the day Father Clement had told her Armand might be alive, Dominie had vested all her hopes in him. Now she asked herself if that was because she'd had no better hope. Or because she had wanted him back in her life, on any terms and at any price.

When they reached the alcove, she swung about to face him.

"Did you mean what you said about wedding me?" she asked in a tight whisper. "Or was it just a ploy to vex Roger and make him withdraw?"

Armand reached for her hand. "You know I would not speak of such matters lightly."

The warmth and gentle pressure of his touch soothed Dominie's wrought-up feelings. Though his views might not always suit her, she knew she could trust him to say what he meant and to do what he promised.

"I know." She squeezed his fingers. "But how *can* you mean it? I thought we agreed it was not possible for us to wed. I would rather make a pact with that devil—" she nodded toward Roger of Fordham "—than to stand by and watch Harwood taken from me, then given to someone who might not even try to protect it."

"I would not blame you." Armand looked rueful but resigned. Resigned to what, though? "Never fear. I did not press my old suit only to offer you a worse arrangement than you would have with our enemy. I will do whatever I must to see that you do not fall afoul of the king by wedding me."

Dominie wondered if her ears were working properly. "Renounce your vow to the empress, you mean?"

She understood, now, what that would cost him.

Armand nodded. "If it comes to that. I hope it need not, but if it does, you have my word I will do what I must to protect you and Harwood."

"And worry about how you will live with yourself afterward?"

Her question provoked a soft, wry chuckle that trailed away in a sigh. "Just so."

Immediately, Armand turned earnest again. "I will be able to live with myself far easier for breaking my old oath than for letting you and Harwood fall into the clutches of that man.''

It heartened Dominie to know that when worse came to worst, Armand could put loyalty ahead of the honor he held so dear. It would not be easy for him, though, and it could not have been an easy decision to reach.

If their positions had been reversed, could she have denied her nature and her duty to do the same for him?

Armand's gaze held hers with bittersweet intensity. ''I cannot deceive you, though, with false promises of assuring Harwood's safety. I will do all I can to protect these lands when St. Maur attacks. I hope I can inspire the people of Harwood to do likewise. But that may not be enough.''

''I know,'' Dominie whispered.

It grieved her to admit less than absolute confidence in Armand's abilities. For almost as long as she could remember, she'd believed he could do anything. Even after he had gone away and she had tried to hate him, something of her old hero worship had lingered.

Her admiration for the man did not rise from whatever other feelings she might have for him. And she was no longer wholly certain what those might be. A part of her mistrusted them, for they urged her to accept Armand's offer when reason told her it would not be the most practical course, nor the surest chance of safety for those who depended on her.

''You once told me,'' said Armand, ''that to sustain yourself and your people, you would do whatever you must and toss scruples to the wind.''

Dominie gave a nod. Her own words, recalled with such faithful precision, carried her back to the spring day when she'd first uttered them. At the time, she'd meant every word, without question. Now something about her defiant declaration struck a sour note within her.

Perhaps scruples, ideals or whatever one called them could not be cast aside as easily as she had tried to convince herself they could. Not even when they imperiled the well-being of those she was duty-bound to protect.

"I understand, now, what you meant," said Armand. "There is much you would sacrifice to insure the welfare of all who rely upon you. That is commendable. In my adherence to high ideals, I fear I have too often been proud and selfish—giving no thought to the price others would pay to keep my honor unsullied and my conscience clean."

The weight of that regret burdened his handsome features, softening the crisp contours of his face. "There is more at stake here than earthly prosperity or survival. If you make this pact, even from the purest of motives, I fear it will taint your soul and all the souls in your keeping."

Her hand still clasped in his, Armand sank down on one knee before her. "Take this chance, I beg you, and I will move heaven and earth to make certain you never regret it."

"Enough!" cried Roger of Fordham. "I have given you ample time to have wedded and bedded the lady, had you been man enough, Flambard. Now I will have my answer."

"So you shall, sir." With a subtle movement of her head, Dominie signaled Armand to rise. "So you both shall."

For good or ill, she had made her choice. Now she must prepare herself to face the consequences.

When Dominie strode back to the high table with a purposeful gait and a resolute air, Armand followed in her wake, bracing himself to hear her decision. At last, he understood the bitterness she had nursed against him for so long. It had been presumptuous of him to make a decision that had affected her so deeply without hearing a word of counsel from her or offering her a word of explanation.

Now that their positions were reversed, she had shown him more consideration than he'd shown her, five years ago. Not that it would make her choice any easier for him to bear if she refused his proposal.

Dominie made a little bow to Roger of Fordham. "I thank you for your forbearance, my lord."

Armand's heart sank. No woman would show such courtesy to a suitor she meant to spurn.

Clearly Roger believed so, too. He composed his sleek, haughty features into an appearance of affability. "I trust you have made a wise decision that will benefit us all."

"I have made the only decision I can live with." Dominie's voice sounded weary but determined.

In spite of how urgently he disapproved of what she was about to do, Armand could not resist an impulse of compassion for her that took possession of his heart.

"Though your offer tempts me sorely, sir, my lord Flambard does have a prior claim. I fear I must refuse you."

Dominie's words refused to have meaning for Armand until Roger gave a grunt of shock and anger and lunged toward the high table. "Daft bitch! Scorn me for this psalm-singer, will you?"

Fortunately for them all, young Lambert Miller had his wits about him. He launched himself into Roger's path with his dagger drawn. "Hold, knave!"

Wat FitzJohn rose from his seat. "Seize him!"

The Harwood men needed no urging. Guards streamed in the door, swarming forward and subduing Roger of Fordham, who put up little resistance.

Perhaps he had never meant to utter the insult and make his threatening move on Dominie. But her refusal must have caught him off guard when he'd been counting on her cooperation.

"Unhand me, fools!" he cried. "I mean your lady less harm than she would do herself, and all of you, by her perversity. Make her see sense if she will heed you, or I vow it will go hard with you in the end."

Would the men of Harwood prefer Roger of Fordham as their master? Armand wondered. And if they joined forces to persuade Dominie, might she heed them, after all?

"Hold your tongue!" barked Wat FitzJohn.

To Armand, it looked as though the guards held their captive tighter than ever. Gratitude for their loyalty warred with alarm over what it might cost them.

FitzJohn turned toward the high table with an eager light in his deep-set eyes that sent a shiver down Armand's back. "Perhaps we should treat our unmannerly guest to Harwood's hospitality for a little longer, my lady? That might make his master think twice before trying to plunder our harvest."

"A fine suggestion," agreed Dominie, before Armand could marshal his wits to protest.

"I came unarmed, to parlay!" Roger's face had grown pale as new cheese and his eyes showed too much white.

He might have far more to fear from his master, should St. Maur discover what he'd been up to.

For the first time since Dominie had announced her decision, Armand found his voice. "The man is right! He came here in peace. It would be the worst kind of infamy to hold him against his will when he wishes to depart.''

''Infamy?'' Dominie turned on him with a glare that might have flayed the flesh from his bones. ''Do you suppose St. Maur would show a jot of concern for such niceties? If we sent that blackguard an emissary, we would likely get the poor fellow back one bloody piece at a time, starting with his severed head.''

The men of Harwood muttered in agreement with her—even the priest. The look on Roger's face betrayed his own poor opinion of his master's honor.

Armand shook his head. ''I doubt St. Maur would observe such conventions, which is all the more reason why we *must.* If we let his dishonorable conduct dictate ours, then he will have stolen something from us more valuable than our harvest.''

He watched them mentally gnaw on his words, knowing he spoke the truth, yet loath to accept it. ''What is worse, we'll have been his willing accomplices in the theft.''

As he fixed his gaze on Dominie, Armand feared that what he must say next would lose him everything he'd so recently gained through unexpected good fortune. She had taught him something of the vivid and varied hues of morality, but there were still a few matters that remained black and white.

This was one of them.

''If I am to be your husband and Lord of Harwood—'' Armand clenched his fist and gently rapped the tabletop with his knuckles ''—I must insist we conduct ourselves with honor in this. If Roger of Fordham is not free to leave here, then…I must depart.''

''Fie, Flambard!'' Dominie fairly trembled with fury. ''You are never more vexing than when you are right.''

Right?

Several mouths fell open among her servants and vassals. Armand gaped with them.

"Aye, you heard me," she snapped. "Do not press my patience by making me repeat myself."

Perhaps because she could not bear the sight of him, she looked at each of the other men in turn, even her enemy. "Respecting the ancient protections of truce and parlay is more than high-flown principle. It is prudence."

Was she trying to convince the others—or herself?

"Even among foes," she continued, her tone growing more certain with each word, "there must be some means for agreement and trust in matters of urgency. Eudo St. Maur *might* not observe them, but if we breach them first, we forfeit any chance to negotiate when we might need to do so."

Leave it to Dominie to make necessity out of virtue! Armand fought to suppress even the faintest twitch of a smile, for fear she would slay him where he stood.

Roger of Fordham showed no such discretion, but cracked a wide grin. "You are a formidable woman, Lady Dominie. We would make a fine match. It is not too late to reconsider, you know. If you think better of wedding Sir Virtue, here, send word to me. Else I regret our next meeting will be under less cordial circumstances."

His grin turned into a lecherous smirk. "I would prefer to have you willing in our marriage bed than at the point of a dagger while your castle burns."

That image sizzled in Armand's mind like raw meat on hot coals. Before he could restrain himself, his hand jerked to the hilt of his sword and a challenge clamored on his tongue.

Before he could say or do anything to break his vow, Dominie spoke. She did not dignify Roger's ugly threat with a reply. Instead she gestured toward the man as if to sweep her hall clean of his odious presence.

"Blindfold him, put him back on his horse, then return to where you found him and set him loose."

While Lambert Miller secured a strip of dark cloth over Roger's face with ungentle hands, she warned him, "Try to burn down my castle, let alone take me at the point of a dagger, and you will find out how formidable I am."

Armand relaxed the death grip on his sword, but dread did not relax its grip on *him*. What if he failed Dominie and Harwood? What if Roger of Fordham's hideous threat came to pass?

The next thing he knew, Lambert and the others had hustled their blindfolded visitor out of the great hall, leaving Armand alone with the woman to whom he was once again betrothed.

An unnatural quiet settled over the big room, so rapidly emptied. The air of regal defiance ebbed out of Dominie, leaving her pale and pensive. She sank onto the nearest chair.

"Dear heaven," she murmured, slowly shaking her head, "I hope we have done the right thing."

Two strides brought Armand behind her. Laying his hands upon her shoulders, he bent forward to rest his cheek against the crown of her head. "Only time will tell if we have done the *best* thing, dear heart, but I cannot doubt we have done the *right* thing."

"I suppose so." She did not sound convinced, yet she tilted her head, nuzzling it against one of his arms. "I fear it will be of little comfort when our nostrils fill with the reek of burning thatch and timber."

"I will not let that happen!" Armand let go of Dominie's shoulders and dropped to his knees beside her chair. "I swear to you, I'll do whatever I—"

Before he could finish, she raised her hand and brought the tips of her fingers to light on his lips with a firm but tender touch. "Do not make a vow that runs counter to one you have already sworn. Otherwise, you will tear yourself apart trying to satisfy them both, and never succeed."

Her too-perceptive gaze held Armand, seeing all his faults and follies, but approving just the same. "Do what you can and be true to yourself. That will be enough for me."

Never, not even when he'd come to the abbey with Baldwin De Montford's death on his conscience, had Armand felt so unworthy.

She lifted her fingers from his lips. "Shall we summon my family and have Father Clement witness our marriage vows? It would be fitting, for he was the agent of your return to us."

How the prospect tempted him! A few words spoken before the good priest, then Armand would have every right to lie with his bride this night. He wanted her as much as he had that day in the bailey when his desire had brought him to his knees. But another kind of feeling for her had grown within him since then.

That feeling made him reply, "Let us not be hasty. I would win your hand in battle against St. Maur. Then we can celebrate with a wedding."

His true reason for the delay, Armand kept to himself. If he was killed routing the Wolf, he did not want Dominie to face King Stephen's displeasure for having wed an enemy.

Chapter Fifteen

"If St. Maur means to attack us," muttered Dominie, staring toward the northern horizon from the watchtower of Harwood Castle, "I wish he'd get on with it and not leave us all holding our breath."

Even the day seemed to be holding its breath.

Until now the summer had been one of dry sunshine, broken by hard but brief spells of rain, often at night. Perfect harvest weather.

Today an oppressive haze hung over the countryside and sultry heat sapped the energy of man and beast alike. Only the flies seemed to thrive on it, curse them! Even from her high perch in the tower, Dominie could not catch a feeble breeze to stir the beads of sweat that clung to her hairline.

The heavy air seemed to wrap around everything, muffling the sounds from below. Out in the pasture, cattle lowed as they rested on their bellies, tails twitching small clouds of flies off their broad backs. A cart laden with sheaves of wheat trundled its ponderous way up the road to Harwood's bailey. Its wooden wheels made a low rumble and the hooves of the stout pony that drew it beat an unhurried tattoo against the hard-packed earth. Even the ringing rhythm of the blacksmith's hammer seemed muted and slowed.

The air had a peculiar, humid pungency, like an old sack of mushrooms or a crock of fermenting ale.

"Is it any cooler up here?" Gavin mounted the last few steps with a lumbering tread.

Dominie shook her head. "Not enough to make it worth the hot climb. Wakeland might be better, on higher ground as it is."

"Not enough to make it worth the hot ride." Gavin flashed an impish grin as he leaned against the half wall that enclosed the tower. "Leave off, Sister. I will not be bundled off back to Wakeland like a babe, just when something exciting may happen."

She'd doubted he would take the bait, but she'd had to try.

"An attack by St. Maur's men will not be *exciting*." Dominie swiped the edge of her sleeve over her brow. "It will be fearful and dangerous and bloody!"

Though meant for a caution, her words seemed to kindle a reckless thrill in her brother's eyes. "The harvest is all but in—what are they waiting for?"

"Let them wait!" cried Dominie, forgetting she had recently wished aloud that an attack would come soon. "I am in no hurry to see them, and neither should you be. You know it will kill Mother if anything happens to you."

"What can happen?" Gavin scoffed. "I'm an archer. Armand has dunned it into our heads a hundred times— as soon as we are engaged in battle, all archers are to take cover and fire on the enemy from there."

"That is all very well." Dominie gripped her brother's hand. "You must promise me, though, if it turns into a rout, you'll stay undercover and hide. Or run back to warn us."

"Aye. Don't squeeze so hard!" The instant her hold slackened, Gavin wrenched his hand away, shaking it. "How could it ever be a rout with Armand Flambard leading us? You don't show much faith in your betrothed, Sister. And speaking of waiting—when are the two of you to be wed?"

She wondered that herself. Their mother had given many broad hints about them solemnizing the match, before she'd finally given up and returned to Wakeland.

"When the time is right," Dominic replied in a sharper tone than she'd intended. "You harp on it worse than Mother."

Like the prospect of an attack from the fens, Dominie looked forward to her marriage with a potent mixture of anticipation and alarm. More than ever, she hungered for Armand's touch, for his company and for the sense of restoration their marriage would bring.

Their confrontation over Roger of Fordham had her worried, though. With Armand as her husband and Lord of Harwood, she and their vassals would be governed by his lofty ideals—whatever the cost. He had promised her he would not make them suffer on account of his old oath of allegiance to the empress, but that was only one matter among thousands that might arise in the years to come.

Back in the spring, she had sought Armand out and offered to wed him even though she'd believed she hated him. All because she'd been convinced he was the only hope for their safety. Now, though she sensed he might pose them all a danger, she cared for the man too much to give him up.

Perhaps she had known more than she realized when she'd told Armand marriage was too vital a matter to taint with foolish fancy.

"Dominie?"

She steeled herself to repel more of Gavin's intrusive questions. Questions to which she had no certain answers.

"What now?"

Gavin pointed north. "What is that?"

Her skin prickled at his words.

"That?" Dominie squinted in the direction of her brother's pointing finger. She could see nothing out of the ordinary.

"Just over that rise. Smoke…or dust."

Dust. Now that she knew what she was looking for, Dominie could see it wafting up in a dull brown cloud from behind a gentle incline.

She might have dismissed it as nothing, but as she watched, something more solid emerged from behind the rise. A horse, moving with more urgency than anything Dominie had seen on that lazy, late summer day.

As she froze, watching it approach the village, she saw no rider. When it drew closer, she could make out a small figure clinging to the beast's back. Somehow Dominie knew this was the signal she had been waiting for…and dreading.

Once again she clutched her brother's hand, this time with even greater force. "Go find Armand!"

When she let go of him, Gavin sprang into action as swiftly as one of his own arrows. His young feet scarcely made a sound as he flew down the stairs three or four at a time.

Dominie followed, holding up the hem of her gown to keep from tripping. Within the castle's stout timbers, the air felt somewhat cooler. But that was not what made Dominie shiver as she hurried down the stairs.

"Armand!"

The moment he heard Gavin call his name in that

excited, breathless voice, a chill slithered down Armand's back.

He turned from his conversation with the miller. "What is it, lad?"

"A…horse," Gavin gasped, bending over and resting his hands against his knees as his young chest heaved. "From the north. Dominie…sent me…to fetch you."

Armand glanced toward the road in time to see a plow horse galloping through the village, carrying a boy younger than Gavin. Exactly the signal he had told Dominie's tenants to send should their manors come under attack.

He sprinted toward the castle, then slowed a little and called back to Gavin and the miller, "Spread the word around the village. Tell the men to muster in the ward!"

Perhaps that order had not been necessary, Armand decided as he approached the bailey gate. Men who had seen the young messenger ride through the village were already streaming toward the castle.

Dominie met him at the gate. Her rich red-brown braids were pinned around her head like a copper crown. Her face was pale and her eyes flickered with fear, but her mouth was fixed in a resolute line.

"Which one?" he asked, knowing he had no need to waste precious breath explaining what he meant.

"Harrowby." Dominie answered almost before he'd spoken the question, naming one of the three outlying manors upon which Armand had most expected the attack to fall. "Young Robert Bybrook. The boy's frightened, of course, but not hurt. They had some warning, by the sound of it."

As well they should.

Armand gave a grim nod. "Then we must hasten to

their aid. Send a rider to Wakeland for all the men they can spare.''

''He's saddling now.''

So he would be. Dominie would have seen to that.

Armand's gaze met hers for a fleeting instant. In that brief flicker much passed between them.

Trust and reliance. Concern for each other's safety. The craving for one more hour of peace in which they could talk over all the subjects they'd avoided of late, holding each other close for what might be the last time.

He could have stood there and looked into her eyes for hours. But duty called them both.

''I must don my armor.'' He could face a thousand foes more easily than he could part from her.

''Let me help you.'' Dominie clasped his hand and drew him into the ward, which buzzed with grim, purposeful activity.

The sluggishness of the day had been seared away by danger.

Men swarmed around the forge, collecting their weapons. Others saddled their mounts, while still others girded themselves with padded leather armor and donned crude helms of iron. Each man moved with a controlled haste bred by repeated drills. No one needed to remind them that a moment wasted now might turn the tide of battle an hour hence.

''See to your horse,'' Dominie called above the clamor. ''I will fetch your armor.''

She slipped away so quickly, Armand had no time to hesitate. The sweet spell of her presence broken, he hastened to the stable, forcing himself to concentrate on the task at hand.

By the time he had saddled his mount, she was back, laden with…

''That is not my armor.'' A faint sense of annoyance prickled through him at the delay it would cause.

''This is better.'' Dominie spoke in a brisk tone that would brook no denial. A hauberk of interlocked mail links jingled as she held it out to him. ''Come, put it on.''

''But—'' a deep chasm seemed to open at Armand's feet ''—this belonged to your father.''

''So it did. His second best. Your father's is too tight for you. It will fit one of the other men better.''

''It might, but—''

''Do not waste your breath reminding me how you and Father fell out. I *know* he would want you to wear this.''

Without waiting for Armand to reply, Dominie pushed one of the sleeves onto his arm.

Now she pitched her voice lower, for his ears alone. ''If you will not raise your sword, then you must be armed with the best we can supply. Forget your pride or your remorse and do this. For me. It will ease my mind, and I need all of that I can get today.''

His throat was too tight and dry for him to answer with words. Instead Armand nodded and forced his lips into a rueful grin of gratitude and submission. He thrust his other arm into the empty sleeve.

Clearly Dominie had expected more of a struggle to convince him. ''It is good to see you show some sense.''

In spite of the fears that weighed on him, Armand's grin widened. The invisible garotte around his throat eased, too.

''And surprising?'' he asked as she continued to help him on with her father's chain mail.

''I would not have said so.'' In spite of the fears that must weigh on her, Dominie's eyes twinkled.

''But thought it?'' Somehow their banter lightened the sense of foreboding that had hung over him during the past fortnight, growing darker and heavier with each passing day.

"Perhaps," Dominie admitted with a look of fond mockery that made clear she cared for him despite their differences. Possibly even prized some of the contrasts between them.

By this time he was fully armed, as were most of his men. Armand dared not delay his parting with Dominie, no matter how he longed to. Pulling his lips taut between two fingers, he blew a piercing whistle.

For an instant, the din in the ward abated and all eyes turned toward him.

"All who are ready, take your mounts and muster outside the walls!" he cried.

The noise and movement swelled again, all the more clamorous for having been stilled. Horses surged through the gate, some led, others ridden, a number with a second, slighter man riding pillion. Once they began to move, Armand paid them no heed.

Instead, he caught Dominie up in his arms and strove to distill a lifetime of tenderness and devotion into one deep, yearning kiss.

She gave a little start, and a squeak of surprise gushed from her lips as Armand's closed over them. Then she reached up to cradle his face in her hands—each slender, deft finger bestowing its own caress. She tasted as sweet as all the ripest fruits of summer drizzled with warm honey and fermented into an intoxicating brew. If he quaffed it every day of a long, long life, Armand knew he would never tire of her special elixir.

He sensed the stares directed at them. He knew it was ungallant for him to kiss her so possessively in front of so many people. But the touch, scent and taste of her made him forget gallantry and every other type of virtuous restraint.

Could it be that blissful indulgence was its own kind of virtue? The notion touched Armand's soul like a shimmering shaft of sunlight, with no substance whatsoever…but all the power in the world.

"Go." Dominie's lips rebelled at forming that one short word that now seemed to her the most loathsome in the language. But duty and will were strong in her. "You must."

That admonition was directed as much to herself as to Armand.

For the sake of everyone at Harwood and Wakeland, she must wrest herself from the secure haven of his embrace and send him off with his ragtag troop to battle a swarm of ruthless, rapacious outlaws. Men who had turned their backs on every ideal Armand had suffered and sacrificed to uphold.

Remembering how she had let him convince her to postpone their wedding, Dominie tasted the bitter brew of regret. It would serve her right if Armand rode off to do battle today, and never returned.

"Aye." He lowered her the short distance to the ground and released her with a sigh. "I must not tarry."

He stooped to kiss her on one cheek, then the other, and finally on her brow. "I will not insult you by reciting a litany of all you must do once we go. You know every bit as well as I."

So she did. Yet, much as Armand's confidence touched her, she wished he would linger to give her every one of those unnecessary instructions.

"Never fear." She let her hands fall from his face, though reluctantly. "I will attend to the stores and to all who seek refuge. You'll see for yourself how well I have managed when you return.'' Somehow, saying those hopeful words aloud helped her believe them.

Armand appeared to savor their sound as well. ''So I shall.''

Gavin ran up just then, with his bow and quiver slung over his shoulder. His light armor looked to have been hastily donned.

''I'm sorry if I kept you waiting, Armand.'' By the sound of his voice, the lad had not stopped running since Dominie had despatched him from the watchtower. ''It took a while to call the last few men from the fields.''

''You have not delayed me any more than my own wish to linger,'' Armand assured him. ''Now, we must fly before the Wolf and his pack bring the battle here.''

He swung up into the saddle of his waiting horse, then reached down to hoist Gavin behind him. Perhaps he read Dominie's thoughts, for he called out, ''I'll fetch this young rascal home to you safe and sound, never fear.''

At a jog on the reins, his mount moved toward the gate with the last of the stragglers.

Dominie hitched up her skirts and ran along beside Armand and her brother. ''See to it that you stay safe and sound to bring him! Do you mark me, Flambard?''

He nodded, and one side of his mouth twitched up at her scolding tone. ''I mark you, lass. Do not fear for me.''

''I'll fear for whom I please.'' Dominie tried to sound tart, but affection sweetened her words in spite of her.

Armand and Gavin both laughed at that.

By now they were through the gate. Whatever invisible tie had bound them stretched taut, then broke. Did Armand also feel a stab of pain deep in his belly when it happened?

If he did, he gave no sign, but bellowed a few orders

to his men, then headed off through the village, where dust had barely settled back onto the road.

Part of Dominie longed to watch after him and Gavin until they rode out of sight. Then perhaps scramble up to the watchtower for a final glimpse.

The notion that such self-indulgence would not be practical did not sway her as it might once have. But Armand was relying on her to do what needed doing here at the castle, and to look to her task without delay.

She would not fail him.

A small knot of village youngsters, near Gavin's age, clustered near the shallow ditch that surrounded Harwood, watching their fathers, uncles and brothers ride off to fight St. Maur's outlaws.

Dominie beckoned to them. "There is much for us to do and no time to lose. Round up as many of your friends as are not needed by their mothers, to help."

"You and you." She pointed at two of the biggest boys, one of whom had a short-legged dog squatting by his feet. "Go fetch the cattle and sheep and bring them into the bailey. Put the plow oxen into the empty horse stalls, like good lads."

"Aye, my lady!" the boys chorused, then ran off.

"The rest of you, round up all the pigs from the village and drive them into the woods, then hurry back to the castle."

One young lad flashed a gap-toothed grin, perhaps over the good fun of chasing pigs, an act forbidden until today.

"My lady," asked a slender girl, "what about the chickens and the geese?"

"Smart lass. Drive the geese with the pigs if they'll go. Leave the chickens to fend for themselves." Dominie winked at the child. "They'll be too much bother."

"Aye, my lady." The girl turned and ran after her

friends, who, like so many young fish swimming against the current to reach their spawning pools, slipped, dodged and wriggled through the stream of villagers now making their way toward the castle.

An old woman in the crowd frowned and shook her head over the children's exuberance. "The young folk fancy this all a lark, the daft creatures. They'll weep before many more days pass, I fear."

Dominie took the woman's withered arm. "All the more reason to let them laugh and run while they may, is it not, old mother? Let us, who know what danger broods, pray for deliverance."

"Pray, indeed." The old woman crossed herself with her free hand and gave a dolorous shake of her head. "For all the good it does the likes of me to pray when highborn folk strive against one another."

"Everyone at Harwood and Wakeland strive against St. Maur's outlaws," Dominie corrected her. "Each of us in what way we can. Now, will you climb up to the motte keep to pass the day, or would you rather take shelter in the bailey?"

The woman pointed a gnarled forefinger toward the forge. "My niece's lad is the smith. I'll be welcome to pass the time there."

Dominie helped her the rest of the way to the blacksmith's cottage. "My lord Flambard has long worked and planned for this day." Was she trying to reassure the gloomy old woman or herself? "Have no fear. He will prevail."

"He *deserves* to," replied the woman. "That I'll grant. But I have seen too many knaves thrive and too many good men come to grief over the years."

Before Dominie could produce a hopeful answer, the old woman sniffed the air.

The sky had darkened since Dominie had looked out from the watchtower. How long ago had that been? An hour at most.

It felt like days.

The heat had not abated much in the meantime, but a breath of wind had begun to stir.

"There's smoke upon the air." The old woman spoke in an eerie, crooning tone. "And blood."

Someone called to Dominie just then, for her decision on what goods could be squeezed into the castle and what must be left behind. The blacksmith's wife emerged from her door. Recognizing her husband's old aunt, she rushed forward to help the woman inside. Dominie was not sorry to part from her.

She turned to answer the question about what to bring and what to leave, grateful for anything that promised to distract her from the chill weight of fear that had settled in her belly.

For the next several hours Dominie did not stop or slow in her duties, until sheep and cattle milled about the ward and all the castle buildings were full to the rafters with villagers as frightened and worried as she.

For their sakes she kept up a false air of cheerful confidence. Soon the danger would be past, she reassured them with every word, look and gesture. Then they could return to their homes to prepare for winter, secure in their full larders and in the conviction that Eudo St. Maur might be evil, but he would never be daft enough to risk another bruising battle against the stout yeomen of Harwood and Wakeland.

At last, when everyone had been fed and had found a spot to sleep, and the first fat drops of rain had begun to patter against the castle timbers, Dominie forced one aching foot in front of the other and climbed to the watch-tower.

The young guard stood tall when he recognized her.

"Anything to report?" she asked, then tried in vain to smother a yawn.

"Naught, my lady," the lad replied. "Fancied I saw smoke to the north a while back, but it might have only been more dark clouds."

Dominie, too, hoped that was all it had been. Now that she had nothing to occupy her thoughts, the old woman's dire muttering about smoke and blood on the air haunted her.

"Go below and get some food. I'll watch for a bit. Not that there will be much to see on a rainy night."

"No, my lady." The boy started down the stairs. "I'll be back straightaway so you can go get some rest."

Dominie did not answer. But in her heart she knew she would not rest until she had touched Gavin and Armand with her own hands and found them unharmed.

And if that time never came? a whisper in her thoughts mocked her. She should have done everything within her power to make Armand wed her before he rode off to battle.

Or at the very least, *bed* her.

Chapter Sixteen

When he first caught a whiff of the smoke, Armand's heart began to pound faster, and his hand itched to close around the hilt of his sword.

All his senses seemed to sharpen. Picking out the plumes of smoke against the brooding gray sky, he could tell they were less than a mile distant. His gaze probed the stands of trees on either side of the road, and soon he was rewarded with a glimpse of men slipping out of cover to meet him.

Armand raised his hand to halt his troop.

"You made good speed, my lord Flambard!" cried Harold Bybrook as he strode toward Armand. "We did not look for you to come for a while yet."

A knot of guilt deep inside Armand loosened a little. He had feared his lingering, reluctant parting from Dominie might have cost them precious time. "That boy of yours made good speed. He'll be a fine knight someday." Armand nodded toward the smoke. "How goes it?

"Just as you planned, my lord." In spite of the fact that it must be his barns or his manor house burning, the master of Harrowby spoke with grim satisfaction. "A body might fancy you had given St. Maur's men instructions.''

"Did St. Maur lead the raid himself?"

"I know not, my lord. Once the alarm was raised, I did all you had bidden me. Sent the boy to Harwood on my fastest horse and the rest of the family after him."

Armand nodded. "We met them on the road. They should be to Harwood by now."

"We loosed the beasts," Bybrook continued. "Then my men and I gathered our weapons and took to the woods. Since then, others have joined us from the neighboring manors. By the sound of it, the Wolf's pack are looting what little they can find."

"Let us hope they elected to sample the beer." Armand gave a gruff chuckle.

That had been one of Dominie's contributions to their plan, bless her devious little heart. Kegs of a potent, strong-tasting beer had been planted at each of the most vulnerable manors, laced with a herb often administered to loosen the bowels.

When he'd protested that it would not be a fair fight, she had rolled her eyes. "Sometimes I wonder if there is hope for you, Flambard. You will not be holding daggers to their throats to make them drink. If they choose to partake of what they have stolen, that is their folly. And you will rightfully benefit from facing drunken foes with their breeches down!"

Armand had laughed until his sides ached. And then he had agreed.

Harold Bybrook pulled a wry face. "Methinks they have."

"Then let us strike while we still have light to tell the outlaws from each other," said Armand.

Word passed down the line, and the men and boys like

Gavin who'd ridden pillion began to dismount with their weapons. Everyone gathered around Armand and listened in silence as he reviewed the battle plan many could have recited in their sleep. Glancing around at their faces as he spoke, he could not help but wonder which of them might be killed or wounded in the coming hours.

"Make prisoner any man who surrenders," he warned them. "Let any who flee into the Fens go." He turned to Gavin and the other bowmen. "Archers, keep to cover and only shoot if you have a clear enemy target. Watch each other's backs. Fight well, but fight with honor. And may heaven protect each one of you."

Most of the men swiftly crossed themselves as they spread out to take their appointed places.

Armand led his column of mounted men along the road at a leisurely walk, halting just out of sight of the manor house. In the distance he could hear loud laughter and shouting. Once again he blessed Dominie for thinking of the beer.

Now, with nothing to do but wait until the archers and the unmounted men were in place, Armand found his thoughts flocking back to Harwood…and Dominie.

He did not dare think what might happen if he and his men failed today. But what if they succeeded? Could he take it as a sign of divine favor? A pardon? The more he reflected on it, the more likely it seemed, and the more impatient he grew to leap into the fray.

One qualm did plague him, though. The fearful certainty that if he yielded to temptation and broke his vow to forswear violence, he would doom any chance for him and Dominie to share a future.

Then a horn blew—the signal for Harwood's archers to release their first volley of arrows. The time for thought had passed. A few of the horses behind him gave eager whinnies and began to move.

Armand swung about in his saddle. "Wait for the horn to blow a second time. Give the archers a chance to do their work."

It must be finely timed. If the horsemen came on too soon, it would complicate the archers' task. If they waited too long, the outlaws might charge the lightly armored bowmen.

Another high, clear note sounded from the horn. Armand and his riders surged forward, but not before he heard the rallying blast cut off too soon.

"Charge!" he cried, in case the arrested signal might confuse some of his horsemen.

Directing his mount with the pressure of his knees, he raised his sword and led the charge, praying he would have restraint enough not to bring his weapon down against another man. Not even if his life were in jeopardy.

For to break his vow would place his soul in graver jeopardy still.

The next while was, in its way, like every other battle Armand had ever experienced—total confusion. Whirling, pounding, screaming, flying confusion.

In the midst of that tempest, with arrows flying, swords clashing and horses rearing, Armand found, to his amazement, that his mad, perilous, impossible vow gave him something to fix upon and hold to. Like a candle in the darkness or a rope over an abyss.

He parried many a sword stroke that day, while smoke from burning wood and thatch rasped his eyes and nose. Once when he feared he must smite one of his attackers or risk being killed, he managed to stay his hand, only to see the outlaw felled by a well-aimed arrow. Neither St.

Maur's men nor his own seemed to realize that while he was in the thick of the fighting, he had done no man harm.

The tide of battle took its time to turn in favor of the Harwood folk.

They were a hardy lot, anxious to defend their homes and harvest. But the outlaws, Armand guessed, must be growing desperate for provisions, having laid waste to so much of the neighboring countryside. The two sides were evenly matched in numbers. But while the Harwood men had learned a little war craft in the past months, the outlaws had lived their whole lives by the sword, and were fit for nothing else. The outlaws were armed to the very teeth, while some of the Harwood men had only billhooks, staves and hayforks for weapons.

Armand's force did have a few advantages, surprise being one of the greatest. It had been so long since anyone had done more than turn tail and run from St. Maur's vicious pack that they had grown lazy and careless. As well, Armand's men benefited from a well-rehearsed plan of attack.

The outlaws, on the other hand, had been caught as Dominie had predicted…with their breeches down.

Still they fought with vicious vigor, possibly outraged that their victims should have the impudence to resist them. Armand had seen no sign of Eudo St. Maur himself. Perhaps his followers feared what he might do to them if they returned empty-handed.

Whatever their reasons, they gave no ground, but slowly the men of Harwood began to gain the ascendency. If they could just continue to press the attack without flagging, Armand sensed that victory would be theirs.

He had just dodged a blow from the mace of one heavy-set outlaw, then ridden out of range, when he glanced up to find Roger of Fordham watching him. The glint of wicked satisfaction in the man's eyes told Armand that Roger had guessed his secret vulnerability.

And he would take delight in exploiting it…to the bitter defeat of Armand Flambard and the men he led.

They had been beaten. All was lost.

That certainty seized Dominie in its crushing jaws when she caught her first glimpse of the Harwood men staggering back home after the battle. Even from high in the watchtower, she could tell their tread was ponderous and labored, as though each step were an effort they could hardly bear to make. Many dragged their weapons behind them.

The horses looked exhausted, too. They had left carrying men on their backs. Now they pulled improvised sledges laden with wounded…or dead.

A tight sob caught in Dominie's throat and she flung to heaven a silent prayer that Gavin and Armand had been spared.

Then she did what she knew Armand would expect of her. She pushed despair aside, squared her shoulders and marched down to the ward, where she gave brisk orders for the cattle and sheep to be driven back out to pasture.

Perhaps, if the outlaws were not too hot on the heels of Harwood's weary defenders, there might be time to herd the beasts toward Wakeland. For now, she needed to make room in the castle for the men.

"Bring brooms and spades," she called, "to shift this dung."

She sent several women to fetch food and ale. Others to bring herbs, hot water and cloth for binding wounds. Anyone who crossed her path or caught her eye was put to work. Experience had taught her that responsibility was the best antidote for despair.

When she could not devise any more chores, or find any idle souls to do them, Dominie could no longer stand the suspense of waiting.

She had already ordered the gates open, and archers to cover the retreat. Now she slipped out of the castle and ran to meet the returning men.

At the edge of the village nearest the castle she came upon her castellan, Wat FitzJohn, leading the first of the horses.

"Did we lose many men?" Dominie braced herself to hear the worst.

"Plenty hurt," he replied in a flat, spent voice. "But none dead...yet."

"Praise God!" Dominie had never made the sign of the cross with such pure thankfulness in her heart. "Then we may yet rally. You must not blame yourselves. I know how hard you must have fought, but they are many, well-armed and vicious as wild beasts."

If anyone should carry the blame, it should be her. Roger of Fordham had offered her a chance to avoid this. Repellant as that choice had been to her, perhaps she should have taken it.

She was so busy condemning herself that she scarcely heeded Wat when he said, "Aye, they were all of that. But we beat them bloody and made them run just the same."

"You did what?" she demanded, grasping his shoulders. "Beat them? Made them run?" Having resigned herself to defeat, the possibility of triumph made her dizzy.

But looking farther down the column, she could see a number of strangers yoked together. Prisoners? Sweet heaven, it must be true!

Wat gave an exhausted nod. "Please do not make me

stop walking, my lady, or I may not be able to take another step.''

Not heeding his plea, Dominie threw her arms around him as tears rolled down her cheeks. "If you fall, I will carry you into the castle on my own back!"

To the archers peering out from the gatehouse she cried, "They have won! The Wolf has had his tail docked! We are saved!"

The archers relayed the good news back into the ward, from whence a great wave of noise began to build. A moment later, women, children and elders came pouring out of Harwood cheering, laughing and weeping for joy. They swarmed down the column in search of their kinsmen, bringing food and drink and warm embraces.

"Dominie!"

At the sound of her brother's voice, she turned, just in time for him to slam into her. The eager collision might have knocked her to the ground, but Gavin latched his young arms around her. For the first time, she felt how strong they had grown from all his bow practice.

She returned his bruising clasp with one at least as hearty, powered by the force of her relief.

"Did you keep your word?" She thrust him out at arm's length and ran an anxious gaze over him from head to heels. "Are you hurt anywhere?"

"A bruise or two," Gavin replied cheerfully. "Hungry enough to eat a hedgehog, spines and all! Apart from those, never better. What a battle it was! I wish you could have seen it. Armand was magnificent! I swear the man was in three places at once. And the way he rallied us for a fresh effort when we began to flag…!"

"Where is Armand?" Dominie looked around, but it was impossible to pick him out of the surging, jubilant crowd. Strange that he had not led his men back to Harwood after leading them away to fight.

"Somewhere back there, I think." Gavin swiped his sleeve across his brow. "I cannot recall seeing him once the battle was over, but I'm certain he's coming."

Coming on his own two feet? Dominie wondered, glancing at the blood-soaked binding on the arm of one wounded men. Or dragged home on a stretcher, bleeding and broken?

"Go find food and drink." She pushed her brother toward the bailey, then turned to battle her way up the road against the current of returning villagers and their welcoming families.

With each step, dread clutched her heart tighter.

Then, suddenly, there he was, cresting the rise that led into the village. He clung to his horse's bridle, Dominie sensed, less to tow the beast along than to keep himself on his feet.

Her own legs would hardly bear her weight as she stumbled toward him. Her heart felt swollen and tender within her breast.

If he had been the only one to come back alive, Dominie knew she would have felt this same wild, sweet elation that pulsed through her now.

She had been wrong, wickedly wrong to call love a foolish fancy. There was nothing capricious or trifling about it. It was as real and necessary as light or air or faith, none of which could be eaten or worn, sown or spent.

Armand glanced up as she approached him.

"I did what you brought me to do." He spoke in a hoarse, weary voice that still pealed with a warm note of satisfaction.

Dominie held her arms open to him. "I would be as happy to have you back if you had not."

His brow furrowed and he gazed at her with a look of bewildered delight that strained her heart almost to breaking. "You would?"

When she could not find her voice, Dominie nodded, hoping Armand would see the truth of her feelings in her misted eyes and her tremulous smile.

As he reached for her, a tiny movement and a flash of bright color made Dominie look down. For a moment she thought the dark spatter on the road might be more rain.

Then she realized it was blood. Armand's.

She let out a cry when he crumpled into her arms. "Someone help me! Lord Flambard is wounded!"

From the blackest depths of sleep, Armand stirred—awake enough for his senses to work, yet not quite able to make his body do what he wanted it to.

His wound pained him far more than it had when he'd taken it from the blade of Roger's sword. Had he not been wearing Lord Baldwin's hauberk, Armand doubted he would have survived the back-slash that had caught him under the left arm. Somehow, that belief heightened his conviction that yesterday's battle had not been just for Harwood's survival. But for his future with Dominie, as well.

Yesterday's battle? How long had he been sleeping?

And what was being done to him? A sharp shaft of pain pierced his wounded flesh, provoking a groan that must have come from him.

"I'm almost done," murmured Dominie. "Try not to waken for a moment longer, dearest."

Where was he? Armand struggled to wrest his eyes open, but the lids were too heavy for his wakening will.

All the things he wanted to know and do swirled in his jumbled thoughts like dead leaves whipped by an autumn wind. Were his wounded men being tended? Would all of them live? Had St. Maur's men rallied from their ignoble retreat in the Fens to launch a counterattack?

Again the pain lanced him. This time he had the presence of mind to flinch from it.

"There," said Dominie, as if she knew he could hear her. "I'm finished. And a fine job I've made of it, if I do say. To think how I used to hate sewing when I was a child."

Sewing…the pain… It all made sense now. Armand's thoughts grew clearer with each passing moment. He tried once again to open his eyes, and found he could.

"I thought you must be rousing." Dominie smoothed a lock of hair off his brow with a sure but gentle touch. "I'm sorry if I hurt you. But that wound needed to be sewn up and I thought it better to do before you woke."

Armand forced a wan smile as he glanced around him. "Where am I?"

"In my bed." She tossed the information off as if it were a trifle.

Perhaps she remembered his protests about modesty on the day she had fetched him back from the abbey, for she fixed him with a daunting stare. "This is where you'll sleep until you are healed, and I won't have any argument."

It was a good deal more comfortable than a pallet on the floor of the great hall, Armand had to admit.

"Where will *you* sleep?"

Dominie shrugged. "There's plenty of room here. You might need me to fetch you something during the night. And we *are* to be wed, after all."

"Good practical reasons." The way she was seated on

the edge of the bed, Armand could graze his knuckles against her thigh without overtaxing his strength. "You have me at your mercy, my love. I have learned enough wisdom to know when I should surrender with good grace."

"Have you, indeed?" She lifted a wine cup and a linen cloth from a small table beside the bed. After dipping the cloth in the wine, she anointed Armand's wound. The sting made him suck in his breath. "At least this will be a more comfortable bed than the last one we shared."

Armand thought back to that first night in Thetford Forest. What a barrier of old hurts and conflicting desires had stood between them! Over the past months they had dismantled that wall, stone by stubborn stone. Until there was nothing to keep them apart.

At least nothing Dominie knew about.

Replacing the wine cup with a small bowl, she began to daub Armand's chest with fresh egg white. The slimy texture made his flesh crawl. But he had been treated for enough injuries over the years to know it would soon dry and seal the wound.

"Can you sit up?" Dominie set the bowl back on the table, then picked up a long strip of bleached linen. "It would make it easier for me to bind your wound."

"I'll try." Armand planted his elbows and gritted his teeth.

Pain slashed through his left side as he forced himself upright…then nearly tumbled back onto the bed when everything around him went into a violent spin.

Dominie caught him in her arms. "I should have let you be. Little wonder you're dizzy, what with the quantity of blood you must have lost."

Squeezing his eyes shut and willing his head to stop reeling, Armand splayed his hands on the mattress to steady himself. Dominie's hair whispered against his cheek. The gentle swell of her breasts pressed against his bare chest, on the side that had not been injured.

Her scent, her warmth and her touch provided a sturdy mooring in his spinning world. When his body roused to her, Armand wondered how he had ever proposed to live a monk's chaste existence.

Practical creature that she was, Dominie did not waste her chance to wrap the linen binding around his chest, while she had him upright.

"There," she said at last. "Not a very elegant piece of work, but it should serve for now."

With one hand on the nape of his neck and the other behind his back, she helped ease him down onto the bed.

She did not pull away once he was lying flat again, but hovered over him. Her hair fell forward, like a veil around their faces, and her lips drew tantalizingly close.

Armand risked opening his eyes again and was rewarded by the most beauteous sight he could imagine.

He opened his mouth to invite her closer, but instead his honor reared its troublesome head. "Now that we have routed St. Maur, I will not hold you to the betrothal Roger of Fordham forced upon us."

"Is that so, my lord?" Her eyes widened. Mischievous green fairy light twinkled in them, and her voice fell to a husky, ravishing whisper. "I regret that I can offer you no such noble clemency."

She drew back the hand from around Armand's neck, her fingertips caressing his shoulder.

"You are mine and I will claim you—" she slid her forefinger down until it poised above his breastbone "—heart—" her hand blazed a blissful trail down over his belly, then slipped beneath the blanket "—and body."

She gave a wanton chuckle when she discovered his

lusty state. ''And unless you are very careful, I may not wait on a wedding Mass to collect what you owe me.''

''I am not feeling very careful at the moment.''

As Armand strained to engage her lips, his conscience protested, but he ignored it. His victory today had absolved him from the death of Baldwin De Montford. There was an end to it!

Or was there?

Chapter Seventeen

Everything she had wanted from life and had striven so hard for was finally coming to pass. As Dominie moved to close the little distance between her lips and Armand's, she gazed deep into his eyes and discovered that the color of love was a noble, shimmering blue.

Eudo St. Maur had been vanquished. The best harvest in years lay safe in barns and larders all over her lands. Soon she would yield to Armand the virginity she had saved for him all these years without ever realizing it.

A groan escaped Armand's lips as he strained toward her.

Dominie pulled away from him, chiding herself. "I should not have enticed you like that when you have just revived from a sore wound, poor man!"

She snatched a cup from the bedside table. "Here, you must drink some of this. It is a mixture of wine infused with herbs. It will ease your pain."

Helping him raise his head with one hand, she lifted the cup to his lips with the other.

Armand gave a droll look of mock suspicion. "You're certain it is not *beer* with herbs?"

"Beer? Never!" Dominie laughed so hard that she let

a few drops of the wine dribble down Armand's chin. "I heard the outlaws slaked their thirst before your battle. I would have given anything to see it. Didn't I tell you? A man cannot fight and shite at the same time!"

Armand managed to swallow some of the wine without choking on it in his mirth.

"I will not deny you were right," he admitted once she had lifted the wine cup away and let him settle back onto the bed. "That gave us a slight but important advantage during the battle. You showed great wit to think of it." His eyes shone with admiration. "Remember what Abbot Wilfrid said the day he bade me leave Breckland to go with you?"

Dominie nodded as sweet tears of happiness welled in her eyes. "I will never forget. He told us that when a man and a woman of great ability work together, much can be accomplished. For all we see the world so differently, you and I have worked well together, have we not?"

"Ah, aye, lass." Armand caught her hand in his. "And accomplished much. I think the abbot knew, then, that I would not be returning to Breckland."

"I have the most marvelous idea!" In her eagerness, she squeezed Armand's fingers harder than she meant to, but he did not seem to mind. "Let us send to Breckland for Father Abbot so he can preside at our wedding!"

Armand considered the idea for a moment, then gave a slow nod of approval. "That would be fitting, indeed. He did much to bring us together, and I believe he will be pleased to see what his matchmaking availed."

"That's settled, then." Somehow the reality that she would soon wed Armand set up a delicious flutter in Dominie's stomach. "I shall send Father Dunstan tomorrow with an invitation. After the trouncing you gave St. Maur's men, I'll wager the road to Breckland will be as

safe as any king's highway in the land. I will dispatch a
small armed escort, just in case.''

She helped Armand to another drink of wine. ''By the
time Father Abbot reaches Harwood and other guests are
summoned, you should be recovered enough to stand and
make our vows.''

''Please God, I will.'' The wine seemed to be taking
effect already. A tightness in Armand's flesh, particularly
around his mouth, had eased.

After several more drafts, his limbs hung loose and his
face bore a sweetly befuddled look. When he spoke in a
dreamy murmur of their wedding plans and the life they
would make together, Dominie was not always certain
whether he was addressing her or simply musing aloud.

''It will be good to see Father Abbot again. A fine
fellow. I always liked him, for all he was reluctant to let
me take full vows.''

Dominie smiled to herself as she lay down on the bed
beside her betrothed. ''I owe Father Abbot my thanks for
that. Since our vassals are no longer in danger of starving,
perhaps we could make a generous endowment to Breckland…have the brothers say lots of Masses for the souls
of my father and Denys.''

When Armand did not answer right away, Dominie
glanced at his face, thinking he might have fallen back to
sleep at last. Instead, she found his eyes open, but with a
vacant inward look that seemed troubled.

''And the souls of *your* parents, too, of course,'' she
added, thinking that omission might have bothered him.

''Another worthy idea,'' he murmured, stretching out
his right arm to wrap around her shoulders and pull her
closer. ''I shall be glad to see Father Abbot again and talk
with him before you and I are married.''

In a wandering, fey voice, Armand kept talking, though

his words made no sense to Dominie. "He will under-stand...probably better than I do myself. He will instruct me in what I should do."

"I'm sure he will," she murmured, hardly caring that she had no notion what he was talking about.

She had not slept a wink the night before, and poorly for over a week before that. The extremity of emotion that had wrenched her heart so far, in so many different directions, had wearied her in a different way. Now with Armand, solid, warm and whole, beside her, and danger at bay for the first time in many months, she could surrender to the seductive lure of sleep.

But could she surrender to the beguiling promise of happiness after it had so often betrayed her?

A few nights later Armand stirred in his sleep to feel Dominie pressed against him, wearing nothing but her shift...a garment that had obligingly ridden up to bare her long, delectable legs and the tempting roundness of her backside.

The way they lay together, him on his back, with her tucked against him, her head pillowed in the hollow of his shoulder, reminded him of the first night they had slept in each other's arms, in Thetford Forest. The feather-stuffed mattress made a far more comfortable resting place than the root-laced ground between the two tall oaks. And there was not the slightest danger of them freezing.

It might have been the heat that had wakened Armand. The cloudburst on the night of the battle had broken the heavy, brooding weather, but inside the closed castle, with Dominie's bed hangings drawn, it remained plenty warm.

On previous nights, he had not noticed, being wrapped in a deep sodden sleep from Dominie's herbed wine. But with his wound healing well, he had been able to fall asleep the night before without taking any wine.

Now he lay wrapped in the close, intimate darkness, savoring the smell of Dominie's hair and the blessing of her presence. If he could fall asleep every night with her in his arms, and wake in the morning to find her still there, heaven could hold few better delights for him.

And if that was blasphemy, Armand Flambard did not care.

The sweet ache of desire kindled in his flesh, spreading from lips that craved her kiss, to hands that longed to fondle her beguiling body. And lower still, to the part of him that reared and swelled with a hot, urgent need. One that would not be denied.

But deny it Armand did, for now at least. He would rather suffer the delicious torture of unsated wanting than wake Dominie when she slept so peacefully.

With him felled by his injury, more burdens had fallen on her shoulders in the wake of the battle. Indomitable as ever, she had tackled each one, refusing to let him be bothered on any account, and leaving his side only when it was impossible to avoid.

She put his generous resolve to the test, though. Squirming sensuously against him, dancing to the provocative music of her dreams. Her soft cheek nuzzled his chest and her hand stroked the sensitive flesh just above his navel, igniting wild flames of yearning in him. Her bare thigh slid over his, forcing Armand to clench his teeth to imprison a keening cry. Fie, if she did not soon lie still, or waken to satisfy him, Dominie might find him a drooling madman by morning!

He almost welcomed the distraction of true pain when her fingers strayed too near his wound. But he could not keep from flinching.

"Armand?" she asked in a delicious, drowsy whisper. "Are you awake, love? Did I hurt you?"

"I have been awake for a while." He tilted his head to graze his unshaved cheek against her hair, thankful he might touch her now with no need to worry about waking her. "My wound is still a little tender, but you did me no harm."

"I'm glad of that." She yawned and rubbed her eyes. "It has eased my mind to hear you sleeping so soundly these past nights." Dominie gave a husky chuckle. "There were times, though, nights when I longed for a better acquaintance with your fine body." She heaved a martyred sigh. "I managed to restrain myself, with great difficulty."

Waves of silent laughter rolled through Armand.

"What is it, love?" She rose on one elbow and cupped his cheek with her hand. "Is aught wrong? Are you having a seizure?"

At her last frantic, whispered question, Armand nearly strangled, trying to stifle a wild bellow of laughter that would have roused all the waiting women who slept in the solar.

He shook his head vigorously, until he could master his mirth to speak. "I am well…almost healed. And that *seizure* was laughter, for I got a taste of your temptation tonight. And potent temptation it was, too."

"Then why did you not rouse me with a kiss, you daft fool?" she demanded in a wayward whisper.

"I wanted to let you sleep while you could. As you did for me."

Armand's voice fell to a tender murmur. "That is love, Dominie. Not a foolish fancy as you once called it, or the healthy needs of the flesh…which I no longer pretend to despise. Just two people who think of each other's safety, comfort and happiness before their own.''

Dominie brought her hand to rest upon his heart. Armand fancied he could feel her pulse beating a lively, tangled rhythm with his. ''That sounds vastly practical.''

She was teasing him, Armand knew, and probably would for long years to come. He would welcome it every time.

''To me it sounds like the most perfect ideal. Will you accuse me of talking like a monk if I say, 'love bears all things, believes all things, hopes all things, endures all things'?''

''On the contrary.'' She stretched up and planted a kiss that might have been meant for his lips, but which fell awry and landed on his chin instead. ''I would say you are talking like a lover.''

''You have heard nothing yet.'' As he had longed to do from the moment he'd woken, Armand reached out to fondle her breast through the light linen of her shift. ''Wait until I begin on the Song of Solomon. How the poor novices used to squirm when that was read to us in chapter.''

A sigh of pleasure gusted out of Dominie, followed by an impish chuckle. ''What about a certain lay brother, Armand Flambard? Did you squirm a little when you listened to those lusty words?''

''Me?'' Armand pretended to take sore offense. Then, breaking into more soundless laughter, he admitted the truth. ''Like I had vermin in the breeches!''

Now both of them quivered in a palsy of muffled mirth that made his wound give a twinge but also made his heart lighter than it had felt in years.

''Vermin in your breeches?'' The naughty little wench

reached down and set her fingers dancing through the thatch of hair at the base of his shaft.

Armand broke into a sweat and very nearly lost control of himself.

When he had recovered to the point where he could trust his voice again, he tugged at the hem of Dominie's shift. "Here now, you have me at a disadvantage, lass. No warrior will abide that if he can help it."

"What do you mean to do about it, Sir Warrior?" Dominie walked her forefinger and middle finger up his arm. "Do battle to strip me of my shift?"

"Would you make your poor wounded champion risk an injury fighting for your favors?" he asked in a mock-piteous tone. "I know right well that if you chose to resist me, you would be a harder opponent to vanquish than some motley outlaw band."

"Sooth!" She stretched her neck up to nuzzle his cheek. "I believe you mean to lay siege to my chastity with your flattering tongue."

"Siege?" Armand murmured. "Now there is a fine idea. And my tongue might be a potent siege weapon."

With only a slight twinge from his wound, he canted himself up on his elbow and flicked his tongue over the soft flesh of her extended neck.

Dominie gave a little gasp of surprise that muted to a purr of pleasure. "What other siege weapons have you in your arsenal, my lord?"

"Why, my lips, of course." He kept them in contact with her skin as he spoke, making his words a series of kisses.

"Mmm, potent indeed."

"And I can always undermine your defenses." Armand slid his hand up beneath her shift to caress the smooth curve of her hip, while he continued to ravish her neck.

"I wonder how long I can withstand such an agreeable

assault before I throw open my gates?'' Dominie spread her legs in an unmistakable invitation to his fingertips. ''And let you make a conquest of me?''

Armand chuckled at her lusty impudence as he kissed his way up to her ear and succumbed to the enticement of her parted thighs.

He was not a vastly experienced lover. Between some youthful stolen kisses and fumbling love play with Dominie and his barren years in the abbey, there had been few partners, all taken for the worst of reasons. A futile effort to forget the one woman he wanted.

In spite of that, he had learned a little about bringing a woman pleasure. And he could imagine more. In the years to come, he would devote himself to intense study of the matter.

''Do not surrender too quickly,'' he whispered, nibbling the lobe of her ear. ''A little resistance of the proper kind will make your eventual surrender all the sweeter... for us both.''

Dominie quivered at the touch of Armand's lips and hands. Why did men waste their time with foolish warfare, when there were such delightful fields of conquest open to them?

''If I yield my shift to you, will you offer me generous terms, my lord?''

''I might, indeed.''

Abandoning her ear, Armand sought her lips for a long, slow, deep kiss that would have vanquished her reluctance...if she'd truly felt any. By the time he finally drew back, Dominie's head was wobbling like a spindle gone wild.

The passion of their kiss seemed to tax his self-control,

for when he spoke, his breath had a ragged edge. "What terms would you have from me?"

Dominie wriggled out of the garment. "I thought you might want to make a survey of the territory you would claim…to discover if it is to your liking."

"I have no doubt it will be vastly to my liking." Armand bent down to bury his face in the cleft between her breasts. "But I would enjoy making closer acquaintance with every inch of you, just the same."

He grazed the side of her breast with his whisker-stubbled cheek on his way to her nipple. Closing his lips over the out-thrust nub, he passed the smooth wetness of his tongue over it again and again, until a gurgle of pleasure threatened to lodge permanently in Dominie's throat.

Meanwhile he stroked the exquisitely sensitive flesh of her thighs with his palm, kindling an almost unbearable longing to have him explore her most secret, intimate places. On every stroke of his hand, she strained toward him, until finally she was rewarded by the most delicate skim of his thumb.

A delirious tangle of sensations caught her—soft and hard, hot and cold at the same time. Armand had known whereof he spoke when he had warned her against playing with fire, that night in the forest. She only hoped they would not burn down the castle tonight, with the heat of their ardor.

Armand seemed intent on it, though, carrying out his delicious threat to explore her in the most pleasing ways imaginable—many of them beyond her imagining. For all that, she did not passively accept this conquest of his, but sated her hands and her lips on the provocative delights of his flesh in turn.

How long this love play of theirs ebbed and surged, built and eased and built again to a more intense pitch,

Dominie could not guess and did not care. Let the cock crow and the castle stir and all the Harwood folk go about their business. She would be more than content to strive with Armand for mutual victory and mutual submission.

Finally, when she was whimpering, writhing and burning in the fever of her need, Armand mounted her with sure but gentle movements. His lips closed over hers to still her cry and to soothe her when he pierced her maidenhead.

"I hope I did not hurt you too much, love," he crooned, nuzzling her cheek.

"Nay!" She clasped him to her. "I have borne far worse and in far less worthy a cause."

"Indomitable," Armand murmured with a fond, warm chuckle, as if it were the sweetest endearment in the language. "Are you ready to continue?"

"Eager," she replied in an urgent whisper, flexing her loins to prove it.

A hoarse growl rose from deep in Armand's throat. "Have you any notion how good that feels to me?"

"If it is even half so fine as it feels to me, then it must be passing delightful."

"Passing delightful." He rolled the words around on his tongue, savoring their rich flavor.

Then, with tightly restrained impatience, he began a rhythmic thrust, hot and slick, that carried her to a blade-sharp pinnacle of sensation and launched her into shattering ecstasy.

Lost in the tempest of pulsing pleasure, she retained just enough awareness to sense Armand's final deep plunge that set him gasping and shuddering in the potent grip of his own release.

They subsided against one another, exchanging soft kisses and barely coherent endearments. Wedded in body as they were already wedded in heart.

Chapter Eighteen

From the first time he'd felt a man's needs stirring in his young body, Armand had craved what he'd just experienced. He had suffered many losses as a consequence of honoring his vow to the empress. But none so bitter as forfeiting the chance to make Dominie his wife. Her presence in his thoughts at Breckland Abbey had been both a comfort and a torment.

Now, as they lay in each other's arms, wrapped in the tipsy haze of sated passion, Armand should have been the happiest and most profoundly fulfilled man in the kingdom.

But he was not.

After loosening its grip on him for a while, the familiar specter of guilt had returned to haunt and taunt him. This time it wore a new and more terrifying face.

Because now he had something to lose.

When Dominie had first confronted him in Breckland Abbey, he had sensed how much she hated him. He had tried to pretend he didn't care. Still, he had shrunk from the prospect of telling her the truth about her father's death and his responsibility for it. Even when it might have dissuaded her from dragging him back to Harwood.

He'd had plenty of opportunities since then to confess, but he'd always found some excuse to keep silent when honor had prodded him to make a clean breast of it. By keeping Dominie in ignorance of what he'd done, he had deceived her into loving him.

But what could he do now?

Having bedded, they must wed. But their marriage would be like a fine stone castle built on the treacherously unstable foundation of a bog. Much as that would grieve Armand, to satisfy his conscience at the expense of Dominie's contentment would be the height of selfish sin.

Had he not said love meant caring more for another's health, happiness and comfort than one's own? Aye, but should not trust and honesty be the cornerstones of a worthy love? Never had Armand confronted a problem that was less black and white. Nor one where the strands of good and evil were so twisted and twined, turning back upon themselves in a tight, stubborn knot.

Dominie's solicitous murmur broke through his turbulent thoughts. "Did our lovemaking aggravate your wound, dear one? I should have bade you wait until it was fully healed...but we had waited so long already."

He would not spoil this happy moment for her, even if he rotted in hell to pay for his well-meant deception.

"I have taken worse—" he teased her with her own words as he held her even closer "—and in a far less worthy cause."

After a low gurgle of laughter, she reached up to caress his cheek. "What ails you, then, if not your wound? Did I do less than a wife ought, to please her husband when they lie together? You seemed to enjoy it well enough at the time."

"No man could have been better pleased!" Armand

chided himself for giving her reason to think otherwise. "What makes you suppose anything ails me?"

His countenance might have given him away, perhaps, but it was still too dark to see.

"You sighed just now." She squeezed his shoulder. "And your muscles are bunched so tight, while mine feel like suet."

The lass was too perceptive for Armand's peace of mind. He could not tell her the truth. Yet he hated having to spin outright lies, however minor, to cover his one great evasion.

"I was only thinking—" he must make his excuse plausible or Dominie would see through it in an instant "—that perhaps we *should* have waited to have our union hallowed. Marriage is a sacrament, after all."

Dominie's hair whispered against his cheek as she shook her head. "Oh, Flambard, I should have known it would take more than one tumble with a maid to cure you of your monkish streak. Do not seek always to blame and punish yourself. This was no passing dalliance for us, but the fulfillment of something we have waited long for. The beginning of a whole life we will share."

Her tone was the sweetest mixture of fond exasperation, forbearance and coaxing. "After all we have been through to find our way to one another, surely our heavenly father will be merciful enough to pardon us for putting the cart before the horse this once. If it will ease your mind, though, we can always try fasting or saying a great many Aves."

If fasting and prayer could have purged the stain of Baldwin De Montford's blood from his hands, Armand would have refused food until he was skin and bones, and knelt in prayer until his knees bled.

"No doubt you are right, my love." He willed his body

to relax, and forced himself to smile, even though Dominie could not see it. Unless he wanted her to guess his secret, he must learn to hide the guilt that weighed on him more heavily than ever.

"Of course I'm right. If you will not take my word, ask Abbot Wilfrid when he comes to bless our wedding."

"Why should I doubt your word, lass?" Armand planted a kiss on the crown of Dominie's head. "You speak with good sense and compassion. For all that, I believe I will take your advice and have a talk with the abbot."

Wise man that he was, perhaps Father Abbot could help Armand find his way through this moral fenland into which he had wandered. And in which he feared he might be lost forever…if he was not already.

Was that truly the only thing ailing Armand? Dominie asked herself the next day when he began to resume his normal activities. Misplaced guilt for surrendering to their desires a day or two before they were wed? It seemed such a trifle to weigh on him so.

And it did weigh on him, though he took great pains to hide his brooding from her. She had not known Armand Flambard for so many years without being able to sense the man's mood.

Part of her bridled at the notion that he should repent making love to her, for any reason. Another part rued the fact that she had urged him to transgress on the ideals he held so dear. Would it have hurt to have waited a little, so they could consummate their union with the church's blessing?

Beneath all of that ran a nagging qualm of suspicion that something besides their lovemaking, or some other

aspect of it, perhaps, was responsible for Armand's uneasy humor.

But what could it be?

Moreover, *how* could that be? He had told her what
was the matter when she'd asked. And Armand loathed
any degree of untruth, no matter how slight. He would
never lie to her.

Would he?

As was her way, Dominie tried to dispel the tiny
shadow of doubt that hung over her by keeping herself
busy. She had no difficulty finding work to do.

There were still a few Harwood men, worse wounded
than Armand, who needed tending. There were prisoners
from the battle whose future must be decided. Dominie
favored keeping them as hostages to prevent St. Maur
mounting a fresh attack. Armand insisted the men must
be turned over to the sheriff of Cambridge, or possibly to
King Stephen himself.

The Bybrook family and their vassals must be cared for
while plans were undertaken to rebuild what the outlaws
had burned. These and many other consequences of St.
Maur's attack clamored for her attention—making certain
the small livestock had been fetched back from the woods,
ordering the ward mucked out after all the cattle and
sheep, restocking the larder.

On top of all those duties, there were preparations to
be made for the wedding. Her mother must be summoned
from Wakeland, and other guests invited from farther
away. The castle must be cleaned and readied to receive
visitors. Food and drink must be prepared for the wedding
feast, which would also celebrate their victory over Eudo
St. Maur.

Though the tasks kept Dominie's worries at bay, they
could not dispel her disquiet altogether. Every time she

caught sight of Armand when he was not aware of her, her heart insisted, yet again, that something was not right with him.

When he noticed her and made an obvious effort to appear cheerful, his counterfeit smiles did nothing to allay her suspicion.

Could his talk of love have been less than sincere, perhaps? Had he tried to convince himself that what he felt for her was more than carnal desire, only to discover otherwise? The more she thought on it, the likelier her explanation seemed…and the more it grieved her.

Dominie told herself not to be so daft. She was not some gently reared child with a head full of romantic daydreams. She was a practical, earthy woman who had, for the past five years, been burdened with the management of two beleaguered estates. She needed a husband with Armand's capabilities for a host of practical reasons.

And if they should take pleasure in their marriage bed, so much the better for them both. More than that was not necessary for a successful union. It could even pose a threat.

Her stubborn, besotted heart refused to heed the practical dictates of her head. She wanted Armand's love, damn it! And she feared she would never be content until she had won it for certain.

As she strode through the ward, checking that it had been set to rights, a cry from the guardhouse jarred Dominie out of her pensive musings. "A lone horseman, coming fast!"

Her insides tied themselves in tight knots. She would be thankful never to open the gates of Harwood to another rider bearing evil tidings. Still, she gathered up her skirts and dashed toward the gatehouse.

Running from the other direction, Armand reached it

ahead of her and clambered up to look out over the timbers of the bailey.

Almost at once came an order in his resonant voice. ''Open the gates!''

The guards rushed to obey, admitting a dappled horse that Dominie recognized from Harwood's stables. With a jolt of alarm, she also recognized the young rider sprawled over his mount's neck, a single arrow bristling from his shoulder. He was one of the party she had despatched a few days ago to fetch the abbot.

She rushed toward him, calling for water, wine and cloths.

''We were attacked…on the old road…two miles back.'' The lad looked no more than a breath away from swooning, but he clung to consciousness with grim determination. ''I was…sent ahead…to summon help.''

''Well done, lad,'' said Armand.

The words had scarcely left his lips before the young messenger's eyes rolled back and he began to slip from the horse's back.

Armand glanced at Dominie. ''See to him, will you?''

The muted glow of absolute trust in his eyes restored Dominie's confidence. She did not waste time on words, but gave a vigorous nod, reaching to support the young man as he slid from his saddle.

Turning away with a swiftness borne of faith in her ability to handle her part in the crisis, Armand bellowed for every available man to arm himself and prepare to ride. He vaulted into the saddle that had been vacated by the fallen rider.

''Armand, no!'' Dominie cried. ''Your wound is not healed. You have no armor!''

He offered no justification, but kept his gaze trained

upon her as he wheeled the tired horse and urged it toward the gate.

Though both her heart and her reason railed against it, she knew this was something he must do. And she knew beyond any doubt that whatever else distressed him, he did love her.

That knowledge brought her little comfort, though, when he might be riding, injured and unarmed, to his death.

This was his fault.

The dire conviction pulsed through Armand's veins in time to the horse's galloping gait. The wind whipped his hair, and each time his horse's hooves hit the ground, it sent a dull stab of pain into his side.

He should have known Eudo St. Maur would not slink tamely away after the first rash, lucky challenge to his reign of terror. To do that would only encourage further resistance, something the outlaw band could not afford.

But Dominie had so wanted to believe that one sound drubbing would rid Harwood of danger forever, Armand could not bring himself to dash her hopes. Instead, he had allowed himself to embrace the seductive wish he knew better than to credit.

If any harm befell the men who had been despatched from Breckland or, worse yet, to Abbot Wilfrid, Armand knew their blood would stain his hands as sorely as Lord Baldwin's had.

He had not ridden far, scarcely out of sight of the castle, when he spied them coming. Three holy men rode in the center of a tight cluster of horsemen, their black cloaks billowing behind them as they fled pursuit on flagging horses. Half a dozen men-at-arms rode behind and on either side of the monks, shielding them as much as possible from direct attack.

Hot on their heels rode a much larger party, some of whom brandished swords. A few mounted archers loosed sporadic flights of arrows. Armand knew at a glance they must be more of St. Maur's outlaws. How large a force did the blackguard have?

Even as Armand rode out to meet them, the outlaw riders urged their mounts to greater speed. They split into two ranks as they overtook the abbot's party, gaining on either side with the obvious intention of surrounding and forcing it to a halt…with deadly consequences.

Armand did not know how quickly reinforcements from the castle might be able to muster, but he doubted they would arrive in time or in sufficient numbers to be of much use.

If he could have ordered his men by thought, he would have told those guarding the clerics not to ride straight for the castle, but to fan out, preventing their outlaw pursuers from closing in on the monks. Either his men were not aware of the danger, or they hoped to reach Harwood before they were surrounded.

Armand knew they could not.

There was only one thing to be done about it. He must turn aside the pursuit, on one side at least, giving Father Abbot and the rest of the party an opening from which to escape the trap.

His horse was flagging, but the speed of those coming toward him was such that they would soon collide. Sizing up the situation at a glance, Armand launched himself at the front-most outlaw on his right.

Perhaps the fellow was too intent on the chase to notice Armand coming. Or perhaps he did not believe a lone rider would dare to engage such a host, head-on. At the last moment, he glanced Armand's way, his jaw slack with surprise, too late to avoid a collision.

The outlaw's horse saw the danger, though. It balked, rearing up on its hind legs. Armand leaned forward over his mount's neck as it drove a wedge between the two parties of oncoming horsemen.

What came next took almost no time. But so many things happened all at once, many of which Armand noticed, that the moments seemed to stretch on and on.

The rearing horse unseated its rider, forcing those coming behind it to swerve aside and check their stride.

A cry from the Breckland party, most likely the abbott, rang in Armand's ears. He prayed it meant they had noticed the breach on their right flank and were veering in that direction to keep from being surrounded.

The instant he cleared the onslaught of thundering hooves, Armand wheeled his horse and set off in pursuit. An intense feeling of relief bubbled up within him when he saw what his desperate charge had wrought.

His men-at-arms on the shattered left flank had fanned out, but so had those on the right flank, just as Armand had wished they would.

Harwood Castle loomed ahead, its gate open just wide enough to let out a line of reinforcements in single file. Armand doubted there could be many more to come, but St. Maur's men had no way of knowing there were not fifty more behind those, ready to make an end of the outlaws they'd already beaten once.

At a signal from the leading rider on the right, the others began to slow their pace and turn aside, while the abbott and his companions bounded toward the safety of the castle.

Suddenly the late summer sun seemed to shine with a brighter golden glow. A yelp of laughter rose in Armand's throat. Even the dull pain in his side was a welcome sensation, for it meant he was alive.

Too late he realized that the outlaws' retreat had sent them back toward him. He made a desperate effort to squeeze through a gap in the noose of men and horses closing around him, but his horse was too exhausted to do what he asked.

As Armand berated himself for letting down his guard too soon, he was surrounded.

A gaunt man whose scraggly beard was shot with gray rode up to Armand. A trio of archers, Roger of Fordham among them, closed in, taking aim. The bearded outlaw cast a smile of disarming charm, and Armand recognized the former Earl of Anglia.

"Why, if it isn't young Flambard!" Eudo St. Maur cried as if they were long-lost kinsmen. He nudged his mount alongside Armand's. "I heard you'd perished at Lincoln, lad." In a bewildering instant, his smile changed to a snarl. "Too bad you hadn't!"

He fetched Armand a clout on the ear that almost sent him tumbling out of his saddle. For such a haggard-looking man, St. Maur dealt a hard blow.

"What did you mean by ambushing my men last week?" he demanded in a menacing growl.

Armand pulled himself erect, shaking his head in an effort to settle his spinning vision. "Your men attacked and looted Harrowby. When did it become a crime for folk to defend their own land?"

"No man who talks to me in that tone lives!" St. Maur took another swing at him, but this time Armand saw it coming and was able to move so the blow glanced off him without doing much harm.

"You mean to kill me?" he asked.

St. Maur smiled again, as if in a rare good humor. No sane man could go from cheer to rage and back so swiftly.

He winked at Armand and shrugged. "You never know."

Before Armand could decide what that meant, St. Maur snatched the reins from his hand. The outlaw earl spurred his mount back toward Harwood, towing Armand's behind him.

"Stay back! Hold your fire!" he bellowed at Armand's men. "We have Flambard, and if you make a wrong move, we will stick him so full of arrows he'll look like a hedgehog!"

The image evidently struck him as funny, for he let loose a great gust of laughter.

By this time Abbott Wilfrid had gained the refuge of the bailey. From the guardhouse, he called, "Do not imperil your immortal soul too far beyond redemption, Eudo son of Godfrey!"

St. Maur laughed harder, but his laughter had an edge hard as flint. "I am already excommunicated, priest. Would you see me doubly damned? Where is that chit of Baldwin De Montford's? She fancies herself mistress of this place. I will treat with her and no other."

Treat? An icy hand clutched Armand's entrails in a fashion it never did when he considered his own plight.

Dominie's voice wafted down from the guardhouse as the outlaws clustered around Armand, and Armand's men kept a wary distance away. "Let Lord Flambard go, St. Maur."

"I will, of course, but in exchange for what?"

"We have five of your men captured when they attacked Harrowby. I will give them all back to you in exchange for Armand Flambard."

"Five for one?" St. Maur stroked his sparse beard.

"Some would call that an overgenerous bargain. He means that much to you, does he?"

"I want your brigands off my hands. I begrudge feeding so many, and they smell to high heaven."

"Kill them then," growled St. Maur. "If they were careless enough to get themselves captured, they are no use to me."

"You cannot mean that."

"Try me." By the flat, cold tone of St. Maur's voice, he could have been talking about five sheep or chickens, rather than men he'd led and lived with. "Bring them here, slit their throats one by one and see if I raise a finger to hinder you."

"What *do* you want, then?" Dominie's tone betrayed the same horrified disbelief that gripped Armand.

She sounded anxious, too, and uncertain.

Armand wished she could summon up a spark of her old unyielding practicality, or even a pretense of it.

"Ransom." A cold, mocking smile curled Eudo St. Maur's lips. He must know he had the upper hand. "I will keep young Flambard here, and take very good care of him…as long as you pay on time each month."

He went on to state his terms—a long and very specific litany of provisions that he wanted from Harwood and Wakeland. They might be able to pay the ransom for a month or two without bringing ruin on the De Montfords and starvation to everyone on both estates.

"Don't do it, Dominie!" Armand cried.

"Silence!" St. Maur struck him in the face.

Armand felt blood gush over his chin, though whether it came from his throbbing nose or lower lip, he could not tell.

"Another word out of you, and you're a dead man, Flambard."

Armand raised his arm to his face to staunch the bleeding. He doubted St. Maur would follow through on the threat, for that would lose him a valuable bargaining tool. Then again, St. Maur had oft proven his spite was master of his reason.

"We cannot possibly yield so much for one man," said Dominie.

In his heart, Armand applauded.

"You'll find a way to pay." St. Maur sounded confident. "For every month you fail to provide the ransom, I will cut off a piece of him and send it to you. I think I shall start with an ear…or perhaps a finger. There are all sorts of *appendages* I could remove, quite painfully, yet keep him alive."

St. Maur gave a lewd, cruel chuckle that made Armand fear for himself as he never had in battle. He knew their enemy was not bluffing. St. Maur had used this system of torture and ransom before, with brutal success.

"I will give you two days to decide," said St. Maur. He told Dominie where to bring the first ransom payment. "If you fail, I will commence sending home your betrothed in pieces. Or if you try something daft like ambushing the men I send to fetch it back, I will begin with a part of him that might get your attention."

If Dominie accepted St. Maur's terms, it would bring disaster on Harwood and Wakeland. And he would die in blood and torment, anyway. What Armand feared most was that out of love for him, Dominie might accept this ruinous, futile bargain.

Somehow, he must stop her.

Then it came to him, like a visitation of grace, and all his fear, all his guilt and all his indecision lifted, leaving only the bittersweet satisfaction that he and Dominie had enjoyed one perfect night of love.

"Think carefully, young mistress," St. Maur called. "And do not make the mistake of trifling with me."

He wheeled his mount and ordered his men back to the Fens. Then he tossed the reins of Armand's horse to one of his men.

In that moment of confusion, Armand saw and seized his chance. He dug his heels into the horse's ribs and gripped its mane.

The beast bolted, ripping the reins from the outlaw's hand.

Armand had no illusions that he could reach the castle alive. All he needed was a moment before one of the surprised archers took aim and silenced him forever.

Just in case the shot did not kill him outright, as he prayed it would, he must make Dominie hate him enough that she would abandon him to St. Maur's cruelest torture.

"I killed…Lord Baldwin!" Armand roared at the top of his lungs. "At Lincoln…I slew him."

He could hear the thunder of hooves behind him, but he ignored it, bawling his sin to the heavens. For years he had kept the truth shut in his heart, eating away at him. Though it meant death or worse for him, a strange wild exultation possessed Armand as he let the demon free.

Then a hot, white ball of pain burst in his head, and Armand sent up one last prayer. For a quick death.

Chapter Nineteen

Dominie watched in numb horror as a swift rider from among St. Maur's party brought the hilt of his sword down on the back of Armand's head. She felt as if Armand's words had done the same to her.

The outlaws regrouped and rode off a ways, leading Armand's mount, and unconscious body, with them. Then Eudo St. Maur turned back, shouting, "Do not heed his raving! The noble fool only wanted to spoil himself as a hostage. Could you abandon a man who would do that for you?"

His question dripped with cloying mockery.

"Shall we give chase, my lady?" called Wat FitzJohn.

Dominie wanted to clap her hands over her ears and bid the whole world leave her alone so she could try to make sense of everything she'd just seen and heard. But there were decisions to be made—difficult ones. Experience had taught her not to shrink from them.

"No." It was the hardest word she'd ever had to speak. "You are too few. It would not be like Harrowby—they are well-armed and on their guard now. They would kill Lord Flambard and who knows how many others."

Making that choice, however disturbing, shook her

from the despairing confusion that threatened to engulf her.

"Look to our defenses," she added, "though I doubt St. Maur will try to take openly what he can extort with treachery. If you need me, I will be in the chapel."

She needed a quiet place to think. She might even try to pray, though she had never been more convinced that God and his angels were all fast asleep.

It was in the chapel that Abbott Wilfrid and Prior Gerard found her, presently.

"My child." The abbott enfolded her ice-cold hands and pressed a kiss on her brow.

Though there was little about the wise, composed cleric to remind Dominie of her rash, robust father, still a sense of paternal concern wrapped around her with its sustaining warmth.

The abbott shook his head. "It grieves me more than you can know, that my brothers and I were the instruments of the evil that has befallen you this day."

"It is not your fault, Father Abbott. If it had not been you, I believe St. Maur would have found some other ruse to draw Armand forth."

She pressed her fingers to her temples. "St. Maur was right, was he not, about what Armand said? He only claimed to have killed my father because it was the worst thing he could imagine to make me abandon him?"

Not finding the reassurance she sought in the abbott's face, she turned to Prior Gerard.

"Never before have I broken the confidence of the confessional, my child." The regret for it burned in his eyes. "In this case, I feel certain Armand would wish it. It was he who gave your father his death stroke at Lincoln. That was what drew Armand to the abbey in search of absolution…but he did not find it there."

The monk's gentle words struck Dominie a painful blow. She wanted to shut her ears to them, but she could not. Too many mysteries became clear in the unsparing light of this truth—Armand's vow to forswear violence, the zeal with which he had thrown himself into rescuing Harwood. Even his poorly disguised remorse for having made love to her.

"In the confusion of battle, Armand did not know it was your father he fought. Only after did he discover the fact, and rue it bitterly."

"So he should!" A seething stew of violent emotions blew off its tight lid. "Armand might not have *meant* to kill my father, but when he joined the empress he should have known he might have to fight a De Montford. If not my father, then his bosom friend Denys. Still he went. That betrayal cut my father's heart out!"

And hers, too.

Since Armand's return to Harwood, Dominie had struggled to put all that behind them. Clearly she had failed, if the fresh, raw anger that blazed in her was any indication.

"If that is how you feel, child," Abbott Wilfrid murmured, "then you will know what you must do." He and Prior Gerard knelt in silent prayer before the modest altar.

Of course she knew what she must do! Dominie wanted to rage at the godly abbot. What choice did she have?

One man's life—or prolonged, painful death—in exchange for so many others? How could she live with herself if she forsook her duty to her vassals that way?

And yet, when she thought of all Armand had done for them, and all he had meant to her, how could she abandon him to torture and death, no matter what he had done? If she did, guilt would eat at her for the rest of her days…the way it had eaten at him.

Pressing her fingers to her temples, she dropped to her knees beside the abbott. "Please, Father, I know what I *must* do, but…is there no other way? You are a wise man. Armand trusts you. Can you give me any counsel?"

The abbott opened his eyes and regarded her with a look of fond compassion. "The only counsel I have to give may not suit a practical woman like you, my child. That is to seek wiser counsel than mine…in prayer."

"How can I be certain God will heed me? All that has happened of late makes me believe he has gone deaf."

The abbot shook his head. "Much that has happened has come to pass because men and women turn a deaf ear to heaven. God may not always provide the answer we want in the way we want it, but if we have the faith to listen and follow where his answer leads us, all will be well."

Did she have that kind of faith? Dominie shrank from the answer to that question. Oh, she attended Mass faithfully, fasted on holy days, gave alms to the poor, kept *most* of the commandments. But her practical nature made it hard to trust in a higher being she could not see, hear or touch, let alone give such a being control over her life.

Now she was desperate enough to try anything—a state of affairs that would surely offend the Almighty if he did deign to listen.

The rote words of the Ave and the Pater Noster would never do, so Dominie fumbled together a prayer of her own, heaping onto it all her fear and powerlessness, all her confusion, all her bitterness and anger.

When at last she rose from her knees, she discovered they were stiff and sore. Strange, for it had not seemed long since she'd begun to pray. Abbott Wilfrid and Prior Gerard stirred from their own meditations and glanced up at her.

"Did you receive an answer, child?"

Dominie thought for a moment. "Yes, Father Abbott, I believe I did."

An hour ago, she could not have accepted such an answer, but now a foreign but welcome sense of peace had settled over her.

A tentative movement at the back of the chapel caught her eye. It was one of her waiting women.

"Lady Dominie, I was sent to fetch you. Your mother has arrived from Wakeland."

"Mother?" Dominie pressed her palm to her forehead. "Dear heaven, of course. For the wedding. Has she heard the news?"

"Aye, my lady, the ward was buzzing with it. That's why I was sent for you. She's not taken it well."

Dominie sighed. "I can imagine. I'll be along in a moment."

What state would Lady Blanchefleur be in when she heard what her daughter had planned?

"I'll listen," she whispered to God. "I swear I will, only please give me strength...or help...or something."

It was dark when Armand's pain woke him roughly.

His side no longer hurt. Or perhaps it did not signify, because his head felt like a quintain that had been used repeatedly for lance practice. The memory of where he was and how he had come to be here broke over him like a cold, suffocating wave. Once again, Armand wished for death.

He was alone, unarmed and injured, surrounded by ruthless enemies who were prepared to torture him to death for sport. Miles of treacherous, tangled Fenland lay between him and any vain hope of rescue. He had hurled that hope away with both hands by telling Dominie the one thing certain to make her hate him.

Yet, bleak as his situation looked at that moment, Armand could not deny a curious sense of lightness in his heart. He was not certain if the truth had set him free, but, looking back, he could see that a lie had held him prisoner.

In an effort to distract himself from the pain in his head, Armand forced himself to take notice of his surroundings. He lay on a pile of straw that smelled foul and was probably crawling with vermin. When he checked to see if he could move his limbs, he discovered that his right ankle was encased in some kind of shackle, secured by a heavy length of chain. Armand did not have even the haziest memory of it being put on him.

Suddenly aware of his thirst, he fumbled about in the darkness, searching for something to drink. But nothing came to hand. It made no sense trying to preserve his life when Eudo St. Maur only meant to take it, piece by bloody piece. But since survival was the only avenue of resistance open to him, he would take it as long as he had a spark of will in his body.

To do less would allow evil to triumph.

All the next day Armand feigned a drowsy daze whenever any of St. Maur's men approached him. After they went away, he used his eyes and ears to assess his place of confinement, praying he might discover some weakness to exploit.

To his surprise and disgust, the first thing he realized was that the outlaws had made their camp in a small priory on an ''island'' of higher, dry ground among the marshy Fenlands. It made a kind of practical sense, he supposed, for the place had been designed to house a community of men.

Though not for such foul purposes.

From the priory chapel where holy Masses had once been sung, Armand now heard gales of drunken laughter. From the chapterhouse, where the monks had once gathered for scripture readings, came the sound of voices raised in anger.

Armand could barely recognize the small room where he was being kept as the sacristy. A finely carved cabinet that had once held censers and sacred vessels of gold and silver had been hacked open and plundered. Some of the outlaws had since gouged obscene symbols into the wood. Armand shrank from imagining the desecration they had wrought on the rest of this holy house.

Hearing footsteps and voices approaching, he sprawled facedown in the straw, the better to feign unconsciousness. He hoped his captors would assume that no man with a functioning sense of smell would do such a thing.

"Still out, I see." A voice Armand recognized as Roger of Fordham's spoke in a vexed tone. "Eudo should have known better than to strike him so hard on the head. What if he dies? We'll have nothing to bargain with then."

The other man gave a dismissive grunt. "With him out of the way, we can take what we want from the manors."

"Take what?" Roger growled. "Didn't you see? They had no more than a week's worth of provisions stored at the last place. And I wouldn't put it past them to have sown what was there with poison. Like that beer."

"Aye, the beer. My bowels haven't moved right since."

"You mark me." Roger lowered his voice as if did not wish to be overheard. "The lady has that whole harvest locked up tight in her castle, and you know as well as I we haven't men enough to storm or besiege it. Especially after last time."

His companion gave a vague grunt of agreement. ''D'ye reckon she'll give over everything his lordship demanded on the first go?''

Roger spat on the floor. ''Has anybody yet? No, she'll have to get a few pieces of Flambard first, to put her in a more reasonable frame of mind.''

''Will she believe what he said, about killing her father at Lincoln?''

''God, I hope not, or we'll be eating each other this winter. Noble fool!'' Roger gave Armand a savage kick that caught him in the thigh.

He bit back a cry of pain and struggled to keep his body limp and inert, as if he felt nothing.

Having relieved a little of his frustration, Roger spoke again. ''We're still going to have to send a party to see if she does pay the ransom, and a sizable company, too, in case the little witch decides to spring a nasty surprise on us. Damn Flambard for teaching those peasants to fight!'' Armand's muscles tightened in anticipation of another kick. This time none came. Perhaps Roger thought better of harming a valuable bargaining tool.

''Five taken prisoner, three dead and a dozen wounded.'' The tight pitch of Roger's voice betrayed his desperation. ''We can't withstand losses like that. Not with winter coming on and the king provoked to action. Eudo should have let Cambridge be.''

''Ye better not let him hear ye say so,'' Roger's companion warned him. ''Or if Flambard dies before his lordship gets to sport with him, it may be yer ears and fingers sent to the lady, instead, for who'll know the difference?''

Armand heard a little scuffle followed by a throttled squeak. Then Roger hissed, ''Eudo had better not hear of *anything* I've said. You mark me, Osbert? Or it will be your traitorous tongue that gets cut out.''

"I didn't mean that!" Osbert's words sounded as if they had no breath behind them. "I was only warning ye to be on yer guard."

"I am never off it."

Roger must have let Osbert go, for he fell to the floor near Armand, coughing and gasping for breath.

"What you say makes a wicked kind of sense, though. If Flambard dies, Eudo can carve up some other fellow his size. And if the lady has stomach enough to deny us still, we can take the boy next."

This time no amount of will could keep a cry from rising in Armand's throat. It emerged from his parched lips as a groan.

"Go ahead and die, Flambard." Roger fetched him another kick. "It seems we may not need you alive, after all."

He gave a harsh laugh in which Osbert joined, relieved perhaps that Roger had found a new brunt for his violence.

The two outlaws wandered off, discussing which men they would muster for the morrow. As soon as they were out of earshot, Armand rolled over and gulped several deep breaths of fresher air.

It was no longer enough for him to survive as long as possible in passive defiance of St. Maur. He must escape to warn Dominie that the outlaws would snatch Gavin next.

Escape? In the back of his mind he could hear Roger's voice mocking him. Even if he could break free of his shackle, even if he could find his way out of the treacherous maze of Fenland, what could he do if any of the outlaws tried to stop him? He had no weapon, and he could not use one if he had it.

His vow shackled him as firmly as iron.

* * *

As she followed one of her outlaw prisoners along a twisted path into the fens, Dominie's right hand closed over the hilt of her dagger. It made her feel a little less vulnerable.

But not much.

She had never in her life done anything so dangerously foolhardy, her practical nature protested. Trust an outlaw to lead her, and a pitifully small band of men who had insisted on accompanying her into the black heart of the Fens to attack the Wolf in his lair? They might all die an agonizing and useless death.

Perhaps, came a soft but impassioned whisper from some uncharted place in her spirit. But perhaps their bold example would stir others to resistance. And perhaps Armand would know she had loved him in the way he craved. Not because she needed him or wanted him, not *because* of anything at all.

She loved him in spite of their differences, in spite of all that had happened in the past, even when he had become a grave liability to everything else she held dear. She could not abandon him to St. Maur's cruelty, even if it meant taking a rash, thoroughly impractical gamble, with stakes as high as her own life...perhaps higher.

The dagger she carried was not to use against the outlaws, but to make a quick, merciful end to herself if she fell into their clutches.

The young fellow who was leading them turned toward her. "We're getting close now," he whispered. "Everyone be on your guard."

Dominie stifled the urge to tell him they had been on guard from the moment they'd stepped outside Harwood's gate. "You're certain there will be no lookouts?"

The lad shook his head. "There used to be, but no one

has ever come here of their own free will. The men grew tired of watching for nothing.''

''I pray that has not changed,'' Dominie muttered under her breath.

She also prayed that the king had received and heeded her message. She prayed that Gavin had obeyed her order not to venture outside the castle, no matter how briefly, no matter what the reason. She prayed her mother would find the fortitude to manage the estates for as long as necessary, as she'd promised.

God had answered one prayer by turning their young guide from the evil path he'd chosen. Dominie conceded that St. Maur's cruelty might have influenced the lad at least as much. When he'd heard that his master had refused to ransom any of the prisoners, the boy had agreed to lead Dominie to St. Maur's camp.

Now he veered off the narrow path, beckoning the others to follow him. Dominie's feet sank into the warm quagmire up to her ankles, then made a sucking sound every time she pulled one out to take a step.

''It's better we go 'round this way,'' their guide whispered, perhaps sensing her fear that he might be leading them into a trap. ''We'll come out at a spot nearer the buildings.''

Dominie relayed the information back, to reassure her men.

From the glimpses she got of the old priory as they slogged their way around the ''island,'' the place looked deserted. Could they truly be that fortunate? Of course, if all St. Maur's force had gone to collect the ransom, perhaps they had taken Armand with them.

At last their guide halted. ''We won't get any nearer than this, my lady. Are you sure you want to do this?''

Dominie nodded as the other men clustered around to

receive their orders. "You have done your part well so far. Wait here as long as you dare to lead us back out. Now, where will we find my lord Flambard?"

"Prisoners are always kept in the sacristy, my lady." The lad pointed toward the spire of the chapel. "There's a rear door, near the altar. It's your best chance for slipping in unseen. Did you bring the chisel and mallet as I bade you, to break his chains?"

Dominie patted a leather scrip on her belt.

She looked around at her men, gratitude welling up in her heart for their loyalty. "We will go together toward the sacristy. Wherever we pass a place of cover between here and there, I will leave one of you. Once we have recovered my lord Flambard, we will retreat by the same path, gathering strength as we go. With good fortune, we may get in and out again without anyone the wiser."

Lambert Miller spoke up. "I think you ought to let one of us go the last leg, my lady. In case there's trouble, or in case he cannot walk."

"I have put you all in danger enough." Dominie thought back over all the ordeals she and Armand had shared during their journey from Breckland. "Trust me, I can get Lord Flambard out if anyone can."

"I hope so, my lady."

Now was not the time to betray the doubts that worried at her. "I *know* so. We have bested Eudo St. Maur once and we will do it again."

Her assurances seemed to hearten them. They gave confident nods and grim smiles, perhaps remembering the battle of Harrowby, when honest vassals had fought rogue knights and emerged victorious.

"Now let us go." Aye, now, before her nerve broke or her practical nature persuaded her it was futile.

It was *not* futile. They had made it thus far, and they would make it home safe again.

"And may God go with us." They would need him.

Balancing stealth and haste as best they were able, Dominie and her small party skirted the outbuildings of the priory. Every hundred yards or so they halted in what cover they could find, listening for any sounds of danger and looking ahead for their next shelter.

By the time they reached the monks' cemetery behind the chapel there were only three of them—herself, Lambert and a young man of the castle guard from Harwood. They left him behind an old stunted yew tree, then picked their way through the grave mounds to the door at the back of the chapel.

"Are you sure you don't want to wait here, my lady?" Lambert asked once again when they'd tried the door and found it unbarred.

"I'll call if I need you. Keep the door ajar. Whistle if you see or hear anyone coming."

With those words of parting, Dominie pulled the door open just enough to slip through. Once inside, she crouched in the shadows, waiting for her eyes to adjust to the dim light. The place reeked of ale and wine...not the holy kind, either.

Dominie strained so hard, listening for the least sound of danger, she could almost feel her ears quiver. But all was quiet. Too quiet.

Her own breath and tentative footsteps thundered in her ears as she made her way behind the altar to the sacristy. That door had been torn off its hinges. At least she would not have to worry about them squealing when she entered. Pale light spilled out through the open doorway into the darkened chapel.

She did not enter at once, in case there might be a guard

watching over Armand. Instead, with her ears still pricked, she peered around the doorjamb.

A sickening void opened in the pit of her stomach when she saw there was no one in the little room. A pile of straw on the floor looked as though someone might have lain there recently. A crust of bread and a small mug also suggested the presence of a prisoner.

Dominie tiptoed into the room, hoping to find some sign that Armand had been here, or perhaps a clue to where he'd been taken.

The mug held weak ale, just a little left in the bottom. Dominie poked through the damp, malodorous straw, but found nothing.

While she was on her knees, however, a gouge in the wall caught her eye. The wood was splintered in one place, as though something might have been torn out.

A shackle, perhaps?

Where was the leg iron their guide had mentioned? The one for which she'd brought the mallet and chisel? If the outlaws had moved Armand elsewhere, they would hardly have taken it along.

Hope warred in her heart with a hundred questions, the most insistent of which was *what now?*

She did not hear the footsteps until it was too late.

She glanced up to find Eudo St. Maur standing in the doorway. He stared at her with a fierce scowl, his shaggy brows knit together in a puzzled look.

Then, as he drew his sword, St. Maur spoke the very words that clamored on the tip of Dominie's own tongue.

''What have you done with Flambard?''

Chapter Twenty

From his hiding place in the small crypt behind the chapel altar, Armand heard the footsteps overhead.

He steeled himself for his escape to be discovered and a search for him begun. He hoped the outlaws would think as he'd predicted and go looking for him in the fens. Once they'd failed in their initial search, he could steal out of his hiding place and try to find his way back to Harwood.

Something about the footsteps in the chapel roused his curiosity, though. They had a soft, furtive sound—advancing, then stopping, then advancing again after a long pause. St. Maur's men would have no reason to tread with such stealth.

Could it be that someone had come in search of him?

Hope battled doubt within him. After a brief but fierce struggle, hope emerged the victor.

Armand reached above his head to raise the trapdoor a crack—enough that he might see what was going on, without calling attention to his hiding place. He was just about to ease it open when another set of footsteps passed overhead. These ones were quiet, too, but with a heavier tread.

What was going on up there?

Knowing there were at least two people in the sacristy, Armand did not dare risk betraying his presence. Instead, he strained to hear anything that might give him a clue about what was happening.

He heard the deep rumble of a man's voice, followed by the cry of a woman.

Perhaps she belonged there—a servant of the outlaws. St. Maur might have a mistress. Or perhaps the woman was not here by choice.

The outlaws tortured male captives for ransom. The thought of what they might do with captive women ignited a blaze of righteous wrath in Armand's belly.

He threw open the trapdoor—or began to.

He had raised it only a few inches, preparing to leap out, when something heavy crashed down upon it. The momentum hurled Armand to the floor of the crypt, stunned.

Overhead, in the sacristy, he heard sounds of a struggle.

Had someone else come to help the woman? Were two of the outlaws fighting over her? Or might two of them be attacking her?

Since returning to Harwood with Dominie, Armand had learned the value of practicality. Practical reason told him the woman might not need his help. He might be outnumbered, even if he had a weapon and the will to use it. He might well be recaptured, then tortured as punishment for his attempt to escape.

None of those considerations could hold him.

Armand threw back the trapdoor, scrambled up into the chapel and ran toward the sacristy, dragging his chain behind him.

For an instant he hesitated at the threshold, bewildered by what he saw.

Eudo St. Maur had his sword raised. Its blade was already smeared with blood. A second sword lay at his feet, dropped there by the young man who was backed into a corner, his right hand held over his left arm. Bright blood seeped between his fingers. Lambert Miller!

As Armand watched, another lad dived for Lambert's fallen sword. Where was the woman?

Then in an instant of anguished clarity, Armand recognized the second boy.

Dominie.

She had come to rescue him, as she had come to another holy house to rescue him from a prison of his own making.

Eudo St. Maur swung his weapon.

Armand had almost no time to react, but in that brief moment he knew what he was doing.

Some vows were better broken and some causes were still worth fighting for.

With strength he had not known he possessed, and aim that must have come from some greater power, he kicked his shackled leg high in the air. The chain bound to his ankle rose like a heavy whip, striking St. Maur's sword and knocking it from his hand.

The momentum of the chain jerked Armand off his feet. By the time he recovered from his fall, Dominie had swords in both hands and the Wolf of the Fens with his back to the wall.

"Spare his life!" Armand cried.

"Why?" Dominie did not take her eyes off Eudo St. Maur. "The scoundrel deserves to die and go straight to hell."

She sounded ready to dispatch him.

"Practical reasons." Armand regained his feet and twisted St. Maur's arms behind him. "We may need him as a hostage to get out of here alive. And I'll wager the king will pay a handsome reward for his capture. Now give me your belt.''

Dropping one sword behind her, but keeping the other one poised to strike, Dominie unfastened her belt and tossed it to him. ''I may make a practical man of you yet, Flambard.''

Armand bound St. Maur's arms behind him with the belt. ''I pray we will have many years together for you to try.''

St. Maur spat. ''You will pay in blood for this, mark me! My men will ravage your lands until there is not a building left unburned or a grain of your harvest unplundered.''

''Let them try.'' Dominie reached for the sword she had dropped and held it out to Armand.

He hesitated for just a moment, then took it from her, knowing that he would use it. Never wantonly. Never with pleasure. But of necessity, to protect the vulnerable and to defend the ideals he still held dear...though no longer absolute.

With their prisoner under Armand's guard, Dominie now turned to Lambert Miller, ripping a strip of linen from her undergarment to bind his bleeding arm.

''Stephen will only let me go again, Flambard,'' St. Maur growled. ''He's as big a chivalrous ass as you are. Then I will not rest until I have had my revenge upon you.''

''Thank you for the warning.'' Armand lifted his sword, pressing the blade to St. Maur's neck, just below the ear. ''We will be ready for you.''

To Dominie he called, ''Can you spare another strip of linen, love? I am already sick of hearing this fellow spew his bile. I'd rather not listen to it all the way back to Harwood.''

* * *

"That was easier than I expected." Dominie glanced back over her shoulder as the rescue party marched in single file over the winding, narrow path that led out of the fens. "It worries me." They had been able to smuggle a well tied and gagged St. Maur back into the Fens without being spotted and challenged. After so many disasters, Dominie mistrusted this unexpected bit of luck.

From his place behind her, Armand reached forward to lay a hand on her shoulder. "Don't fret yourself over it. I overheard Roger of Fordham talking to one of the other outlaws. He made it sound as though they could not spare many men to stay behind when they went to check on the ransom. Few able-bodied ones, at any rate."

Dominie breathed a little easier for hearing that.

After they had walked a little farther in silence, Armand spoke again. "Why did you come for me? Did you not hear what I said when St. Maur made his ransom demands?"

"I heard." Dominie kept her gaze fixed on the path ahead. "At first I did not want to believe it, but Prior Gerard told me you had confessed to him."

In truth, it was more than the fear of an outlaw ambush that made her uneasy. When she had decided she must go to Armand's aid, she had imagined it a lost cause—finding Armand already dead, perhaps, or the two of them being killed during the attempted rescue. She had not reckoned with them returning to Harwood and going on with their lives.

As if nothing had changed between them.

"But if you heard...and believed, why did you come for me? Why don't you hate me?"

"I...don't know the answer to either of those questions, Armand. I had to try, that's all. I *had* to. As for hating you, I cannot lie—it does grieve me to know my father perished at your hands.''

"No more than it has grieved me these five years.''

"I know. And that makes a difference, somehow.''

"I should have told you.'' Armand heaved a sigh. "The moment you found me at Breckland, I should have told you. I gave myself dozens of reasons for keeping silent, but the truth was I couldn't bear to have you hate me.''

Dominie could not let him take all the blame for that. "It cannot have been easy to tell the truth when I was forever harping at you to hold your tongue over this or that.''

"I convinced myself I was sparing you knowledge that could only hurt you. But in my heart I knew I was the worst kind of pretender—always talking of lofty ideals while I was keeping a secret like that from you.''

"You did tell me at last, when it mattered most of all. And on my account you broke your vow not to use violence.'' Dominie glanced back at Armand. "What made you do those things?''

He shrugged. "As with you, I had to. To have watched you come to harm while I hesitated would have been as bad as attacking you myself.''

Acknowledging his answer with a fleeting nod, Dominie fell silent again. Armand had said nothing about love. That was what she'd truly wanted to hear, though she chided herself for such foolishness.

She kept the questions that plagued her at bay until they had emerged from the fens.

The horses her party had left behind were still there, grazing placidly. They had brought one extra in the hopes of bringing Armand back with them. But they had not reckoned on taking prisoners.

"Put St. Maur on my horse,'' Dominie ordered the men

who were guarding him. "I can ride pillion with my lord Flambard. Go quickly in case we are pursued. We will catch up with you."

The men mounted and set off for Harwood with their captive.

When Armand prepared to climb into his saddle, Dominie laid her hand on his arm to stay him. One question burned in her thoughts. If she did not ask it now, she might never find the courage. She needed to see his face when he gave her his answer.

"I need to know something, Armand, and I must have the truth from you, no matter how much you think it might hurt me."

His face was already pale, beneath smudges of dirt and a dark shadow of whisker growth. Now it grew paler still. The cuts and bruises on his face made Dominie long to wash, anoint and bind them. The furrows in his brow called to her lips to kiss them away…whether or not she truly had the power.

Armand gave a dispirited nod. Did he guess what the question would be and did he shrink from answering it?

"The truth," he agreed.

Dominie's throat went dry and dismay gripped her, as potent in its way as what she'd felt when Eudo St. Maur had caught her in the sacristy. Worse, perhaps, since this was not mixed with righteous fury.

"Did you offer to wed me—" she could not meet his gaze "—and all the rest, as a way of atoning for my father's death? Was I only a penance to you?"

The silence that greeted her question seemed to stretch on and on. Did Armand's answer lay in that silence…? Dominie's heart contracted into a tight, impenetrable ball—the way it had been before Armand came back into her life and coaxed it to open again.

"Ha!"

The burst of laughter made Dominie jump. She glanced at Armand's face to make certain it had come from him.

Indeed, he was laughing. But in the strangest way she had ever heard. His laughter sounded as though it held a great many strong emotions, none of which was amusement or joy.

"Like my years in the abbey, you mean?" His laughter died away, leaving a mist of tears in his eyes. "No, Dominie. It was nothing like that. Do you not remember how hard I tried to resist my desire for you?"

She did. She remembered also how puzzled she had been by the intense struggle she'd sensed within him. Too intense for what she thought had been at stake.

Armand pushed back a lock of hair that had fallen over his brow. "I only offered to wed you when Roger of Fordham left me no choice. Or so I told myself. In truth, I wanted you for my wife more than anything, though I knew I did not deserve the happiness you were sure to bring me. It was only after we battled St. Maur's raiding party that I began to think otherwise. After we lay together, I knew I had deceived myself."

"So you *did* love me?"

"*Do* love you," he corrected her. "*Will* love you…as long as my soul endures."

"And I you." The words left her lips before Dominie had time to think. But when she spoke them, she knew they were true.

She leaned toward Armand, pressing her brow to his chest.

He enfolded her in a tender but loose embrace, as if doubting his right to take such a small liberty. Or perhaps to make it easy for her to pull away…if she wished.

"So," he murmured, his chin resting on the crown of

her head. "We love each other in the ideal way I once dreamed. We do not live on some ideal plane, though, where we may please only ourselves. We live in a dangerous, demanding world and our decisions affect many other lives. I fear it would be impractical for us to wed."

His words uprooted the fragile seedling of hope that had begun to grow in Dominie's heart.

She did pull away from Armand then, far enough to look him in the eye, but not so far that he must let her go. "Why impractical?"

"Could your mother and brother accept me as your husband, knowing your father's blood is on my hands? Could the people of Wakeland suffer to have me as a neighbor?"

"It may not be easy, but I believe they can. You did not—" she stumbled over the word, still not fully able to grasp it "—kill my father out of malice. If you had seen his face that day you fought, I believe you would rather have taken your own death blow than knowingly do him harm."

A look of pain twisted his face, and a single tear rolled slowly down his battered cheek. He moved his head in a barely perceptible nod.

As Dominie lifted her hand to wipe away that tear, a thought blossomed in her mind that seemed to come from elsewhere. "Then might it be that my father recognized *you* that day at Lincoln and did the same? Do not belittle the power of forgiveness, Armand. It may not grow quickly, but it can yield a hardy crop if you tend it with patience."

Could it be? Armand sought the courage to believe what Dominie had said. Might absolution not come in a vast, breathtaking waterfall, scouring guilt away by the power of its outpouring? Might it come rather as a trickle, eroding the stubborn stone of self-blame with its unfaltering constancy?

Armand looked within himself to find his burden of guilt had already begun to wear away.

He could not give Dominie an answer in words, for he was too overcome to speak. Instead, he lifted her off the ground and kissed her with all his love. The old and the new. The ideal and the practical. And the promise of what would grow between them in the years to come.

When at last they drew apart, Dominie lofted him a grin of her old playful impudence. "We had better mount and ride before the others fear foul play and come in search of us."

"Very well." Armand climbed into the saddle and hoisted her up behind him. "There will be plenty of time for kissing later."

"Time for kissing." Dominie's arms wrapped around him in a close embrace, her cheek resting against his back. "And many other pleasures."

Armand would have wed her the moment they arrived back at Harwood, but Dominie insisted they wait until the next day, so his wounds could be tended and they could both be suitably bathed and attired.

One private preparation Armand made was his confession to Prior Gerard, in which he admitted to lying with Dominie before they were married. He also confessed that he had broken his vow to abstain from violence. The good prior granted him absolution with a token penance.

Lady Blanchefleur and young Gavin both gave the marriage their blessing. Armand sensed a blight in their old feelings toward him, especially from the boy, who finally seemed to view him as something less than a marble paragon. That, Armand decided, was no bad thing. He trusted what Dominie had said about the healing power of forgiveness to grow a new, stronger bond with both of them over time.

He and Dominie made their vows at the chapel door, then celebrated their marriage with a wedding Mass. Armand's heart swelled with pride and love whenever he looked at his beautiful, passionate bride, her unruly tumble of rich auburn hair adorned with a ring of late summer flowers.

The wedding ceremony was followed by a more bountiful feast than Harwood had seen in a great while.

They were in the midst of drinking toasts, with merry music piping in the background, when a watch guard appeared behind the head table looking anxious. "My lord, my lady, King Stephen is at the gate with a large host, demanding entry and speech with you."

Armand rose from his seat, stifling a sigh. It seemed to him that moments of happiness were as fleeting as the beautiful blossoms in Dominie's bridal wreath, while troubles flourished like noxious weeds.

Then Dominie rose, too, catching his hand in hers. "We will both go to receive his Grace's good wishes on our marriage."

Though he doubted that was the reason for King Stephen's sudden appearance, Armand squeezed his bride's hand. The support and comfort of a loving spouse would enrich the happy times while sustaining a body during times of trouble.

Thus heartened, he escorted Dominie out of the castle, down the sloping drawbridge to the ward. As they descended, Armand caught sight of the king's army. Had Stephen gotten wind of their betrothal and come to take Harwood out of "enemy" hands?

The guard had run ahead of them to open the gate. By the time Armand and Dominie reached the ward, King Stephen and a small party of men-at-arms had ridden in.

The king dismounted with stiff movements. Though still a handsome man of imposing presence, he looked a good deal older and thinner than when Armand had last seen him.

Glancing at Dominie's bridal attire, the king broke into a smile of renowned charm. "Have I interrupted a wedding? I must beg your pardon if I have."

Before Armand could reply, Dominie swept the king a deep curtsy. "The wedding ceremony has already taken place, my lord, but the feast has just begun, if you would join us."

The king's smile broadened as his gaze rested on her. Armand could hardly blame the man. He himself had been grinning like a fool all day.

"I believe I will accept your invitation, my lady. We have much to celebrate."

When Armand raised an eyebrow, the king explained. "Your wife sent me a message yesterday, saying where I might find a large party of Eudo St. Maur's men. I am pleased to report the ambush was a perfect success. However, when one of St. Maur's lieutenants led us back to their camp, the slippery scoundrel had already fled. Still, his power is broken and law may return to this corner of my kingdom."

Dominie gave Armand a none too gentle nudge with her elbow.

He cleared his throat. "Your Grace, *I* am pleased to report that Eudo St. Maur is our prisoner, though we would be honored to surrender him to you."

The offer gave him a twinge of worry after St. Maur's threats of revenge.

King Stephen allayed his fears. "I shall be glad to take him. I should never have let him go the first time, but I felt I owed him some clemency for his past service. I now owe it to the good folk of Anglia to protect them from his blight."

Armand and Dominie exchanged a look of relief.

The king continued, "I am in your debt, sir. Flambard, is it? Son of the Flambard who once held this estate?"

"Aye, Your Grace." He bowed. "Armand Flambard."

The king's brow creased. "You declared for my cousin the empress, did you not, Flambard?"

"Aye, Your Grace, and fought at Lincoln. I was younger then. I felt that honor required me to keep the vow of loyalty I had sworn before King Henry and his daughter. I have since learned that honor can be tempered by practical concerns without being compromised. I pray you will not punish my wife for my actions. If you will allow her to continue holding Harwood in her own right, I will be content to remain her consort."

"Could you bring yourself to swear fealty to me?"

Before Armand could choke out the words, Dominie spoke in a firm voice, "No, Your Grace, he could not. Nor would I want him to. I have seen these past years what happens when men let their honor and virtue erode."

The king gave a rueful nod, remembering, perhaps, the oath he had been first to swear, all those years ago. "There are those who say I thwart my own cause through too much care for honor. As I said, I am in your debt for capturing Eudo St. Maur and for delivering his band of brigands into my hands. If I reward you with more land, can you at least promise not to take up arms against me in future?"

Armand dropped to one knee. "That I can do, Your Grace, with a willing heart."

"Good." The king beckoned him to rise. "That is settled then. Let us go to this feast of yours and celebrate fine harvests, of many kinds."

"Aye, Your Grace." Armand prepared to kiss his bride the moment the king's back was turned. "Fine harvests, and new beginnings!"

* * * * *

Savor these stirring tales of romance with Harlequin Historicals

On sale May 2004

THE LAST CHAMPION by Deborah Hale

Once betrothed, then torn apart by civil war, will Dominie de Montford put aside her pride and seek out Armand Flambard's help to save her estate from a vicious outlaw baron?

THE DUKE'S MISTRESS by Ann Elizabeth Cree

Years ago Lady Isabelle Milborne had participated in her late husband's wager, which had ruined Justin, the Duke of Westmore. And now the duke will stop at nothing to see justice served.

On sale June 2004

THE COUNTESS BRIDE by Terri Brisbin

A young count must marry a highborn lady in order to inherit his lands. But a poor young woman with a mysterious past is the only one he truly desires....

A POOR RELATION by Joanna Maitland

Desperate to avoid fortune hunters, Miss Isabella Winstanley poses as a penniless chaperone. But will she allow herself to be ensnared by the dashing Baron Amburley?

eHARLEQUIN.com

For **FREE online reading,** visit
www.eHarlequin.com now and enjoy:

Online Reads
Read **Daily** and **Weekly** chapters from
our Internet-exclusive stories by your
favorite authors.

Red-Hot Reads
Turn up the heat with one of our more
sensual online stories!

Interactive Novels
Cast your vote to help decide how these
stories unfold...then stay tuned!

Quick Reads
For shorter romantic reads, try our
collection of Poems, Toasts, & More!

Online Read Library
Miss one of our online reads?
Come here to catch up!

Reading Groups
Discuss, share and rave with other
community members!

For great reading online,
visit www.eHarlequin.com today!

INTONL

FALL IN LOVE WITH
FOUR HANDSOME HEROES
FROM HARLEQUIN HISTORICALS.

On sale May 2004

THE ENGAGEMENT
by Kate Bridges

Inspector Zack Bullock
North-West Mounted Police officer

HIGH COUNTRY HERO
by Lynna Banning

Cordell Lawson
Bounty hunter, loner

On sale June 2004

THE UNEXPECTED WIFE
by Mary Burton

Matthias Barrington
Widowed ranch owner

THE COURTING OF WIDOW SHAW
by Charlene Sands

Steven Harding
Nevada rancher

Visit us at www.eHarlequin.com

HARLEQUIN HISTORICALS®

COMING NEXT MONTH FROM

HARLEQUIN
HISTORICALS®

- **THE COUNTESS BRIDE**
  by **Terri Brisbin,** author of THE NORMAN'S BRIDE
  Count Geoffrey Dumont must marry to secure control of his lands
  in France. Though she's completely unsuitable for a man of his standing,
  Geoffrey knows that Catherine de Severin is the only
  woman for him…so he kidnaps her! Will he convince Catherine
  to elope with him before they are caught?
  HH #707 ISBN# 29307-0 $5.25 U.S./$6.25 CAN.

- **THE UNEXPECTED WIFE**
  by **Mary Burton,** author of THE LIGHTKEEPER'S WOMAN
  Everyone in Matthias Barrington's tiny Montana town knows that
  he needs a wife. And since the struggling single father refuses to find
  a bride, the townspeople take matters into their own hands and find
  Abby Smyth, mail-order bride. Though Matthias has vowed never to
  remarry, would he deny his sons a mother…and deny himself a second
  chance at love?
  HH #708 ISBN# 29308-9 $5.25 U.S./$6.25 CAN.

- **A POOR RELATION**
  by **Joanna Maitland,** author of RAKE'S REWARD
  To avoid fortune hunters, heiress Lady Isabella Winstanley allows
  the ton to believe she is an almost penniless poor relation. When
  Leigh Stansfield, Baron Amburley, meets Isabella at a ball, he falls for
  her disguise, but thinks she's greedily trying to snag a wealthy husband.
  As Isabella finds herself attracted to Amburley, how can she show him
  she's not a wanton gold digger without giving away her secret?
  HH #709 ISBN# 29309-7 $5.25 U.S./$6.25 CAN.

- **THE COURTING OF WIDOW SHAW**
  by **Charlene Sands,** author of WINNING JENNA'S HEART
  When Steven Harding finds Gloria Mae Shaw lying unconscious next
  to her dead husband with a bloodied knife in her hand, he takes her to
  the one place no one would ever think to look for her—his mother's infa-
  mous brothel. Steven's not sure if she's guilty of murder and Gloria
  has no memory of the night in question, but a secret from Steven's past
  compels him to protect her.…
  HH #710 ISBN# 29310-0 $5.25 U.S./$6.25 CAN.

KEEP AN EYE OUT FOR ALL FOUR
OF THESE TERRIFIC NEW TITLES

HHCNM0504